W9-COE-723

JOANNA

JOANNA

Rosemary
Upton

Guideposts®
CARMEL • NEW YORK 10512

This Guideposts edition is published by special arrangement with Harold Shaw Publishers. It was originally published under the title *The Court and the Kingdom.*

Copyright © 1993 by Rosemary J. Upton

Scripture quotations are taken from the King James Version of the Bible.

All rights reserved. No part of this book may be reproduced or transmitted in any form or by any means, electronic or mechanical, including photocopying, recording, or any information storage and retrieval system without written permission from Harold Shaw Publishers, Box 567, Wheaton, Illinois, 60189. Printed in the United States of America.

ISBN 0-87788-159-6

Cover design and illustration © 1993 by David LaPlaca

Library of Congress Cataloging-in-Publication Data

Upton, Rosemary J.
The court and the kingdom : a novel / by Rosemary J. Upton.
p. cm.
ISBN 0-87788-159-6
1. Bible. N.T.—History of Biblical events—Fiction. 2. Jews—History—168 B.C.-135 A.D.—Fiction. 3. Man-woman relationships—Israel—Fiction. 4. Jesus Christ—Fiction. I. Title.
PS3571.P54C6 1993
813'.54—dc20 93-4224
CIP

To
all the Joannas who balance marriage
and following their heart's desire,
and
all the Chuzas who must finally choose
between the Court and the Kingdom

HERODIAN FAMILY

A Partial Genealogy

3 B.C.—A.D. 37

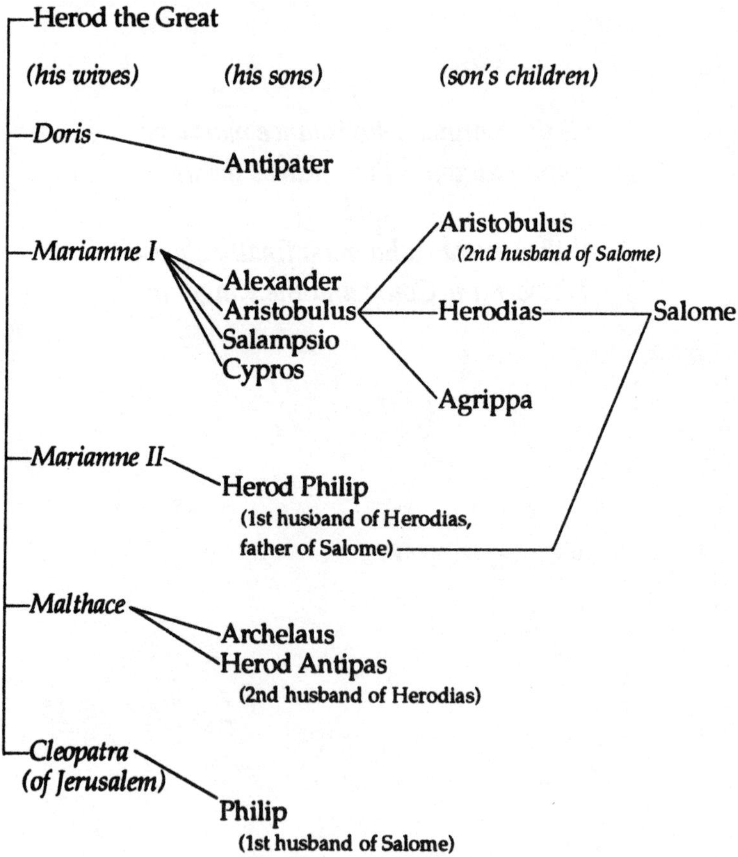

The wives of Herod the Great are in italics.
He had five other wives that are not listed here:
Pallas, Phaedra, Elpis, and two others that are unknown.
Herod the Great had ten sons. Nine sons are listed.

MAJOR CHARACTERS

*Joanna, wife of Chuza
*Chuza (Cuza), Herod's steward
*Susanna, follower of Christ
*Herod Antipas, ruler in Galilee
*Herodias, Herod's second wife
*Salome, daughter of Herodias
*Manaen, schooled with Herod at Rome
*Agrippa, brother of Herodias
*Cypros, Agrippa's wife
*Jesus the Christ

MINOR CHARACTERS

Beth, mother of Joanna
Samuel, father of Joanna
Rabbin Kesil, Samuel's friend
*Arabian princess, Herod's first wife
*John the Baptist
Emis, Joanna's servant
Lia, Susanna's servant
Monaea, Beth's servant and Joanna's "mother"
*Aristobolus, brother of Herodias and Agrippa
*Philip the tetrarch, half brother of Herod
*Joseph Caiaphas, high priest at Jerusalem
*Mary Magdalene
*Miriam of Jerusalem, follower of Christ
*Salome, wife of Zebedee
*Zebedee, father of James and John

*** *denotes real historical persons***

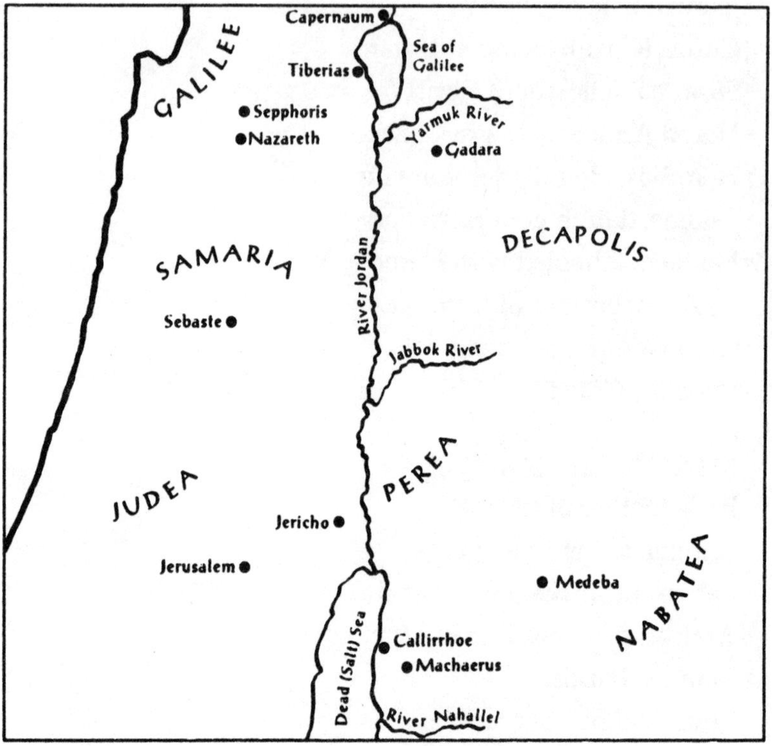

Capernaum
Sea of Galilee
Tiberias
GALILEE
Sepphoris
Nazareth
Yarmuk River
Gadara
DECAPOLIS
SAMARIA
River Jordan
Sebaste
Jabbok River
PEREA
JUDEA
Jericho
Jerusalem
Medeba
NABATEA
Dead (Salt) Sea
Callirrhoe
Machaerus
River Nahallel

Dear Reader,

A year of research was accomplished before a word of *Joanna* was written. The historical facts are influential in almost all the fictional events. Primarily it is the story of Joanna and Chuza, of Herod's court, but includes many other prominent figures of the Galilean seat of power.

For your information an Author's Notes section is provided at the end of the book. Check it by chapter if a question comes to mind. You might be delighted to learn some of the little-known facts of those times.

Now, may you enjoy stepping into the past, meeting the characters, and walking in their sandals.

Rosemary Upton

Acknowledgments

My thanks are extended to those who read portions of the manuscript and commented on the content: Norman Rorher, Rev. John Warren Steen, Margie Starkey, and Kistler London.

Special thanks go to Beulah Tate, who shared her sources of knowledge on ancient tradition, becoming a chief encourager, and grammarian to the completion of the manuscript, and to my husband, Hugh Upton, for his practical help and faith in this project.

My gratitude is extended to Dr. Paul Maier, novelist, theologian, and professor of ancient history at Western Michigan University, who gave of his valuable time to read the manuscript and comment on the historical research.

To each one I am most grateful.

Prologue

After the death of Herod the Great in 4 B.C. Jewish rebellions erupt throughout Judea and Galilee while Rome decides which son of Herod will succeed him on the throne. Under orders from Caesar, Syrian forces with Nabatean (Arabian) auxiliary troops squelch the insurrection. They burn the palace at Sepphoris, the capitol of Galilee, to rout Judas, son of Hezekiah, who had seized its arsenal and made it his stronghold.

PART I

THE COURT

3 B.C.–A.D. 23

Chapter 1

Samuel was torn between his concern for Beth, who lay in agony on her mat, and the battle that waged outside in the city streets. A reflection of fire danced upon the walls of the chamber, mocking his prayers to the Almighty One and adding to the fear-charged atmosphere.

From the window he could see the palace only a short distance from his own residence. It burned like Gehenna itself! Or hell, if one believed in such a place. Flames leapt high in the air as if they were claws scratching at heaven. Smoke billowed above his beautiful city of Sepphoris. The heat and energy closed about the four occupants of the room like a vise, and the smell oppressed both nostrils and lungs.

Beth, soaked in perspiration, was doubly tormented. She was now more than thirty hours in labor. The midwife crouched beside her in the shadowy room, feeling more than seeing the progress of the new life fighting to be born.

"Soon," she whispered to the woman of forty, whose face twisted in pain. "It will be over soon." Her eyes refused to give any message to the eyes of the young woman bathing her mistress's forehead, even though they implored her. The servant, Monaea, dipped the cloth again.

Samuel overheard the midwife's reassuring words and turned from the window to come to Beth's side. He would not let the midwife keep him from her. Customary or not, these were extenuating circumstances. They had been forced by the raging flames and, in danger for their lives, had fled to the farthest room of his opulent home—a barren corner, the safest place within these walls.

Was there any safe place? Perhaps they were all as good as dead. If so, what did it matter to a Sadducee, such as himself, who did not believe in eternal life and rewards, to defile himself with his wife's birthing blood? There is nothing beyond the grave anyway, and if they should live he would fulfill the requirements for purification according to Levitical law. In all honesty, it was not only by circumstance, but by choice that he remained by her side as she struggled once again to give life to a child that was the two of them become one flesh, his only posterity.

Beth clasped his hand in superhuman strength, crushing the bones of his knuckles together. It was the grip of a man, not a tiny woman. Her face gleamed oily and wet with mingled tears and sweat. She tossed her head from side to side, strands of long dark hair sticking like webs against her skin. Her teeth were clenched.

Beth refused to scream in response to the gripping pain. *Was this dream-terror?* she wondered. The crazy reflections on the wall made grotesque figures that seemed ready to pounce and devour her. And the noise, the yelling, was it in her mind, or as it seemed, outside in the streets?

"What's happening?" she managed to ask, although her teeth chattered when she did not clench them. "All the noise . . ."

As he bent over her, Samuel's face seemed older than his forty-five years. It sagged unnaturally and was etched with worry.

Her eyes held his relentlessly. Should he tell her? Didn't she have enough to dwell on right now? She shouldn't be concerned with anything but the child. He looked at Monaea as if to find the answer in her beloved servant's fearful eyes.

"Tell me," Beth demanded.

Samuel chose his words carefully. "King Aretas of the Nabateans has entered the city to—to liberate it from the insurrection of Judas the Galilean."

"The Arabians," she moaned. "What will happen to us?"

"We'll be all right. We're innocent of any involvement in the revolt."

Technically true, he thought, *but how do those who plunder know? And what about the spreading of the fire?* He wished they could leave the city as others were doing. Yet, the sound of neighing horses, the clash of swords and screams, denied the safety of such a move. Perhaps they were better off here.

A door burst open. Framed in the entrance stood an Arabian warrior, his face and body undiscernable except in silhouette. Behind him Samuel could hear other soldiers stomping about and his servants scrambling to get out of their way. From the direction of the stables below came the sound of horses being moved and their protesting whinnies.

They are taking what they want, he thought. The gold and silver ornaments throughout his home would be gone. *Well, let them take what they will!* But his fear for Beth created an anger that wouldn't be contained. He jumped to his feet.

"Why do you come here?" he demanded. "We are loyal to Rome and have nothing to do with sedition. Get out! Have you no concern for a woman whose time is at hand?"

The warrior faltered for only a moment. He evaluated the scene before him, then turned and left.

The bawling of the newborn infant drew Samuel to his knees near the mat again. The midwife lifted the child, a mass of trembling, slimy humanity onto a clean linen cloth and placed it in the new father's hands. The squirming baby was red and angry, as angry as Samuel had been only a moment before. Expertly the midwife tied the twine about the cord and snipped. Then she turned her attention to Beth.

Samuel held the screaming child high to the Almighty and began to laugh in hysterical relief, hearing himself as though his voice was part of the ghastly chaos around them.

"A live child! Praise the Creator of the heavens and the earth!"

"My lord," the midwife called to him. The emergency in her voice interrupted Samuel's momentary relief, and tension swirled around him again. He looked at the silent, exhausted form on the mat. Monaea still knelt at Beth's head, cradling her face.

"Give Monaea the child, my lord," the older woman commanded. "She knows how to cleanse it with the salt."

When he had released the baby to the young servant, the old midwife drew him aside. The permanent frown on her wrinkled face deepened. "She hemorrhages," came the hoarse whisper. "I can't stop the flow. If you wish to speak to her you must do it now, before she falls into the deep sleep."

No! It can't be true, he thought. What was she saying? Yahweh had blessed them with a live child. There were times, when the others had issued from her lifeless, that he knew she wanted to die—but not now. He would tell her—she must know—the child lives!

He knelt beside her, holding her small hand almost as tightly as she had held his. "Beth. Beth."

Her eyes fluttered open and fixed him with a look of desolation.

"The child lives, Beth. It lives." His eyes implored her to respond. A wan smile rewarded him.

"Is it a boy?" she asked, barely audible.

Samuel hesitated. "It's a strong child with a healthy cry." He fought the choking grip of fear in his throat. She must not know her danger. She must fight to live.

"Your eyes swim with disappointment," Beth accused.

"No, my love, with joy."

"Is it a son then?"

He wished with all his heart that he could say it was a boy, not for himself, but for her. She must not slip away from him thinking that she had disappointed him.

"Yes, Beth, we have a fine son."

The old midwife looked at Samuel, startled. His eyes bore into hers, commanding silence. Beth sighed and closed her eyes.

"She sleeps, my lord," the midwife said. "I don't know if we can arouse her again."

Samuel was trembling. A part of him wanted to shake her awake, demand her well-being, and another part wanted to clutch her to himself, denying the unseen power that took her from him. Why would God give them four dead children in succession and now turn the joy of a live birth into sorrow? Samuel's soul was as ravaged as the city of Sepphoris.

❖ ❖ ❖

"And what will you name her?" the rabbi asked when Monaea had retreated from the room with the sleeping child.

"Joanna," Samuel answered.

"God is gracious?" he questioned, translating the infant's name.

"If we can't believe that, we have no hope," Samuel said.

"You have a strong faith after all," the rabbi declared.

"Rabbin Kesil, can you say that in view of the debates we've had concerning the Holy Scriptures?"

"There is room in Judaism for individual thought as long as we uphold the Law of Moses," the rabbi said. "I have always found our discussions disturbing, but stimulating."

Samuel stroked his thick, dark beard. His shaggy brows knit together on his broad forehead. "I've cherished our friendship for many reasons, Rabbin Kesil, but never more than in the wake of this political storm." He glanced about his home, stripped of rare carpets and fine metal objects. The walls were discolored by the smoke that had smothered the city as the Herodian palace became a stone shell of flaming ruins.

The faction of Jews loyal to Rome had been caught in the middle and suffered the devastation that covered Sepphoris even as those who had revolted. Samuel was grateful that his house still stood. Some of his servants had hidden and had escaped being taken as slaves by the Syrian army and their auxiliary Arabian troops under

Aretas the Nabatean. Losing the goods of one's household to plundering hordes was infinitely better than losing one's freedom—and many of the residents of Galilee's capital city had lost both goods and freedom. Those guilty of the insurrection under Judas, or even of sympathizing with the Jewish revolt, were reduced now to slavery. In southern Palestine it was worse. Two thousand Jewish rebels in the province of Judea had been crucified for sedition.

Varus the Syrian held control until Caesar finally named which son of Herod the Great would rule. Since the death of the Jewish king, there had been many revolts and much unrest while his numerous sons contended for his throne, albeit under Roman authority.

"The political storm will not be over if Caesar names Archelaus king," Rabbin Kesil predicted. "He is worse than his father. However, Antipas and Philip are rather young to handle such a high-spirited nation."

"A terrible time to raise a child," Samuel said, "especially a girl."

The rabbi pulled at the long coil of hair at his ear thoughtfully. His closely set, squinting eyes gave the impression of continual scrutiny. "You will marry again and produce a son and heir," he said, misunderstanding Samuel's remark.

"I'll never marry again," Samuel declared. "The Almighty has smiled upon me once and frowned too many times. Joanna will be my heir."

"Nonsense . . . "

"I've studied the Scriptures," Samuel pressed on. "The ancients, according to Leviticus, sometimes named their daughters as heirs."

"It is not customary," Rabbin Kesil said. "And extremely unwise. She would be prey to those who hold fortune above all else."

"My Joanna will be wise," Samuel said with confidence. "I shall see to her education and her skills in the ways of commerce."

The rabbi's eyes narrowed even more. "And she will remain a virgin?" he asked in disbelief. "Where would be the future for your accomplishments then?"

"She will marry well—and give me a grandson for an heir," Samuel declared. Then he laughed at himself. "The child is still an infant, and my fortune is nearly depleted! It will take years to mold the child and rebuild the business, but in time I will do both!"

Chapter 2

The kingdom was split. Augustus Caesar divided it between three sons of Herod the Great. Archelaus, the oldest, was given Judea with the promise of the title *king,* if after a given time, he ruled well. Antipas, his younger full brother, who was favored by the Syrian governor, was given Galilee and Perea. Philip, a younger half-brother, was given the territory of Batanea, Trachonitis, Iturea, and Auranitis.

Antipas was in his early twenties when he began to rule in Sepphoris with the strength of Rome behind him, practically applied by Syrian forces. An influx of Arabians was grimly tolerated. Uncertainty was the mark of the times, but slowly the young tetrarch began to rebuild his domain. It was rumored that he relied heavily on advice from his middle-aged steward and other financial ministers, while depending upon the auxiliaries to train his own cohorts. Except for minor scrimmages on the Perean border from Bedouin raids, Galilee began to relax under the new rule.

In time, Samuel rebuilt his fortune, trading in fine metals of gold and silver. Valuable home furnishings were replaced, and a toddling Joanna was allowed to place her fingerprints on any object, regardless of value. Monaea was instructed to remove the child from Samuel's presence only by signal from him, and that signal was never given unless she was tired or misbehaved.

Rabbin Kesil became accustomed to Joanna's golden curls bobbing in and out of view by Samuel's knee as they talked. Business associates, Jews and Gentiles alike, were no longer astonished to see the amber-eyed girl climb into her father's lap and watch them intently from under thick, dark lashes. What did she absorb of their discussions concerning events at Rome or Jerusalem?

She was often present when he planned business transactions with his steward, Helek. Samuel reasoned that Joanna would learn more by observation than he could ever teach her, and he was rewarded when the child reached an age to ask intelligent questions about what she heard. Helek was like a grandfather to her, patiently answering each query, no matter how trivial, for she delighted him with her growing awareness.

Joanna couldn't remember how her father conveyed the fact that business was "personal" and not to be discussed with her best friend, Susanna, but early in her training he did. She knew that Susanna didn't have a similar kind of relationship with her father. Joanna would never jeopardize her trusted position, for she was smug with the knowledge and recognized its advantages. At an early age she could carry on a conversation with anyone who crossed the threshold of Samuel Bar Simeon, and she acquired a reputation for being personable as well as beautiful.

When Joanna was four, Antipas began a complete rebuilding of the city of Sepphoris, in addition to the Herodian palace. It took years in the developing. Included in the architectural plans was a magnificent waterworks that would make Sepphoris the flower of Galilee.

Masons and carpenters worked for years, coming from the Galilean cities surrounding the capital—from Cana and especially from Nazareth, which was only four miles to the northeast. With plenty of water, Samuel decided to build a terraced garden adjoining the main room of his prestigious home. Joanna was ten years old, and she watched the workmen with fascination.

When the masons had laid the rock paths, installed the sundial, and mortared the rocks for the gardens, the nurserymen planted an abundance of flowering shrubs. The brilliant colors and varieties turned Joanna's city home into an exotic paradise. Samuel included a stone bench secluded by juniper trees. This became Joanna's "house," her own miniature dwelling, where she could play at being a grown woman. In time, this place would evoke memories of events that would kindle emotions of both ecstasy and despair. Right now it was a special place that Samuel would never have thought to provide. The fantasies of a little girl were outside the understanding of a father. Monaea understood. Monaea always knew when Joanna wanted to be alone. Joanna often wondered if perhaps her mother had been like Monaea, only more beautiful, of course.

Samuel did think to include a game-slate. He built it into one of the low stone walls. Once, Rabbin Kesil had arrived while they were playing.

"You spend your time in child's games, my friend?" he mused aloud.

"She thinks it is a game, but it is teaching her the competitive skills for life. You'll see!" Samuel said.

The carpentry work to finish the project was minor, only some lattice work and support beams to create the transition from indoor to outdoor living. For this Samuel engaged a mild-mannered man from Nazareth who brought his young son. Joanna was intrigued by the boy, who was about thirteen. He was most serious about his apprenticeship. When she spoke to him, he answered, but never stopped his task for a moment.

"You do exacting work," she commented, borrowing a word from her father's vocabulary.

"Thank you. My father trusts me to do my best," he said. His eyes studied the plumb-line. Thick, light brown hair capped his forehead. Soft and slightly curly, it was cropped above the brows to keep it from falling in his eyes as he worked.

"What's your name?" she asked.

"Jesus," he answered.

"That's a common name," she remarked without intending to offend him. "I know several boys named Jesus. Jesus what?"

"Jesus Bar David."

"Oh, I thought you would say, Jesus Bar Joseph. I thought the carpenter was your father. And I know my father spoke of him as Joseph."

Jesus smiled. "His name is Bar David too," he explained. "We are of the house of David."

She laughed. "You mean David the king?" Then in disbelief, "Are you telling me that you are a prince pretending to be a carpenter?"

He smiled. "We are descendants of David," he said again.

"There must be any number of you!" she stated. "It's been generations since David ruled."

He appeared busy and didn't answer.

"Do you know that Archelaus was just removed as ruler in Judea?" she asked. "Caesar has banished him to Gaul!" She flung her arms wide to indicate a faraway place, pleased with her knowledge of political affairs. "A Roman governor has been appointed. But Father thinks that Antipas will someday be king."

Jesus nodded.

It annoyed her that he knew. Susanna had been surprised when Joanna told her. But then, Susanna was young and rarely knew anything important. Jesus was older, and even though he was only a carpenter, he probably went many places.

"Did you go to Jerusalem for Succoth?" she asked.

"Oh, yes."

"My father and I stayed in a booth this time," she shared excitedly.

"We stay in a booth," Jesus said. "We camp with all of our relatives."

Joanna looked away. He had scored one on her as sure as if they had been at the game-slate. *I wonder what it would be like to have sisters and brothers and cousins,* she thought wistfully.

❖ ❖ ❖

When Joanna was twelve, Samuel took her to Greece and Rome for the first time. She had studied their history, languages, and politics as well as her own ancient Scriptures and the Mosaic Law. She had been tutored far beyond most girls of her age.

When she was fourteen, Samuel escorted Joanna to the Herodian palace for a banquet given by Antipas, who was often referred to simply as Herod or Herod Antipas, in anticipation that he would one day be named king. It was Joanna's first time inside the monstrous structure. Although recently renewed, it looked old, for it was made of large dark stones that were softened little by the oriental fixtures and furnishings. It was not to be compared to the magnificent buildings of Athens and Rome.

Her attention wasn't drawn to the surroundings, since they failed to impress her, but she waited impatiently for her opportunity to meet Herod Antipas. Although she had met many important people in her brief span of years, she had only seen the tetrarch from a distance when he left or entered the capital city and his entourage marched by her father's home.

Her heart fluttered disturbingly when the the tetrarch greeted her.

"So this is the beautiful woman who graces the home of Samuel Bar Simeon," he said. The ruler, who was now in his mid-thirties, was handsomely groomed after the fashion of Rome. His dark eyes played familiar games with hers. After all, he was unmarried.

"Yes, my lord," she answered. Then realizing that her response sounded pompous, she faltered. "I—I mean—you're so kind, my lord." Her face flushed and her hand sprang to the gold necklace about her throat.

He laughed with delight. The twitching smile was easy to see on his clean-shaven face. Dark eyebrows arched. "I've heard it rumored that nothing daunts the composure of Joanna of Sepphoris. I'm flattered to have cracked that facade. Cool restraint is never so becoming!"

Joanna held his remarks to her heart for months afterward, rolling them over in her mind for obscure meanings. Was he teasing her? Was he only making her relax? Did he like her? Was she really so beautiful? So graceful?

Samuel observed the change in his daughter and realized that she was becoming preoccupied with daydreams. He was proud of her. The darling little girl had turned into a lovely replica of Beth. Golden curls had been replaced by long chestnut swirls with golden glints. The amber eyes were sheltered by long, dark lashes against a golden olive complexion. Her body, so rounded at twelve and so tall and thin at thirteen, was now both rounded and thin in the most pleasing places. She was a woman.

It was time for him to consider a proper husband.

Chapter 3

Susanna absently twisted an ornament on her gown. Today she would take the most serious pledge that she would make in her entire life. In a matter of moments she would be sealed unto Jacob Bar Saul for life. It was her betrothal, but the promise was as binding as the wedding that would be celebrated a year from now. She felt alone, yet she stood in an arc with her groom, parents, and a few family friends.

She had always thought Joanna would be first. Her self-assured friend was so much older and wiser. Well, a year older anyway. She shook herself mentally and thought, *Silly child, you can't expect Joanna to lead you everywhere you go! At least she's here to witness it.*

In a way it was nice to be experiencing something before Joanna did. Joanna was always acting so smart. Susanna's dark eyes met her friend's. *I wonder what she's thinking now?* Her friend didn't seem to approve of Susanna's betrothal. *Maybe she's jealous.* Susanna knew the contract was very desirable; her father had told her so.

Joanna smiled reassuringly, trying to read the thoughts she saw in Susanna's luminous eyes. *How pretty she looks, and so much older with her hair caught into a net of tiny pearls.* The pearls nestled in her long raven hair like stars in the midnight sky. She was dressed elegantly for her betrothal in fine white linen with blue and gold threads interwoven to form a delicate pattern along the edge. Susanna was the daughter of a textile merchant, and Joanna knew that when it was time for the wedding, her bridal dress would be unmatched in all Galilee!

Jacob Bar Saul, the bridegroom, was a wealthy shipping magnate from the city of Caesarea. He was fifty-five. As they stood together, Susanna looked petite and childlike with her round face and large, dark eyes. Jacob was an attractive man, but he was old, as old as their fathers. Joanna, yet unbetrothed, was now fifteen. Susanna was fourteen. Sometimes a girl was betrothed much younger if her parents were anxious to settle the matter.

Susanna seemed happy. She didn't appear to share Joanna's worries. *Surely Jacob is kind,* Joanna thought. His face showed kindness, and he had kept until death the covenant of his youth with a first wife who was barren. He would be good to Susanna. What more could a girl expect? *Why do I always want more?* Joanna thought.

She glanced at the small group assembled. Susanna's parents, her young brother Abraham, Joanna's father as the "bride's witness," and Jacob's "friend of the bridegroom" stood in a half-circle on either side of the couple. A glass of wine had already been offered, and they sipped it solemnly. A meal would be served after the vows were said. Servants collected the wine glasses, and Jacob proceeded to present the contract. A bride-price, or *mohar,* had already been agreed upon. Now it was time for the ring. Joanna's breath caught in her throat. *If my excitement is so great, how must Susanna be feeling?* Susanna's dark eyes were lowered discreetly as Jacob slipped the ring on her finger. Then his deep voice repeated the ancient vow, "Behold, thou art consecrated unto me by this ring according to the laws of Israel."

There, it was done. Now it could only be undone by a writ of divorce and disgrace. It was so brief a moment to effect such a change in their lives. *How will our friendship change?* Joanna couldn't help wondering. They would live miles apart. *But not yet. Not for another year,* Joanna reassured herself. *Susanna and I can still be companions for another year until the wedding is celebrated.*

❖ ❖ ❖

Susanna rolled the dice and squealed her delight. She was disgustingly smug, Joanna thought, as she watched Susanna toss her black hair over her shoulder. It wasn't because she won the game! She had been self-satisfied for weeks now.

They sat in Samuel's garden surrounded by lush foliage and flowers. The polished stone game-slate was set in the cubit-high rock ledge that separated the stone path from an oasis of plants and shrubs. The girls perched on either side. Susanna's cheeks were pink from the warm sun and her excitement, lending vivid beauty.

"You know, Joanna, I still can't believe that I'm betrothed. Would you have thought that I would marry before you did?"

"You aren't married yet," Joanna reminded, "Besides, don't you think that I could be betrothed if I wanted to be? There's a lot to be considered before making a proper match."

Susanna glanced at her with dark eyes snapping. "You sound like you're taking part in the arrangement."

"Why not?"

"Oh, Joanna, don't be silly. Your father may favor you highly, but I'm sure that he's too conventional for that."

"What would you say if I told you he had chosen someone and I said no?"

"I wouldn't believe you."

"Well, I didn't actually say no. I just reminded him how lonely he would be without me and that maybe there would be a better match should we wait."

"Joanna, I don't know how you always manage to have your way! I wouldn't even try." She smiled in awe and turned the newly acquired gold ring on her finger. "Besides, my father has chosen a fine man, who is highly respected. It will be an honor to be his wife. Everyone will hold me in great esteem, and I will have a lovely home and many servants."

Her little speech was more than Joanna could take. She remembered the betrothal ceremony. Jacob Bar Saul was a childless widower. Before she realized what she was saying she spoke her uppermost thoughts.

"He's only interested in having a son."

The remark did not seem to bother Susanna. "Of course. So am I. Maybe he will be the Messiah."

"The Messiah is to be born of a virgin," Joanna reminded with disgust.

"So some claim," Susanna retorted. "Well, maybe you'll be the mother of the Messiah!"

❖ ❖ ❖

An endless moodiness had settled over Joanna. As the months slipped by, she felt as if she were marking time. It was Susanna who waited. Why should it have any effect on her?

Then Helek died, and although he had grown old and was ill for some time, the loss was painful. Her spirit rebelled against the changes in her life—changes over which she had no control. She continued to mourn him for weeks in deliberate sorrow.

Then, as if her spirit had become bored with sadness, a restlessness took over. One evening at dusk, she headed for the upper court of her home. Alone, she would watch the city transform itself from the hustle of daylight activities to solemn prayer, as one by one soft oil lamps became visible on the rooftops.

Samuel preferred the garden for his meditation. It was easy enough to face Jerusalem wherever you were, although Joanna failed to see the necessity. She had stopped formal prayer some time ago, when she was about twelve.

Helek's illness had rekindled a desire to pray, but her efforts were wasted! Her father said that Helek was old and that he went the way common to all mankind, according to the Scriptures. Afterward,

Joanna found even less reason to talk to the Almighty. That she should spend time in simple worship and recognition of him for who he was did not occur to her.

From the latticed colonnade that paralleled the garden, a stone stairway ascended to the upper court, hugging the outer wall of the main house. When she reached the top, twilight had painted the whole city in smoky hues of blue and gray, with a feather brushing of pink. A hush had settled on the land.

Not ten feet away stood a young man she had never seen before. His arms were folded across his chest, and his expression was one of contented preoccupation. She studied the dark complexion and thick dark hair. It swept back from his face, yet covered the ears and seemed as one with the thick beard. His profile was distinct. She expected an unhesitating nature. He was pleasant to look at, and she was disappointed when he became aware of her presence.

His eyes conveyed his pleasure in her as well. It did not surprise Joanna, for she knew that she was attractive to men.

"Who are you?" she asked bluntly. She disliked being taken off guard and feeling like an intruder in her own home.

"Your father's new steward," he replied. He was self-confident without arrogance.

"Quite a responsibility for one so young," she remarked with superiority. "Helek was much older."

"And in the manner of the elderly, he's gone to final rest." His eyes smiled. "I come highly recommended. I've passed your father's scrutiny, Miss; now must I pass yours?"

So he didn't like her reference to his age! Because she was younger herself, or in his opinion too presumptuous of her father's affairs? How could he know the liberty Samuel had given her?

"Of course not." She shrugged and turned to go. Why had she bothered to talk to him in the first place? She was annoyed. Was it him, or herself, or maybe just the circumstances? She wasn't sure, but he was much too confident. She stopped and faced him again. "How do you know he is my father? I could be his wife."

"He told me that he had an inquisitive daughter."

Now it was clear by the smile in his eyes that he was amused by her. Resentment swelled within her. The other servants knew their place with her; she would see to it that this one did too.

Later she learned that the young steward's name was Chuza and that he was some sort of genius, a master of economics. He had been born and raised in Nabatea, of Bedouin parents, but his uncle, who made his home here, recognized his potential and persuaded Chuza's father to allow him to be schooled in Galilee. He had lived in Sepphoris for ten years.

It was not long before Chuza was dining with them as Helek had. This was typical of Samuel. His cosmopolitan nature made him liberal in his contacts and dealings with Gentile merchants. Joanna was accustomed to mingling with the Jewish elders of the Galilean Sanhedrin, which convened in Sepphoris, as well as Greek businessmen and Roman officials. How her father managed to keep his basic Jewish beliefs was hard for her to understand. *Tolerance* was a word that he used to describe that relationship, but she never dreamed that it could include a Nabatean.

"I don't know why my father hired you," Joanna blurted one evening as they waited for Samuel to join them for the evening meal. She had a habit of beginning a conversation right where her thoughts were. "He should hate you."

Chuza's startled brown eyes almost made her laugh. "I mean," she added, "after what your people did to us!"

"During the Jewish revolt?" he guessed.

"Of course. Do you know that they stripped our house bare? They invaded our home while my mother was—was—dying!"

"They were enlisted by Rome to squelch the rebellion," Chuza defended. "Besides, that was fifteen years ago. I was only twelve and back in Nabatea."

"Did you know about it?" Joanna's tone was still accusing.

"Only later. My uncle told me about it when I came here. He thought I might find prejudice." The smile played about his eyes again. "But I'd hardly expect it from someone who can't even remember the uprising, Joanna."

She liked the way he pronounced her name with the slight Arabic accent. She hadn't thought about whether she liked her name before, but when he said it, it sounded unique, like something precious and delicate. An uncomfortable emotion stirred within her, one she had difficulty understanding. His eyes became serious again and her heart wrestled with her mind over the necessity of the offensive verbal games she played with him. She failed to think of a quick retort.

"Every nation has its uncivilized people who are ignorant and uncontrollable in time of war, Joanna," he spoke gravely. "Many of my people are highly educated, such as my Uncle Abdul."

"And you."

"He has seen to it," Chuza answered with a measure of pride. "Abdul has made his living well in Galilee. I will too. There is such a mixture of nationalities here; it would not be so easy in Judea."

"My father treats all men the same."

"It would be hard to find a successful man who alienates himself from most of society."

Joanna pondered the remark. Was that the reason for her father's tolerance? Because it was good for business? Samuel was passionate in his own interpretation of Judaism. His lengthy debates with Rabbin Kesil proved that. He was a Sadducee, for the most part, while the rabbi was a Pharisee. Yet they sparred with mutual respect, unlike some, such as Susanna's father, Obed, who became upset with anyone who disagreed with him. Samuel reserved his debates for Rabbin Kesil and did not discuss religion with his other associates, Jews or Gentiles. She was glad that he was more open-minded than Obed Bar Dan. Susanna could never discuss ideas with her father as Joanna had been taught to do. On only one thing Samuel was unbending. Joanna could voice her opinion on religion as long as she upheld the Law of Moses.

On questions of business, it was stimulating for Joanna to find that expressing her thoughts deepened Samuel's respect for her logic. The only thing he would not accept was if she offered no opinion.

Lately, in an effort to develop her economic understanding, he had provided an allotment for her to use. Since the amount was minimal, failures were not disastrous and when she did make an error in judgment, he would show her the ways in which he had been sure her choice would be faulty. But Samuel allowed Joanna to fail, and the lesson was well learned.

This "gaming with investments" was appalling to Susanna's father, who thought that teaching Joanna to control her own funds would do her an injustice in the end. Once she had heard the two men discussing it, and now their words repeated in her mind.

"Isn't it better to arrange a stable and secure marriage, rather than to trust Joanna's abilities to manage wisely?" Obed said. "What woman is capable of keeping herself from the exploitation of men, who hold the reins in world affairs?"

"I intend to make her my heir as the Levitical Law allows," persisted Samuel, "and to arrange a secure marriage as well."

"Then choose her husband carefully," warned his friend, "for you will make him rich."

"I will be able to esteem him as a son," Samuel spoke confidently. "He will be one whose own wealth is assured, so that my daughter's virtues will be his highest gain. Why do you think I deliberate so long?"

Joanna was preoccupied with her memories, and she was unaware that Chuza had greeted Samuel as he entered the room for the evening meal.

Chapter 4

Susanna was busy with her plans for marriage and ever eager to tell Joanna the latest development in the arrangements.

"Can we talk of nothing else?" Joanna asked.

"Well, I thought you were interested."

They were playing knucklebones in Samuel's garden. Susanna's face was puzzled. Joanna didn't care. The thought that there were still three months yet to wait until the year of betrothal was over wearied her.

"I'm going home then," Susanna said, jumping up. When Joanna made no further comment, she left. Joanna stayed where she was, staring at the dice. The game wasn't over yet. Who could say who would have won? What did it matter anyway?

She picked up her lyre and began to play a melancholy psalm. As the last strains of the music died, she heard Chuza's voice behind her.

"Your friend didn't stay long."

"No, she's very busy with her wedding plans." She fumbled to put aside her lyre. Her heart had begun to beat abnormally. She could feel the heat in her face. For some time now she had found it difficult to look into Chuza's dark eyes without losing her pattern of thought and becoming flustered. It unnerved her. She was used to being in control and felt out of control in his presence.

Her change in attitude toward him had come subtly. He remained remote and businesslike, but in his eyes she saw something more than the casualness he portrayed. His smile no longer assessed her as an amusing child, and Joanna was heady with the knowledge that she also affected him. There was no longer any desire to challenge him.

"Your father told me that we would be dining on the upper balcony this evening."

"Oh, what makes today so special?"

Chuza smiled. "I'm sure I don't know. Perhaps it's the promise of a lovely sunset." He looked toward the sky, which was already pink-orange clouds against a brilliant blue backdrop. There was a stillness in the air, and it was as if they were suspended in the heavy scent of the flowers around them. They walked to the other side of the garden to climb the steps to the upper court, the place where she had first met Chuza and resented his being there to take Helek's place.

Sepphoris, the beautiful "ornament of Galilee" came into view. Samuel already occupied one of the reclining benches on the porch. Joanna was aware of the roundness of her father's stomach. Chuza was so lean. Samuel had a round face, and his beard was startlingly black and white. Two broad silver stripes followed a line from the corners of his mouth to the end of his neatly trimmed beard. His bushy brows always needed a combing.

He greeted them from his couch—a bit jubilantly, Joanna noticed. There must be an investment of sizable proportions to excite him so much. She dropped down on the huge cushion placed at the side of her father's bench. This was typical of the intimacy they shared. She rested her elbow on his bench and they clasped hands in greeting. The low table, laden with more delicacies than three could eat, was between them, within reach of them all.

Two servants, one carrying the basin and the other the pitcher of water, completed the ritual of washing hands. No water would touch more than one pair of hands, but would be poured freshly on each. Then Samuel, beard in motion, gave the blessing in a monotone.

"Blessed art thou, King of the Universe, who bringest forth food from the earth."

Conversation began as usual, centering upon the happenings of the day. Finally Joanna sensed that her father was approaching the real news. He had met with Jared Bar Seth, and they had discussed a contract, not openly, of course. But in the manner of good Jewish judgment, they had sparred verbally. Now a more formal approach was to be expected.

Joanna had stopped listening carefully. With her father talking and Chuza so intent on what he was saying, she had an opportunity to watch the young man. She liked his dark eyes the most, with their thick, black brows knit in such serious pondering. But his beard was fascinating, too. It had a sable look about it and promised softness to the touch.

Her first indication that something was wrong came from a change in Chuza's expression. In a moment it moved from intent to wary and then melted into depression.

"And, of course, I would have you, Chuza, to act as friend of the bride."

In confusion Joanna sorted out what was taking place. It wasn't a merger in the usual business sense. Her father had found a suitable bridegroom. There had been others considered, but this time he was more excited than he had been before. She looked at her father, who was busy twisting a large grape from its stem. Her eyes met Chuza's. They were full of hopelessness.

So, she thought, *his feelings are as deep as my own.*

❖ ❖ ❖

Joanna had not done so daring a thing before in her life. Waiting until the household was well past the hour of sleep, she cautiously made her way through the passageway with only the dim light of a small oil lamp in the alcove. If she encountered anyone, she had already decided to pretend to be sleepwalking.

What if he weren't there? But she was sure that he would be. Out in the open colonnade, she could see the shadows of the garden trees and the faint outline of open skies. There was little moonlight. The stone path was hard to follow without causing noise. She headed for the three juniper trees that secluded the marble bench by the sundial. As she rounded the shrubs, Chuza's shadowy figure rose quickly from the bench and enveloped her in his arms, clasping her so tightly that she nearly lost her breath.

"You came!" he whispered into her ear.

She clung to him, feeling protected after her lonely night walk. "Of course," she answered, aware of the strong masculine scent of him and the strength of his arms. They stood holding each other, more in desperation than in tenderness. She felt the softness of his beard against her cheek and thought of how often she had desired to touch it. They had never so much as touched hands before, and now they were reluctant to let each other go.

He pulled her down to sit beside him on the bench. She could feel the cool marble penetrating her night garment and gave a shiver, partly of nervousness, partly of chill. With one quick move he enclosed her with his cloak. She wished that she might stay there forever, commanding time to stand still, that they would never have to face tomorrow. Like two refugees from dawn, they huddled and kissed and talked. It was as though they would fill a night with a lifetime of loving. Finally he held her away from him and looked into her eyes. Joanna's face was illumined by daylight's first rays.

"This is senseless; he would never consider my contract."

"He loves me," she reminded. "He's never denied me anything."

Chuza was sure she spoke the truth. How could Samuel resist? Even a father must feel the wonder of Joanna. Those amber eyes generated more love than he ever imagined. He felt their promise to submerge him in a pool of ecstasy for the asking.

"I'll speak to him before I do anything else. I only wish I had spoken before Jared Bar Seth."

"No. Let me talk to him first. I'll persuade him to understand our feelings. Then you can approach him at dinner tonight. You'll see; everything will be all right."

❖ ❖ ❖

Samuel's face took on the characteristics of a pomegranate. The twist of his mouth looked as if he had tasted one. Joanna steeled herself against the tidal wave of anger that loomed before her. Finally she watched his face melt into natural flesh tones once more.

Instinctively she knew that he was calculating his next move. She had played enough games with him to know how his mind worked. But she knew that she too possessed a sense of strategy.

"So you are in love with Chuza," he said with measured lightness, as though it were a poor joke.

She nodded, her amber eyes wide and unflinching.

"The daughter of a fine metal merchant is in love with her father's steward." His voice was strained control.

"And he with me, Father," she said defensively. Why did it sound so ridiculous when he said it?

"Of course; why not?" Samuel tapped the tips of his fingers together, purposely assuming a relaxed posture.

She was puzzled. "Are you saying that he is interested in making his position better?"

"Not only that, but his finances too." His wiry brows lifted for effect.

"You are so used to thinking in terms of political and financial contracts that you don't even care how I feel," she accused.

"Feelings come and feelings go." He shrugged.

"You once told me that you loved my mother."

"I did, although I didn't meet her until our betrothal. You see, true loving comes with time and shared experience. You will understand once you are married to Jared Bar Seth." It was a dismissal of the subject.

"Father, I told you. I will not agree to a marriage with Jared Bar Seth." Tears of frustration sprang to her eyes. "I will marry only Chuza."

"He has not seen fit to approach me." Samuel cited one more reason for his unworthiness.

"Because I convinced him not to talk to you before I did. I knew you would react this way."

"Then you admit I have just cause." Samuel trapped her.

"I didn't say that." She sensed that she was losing ground. "I knew that the money would come into it. Oh, Father, look how much Chuza has saved you in these past months. You've told me how brilliantly he negotiates, how much you depend on him."

"He is smart," Samuel agreed. "I didn't know how smart! Tell me, Joanna," he asked cynically, "who will act as friend of the groom?"

"You make light of the matter when it is the most important thing in life to me."

"How am I to respond? You're a foolish child. It's time that you grew up and realized that all of life is not a playground. It's my own fault for spoiling you."

"My happiness always mattered to you before."

"And you always trusted my judgment when it came to what would bring you happiness," Samuel reminded.

"But I'm a woman now."

"A child in a woman's body. What do you know of disappointment? Haven't you gotten everything you ever wanted?"

Joanna raised her chin and looked away.

"Your mother and I knew great disappointment. We lost three children before they could be brought to the fullness of time. Then a son, born dead."

"Yes, I know." She hated what he was doing to her. "My mother gave her life to deliver me, and you won't let me forget that."

"Don't you see? It's my deep love for you that gives me such concern." His voice dropped to barely a whisper.

Joanna's emotions drained her resolve. She avoided his eyes, fighting a rush of tears.

"Joanna," he pressed gently, "this is just the desire that sometimes possesses a young woman."

"You think our love is just some silly feeling that can be put aside." Joanna shook her head.

"Have you given so little thought to circumstances that you would think I could welcome a foreigner as a son or half-breeds as my heritage?"

"That's the real reason, isn't it?" The bonds of sentiment snapped, and resentment took its place. "Because he's Arabian!"

"We are children of faith," Samuel reminded. "The faith of our father, Abraham."

"He's a son of Abraham too."

"Through Ishmael—not the son of promise—not Isaac. Don't you know that the Nabateans have left the true God and worship pagan gods?"

"Father, you've always shown tolerance. You've welcomed him to our table."

"But I would not sit at his! It would be defilement for a Hebrew to eat unclean food. Would you like to think that you could not invite your father to the home of your marriage?"

"To come or not would be your choice," Joanna bristled. She recognized his hypocrisy.

"It's a choice I will not need to make." His voice was hard; his eyes narrow, under the bushy brows. "I've never required your obedience before; I've never had to. But if I must, I will."

Joanna's face flushed with anger. "I will not agree to the betrothal, and if you force me, I shall be unfaithful to my vows at the first opportunity."

"You talk like a common harlot!"

"I'll be Chuza's wife, or you'll see me stoned!" It was a rash declaration, and Joanna felt herself propelled down the steep incline of such a decision.

Her statement was a sword between them. Samuel didn't move. His daughter's will had not shown itself so strongly since she was a toddler. Then he had delighted in her determination toward independence. It proved that she had an unquenchable spirit, but there were times when her best efforts went down to defeat and she sprawled upon the floor, ringlets of golden curls flung in a mass on the carpet, and her feet would beat out her frustration.

The tantrums always ended. He simply ignored them, and when she was exhausted she would seek his consolation. Samuel spoke calmly.

"There will be no contract with Chuza."

A stranger sat before her. She had seen the cold, penetrating eyes before, but their fury had never been directed at her. She felt the first wash of clammy fear.

Chapter 5

Nothing in Joanna's upbringing had prepared her for the time when she could not reason with Samuel. She was shocked to discover that Chuza was dismissed from the household and his position without further consideration. For weeks she used every persuasive device she had absorbed in her years of watching Samuel in his business practices. Finally she resorted to emotional female tactics, so foreign to her thinking, but which she felt would be effective because of his love for her.

Samuel was as immovable as the Herodian city walls.

Meanwhile, no word came from Chuza. She was certain that he had returned to Abdul's home, and she could not believe that the strength of their confessed love or his determined nature would allow him to accept Samuel's verdict. He must have tried to reach her and couldn't.

When she made her decision, it was so easy that she wondered why she didn't do it sooner. Samuel had made it clear that he would not allow them to see each other. Joanna was stubborn, but she had never been rebellious, and she knew Samuel did not take her threat seriously. However, her father was smart enough to let matters rest before insisting on the betrothal with Jared Bar Seth. From time to time he urged, but never coerced.

One morning Joanna arose, dressed, and calmly left the house, taking nothing with her. She walked to the Arab sector of the city and inquired for the home of Abdul. With this impulsive act begun, she moved as in a dream, concentrating on one objective—to be with Chuza.

The air was cool and damp from the dew. The sun cast a pinkish glow on the stone pavement as she walked. Early morning sounds of the city coming to life were comforting. A braying donkey stubbornly resisted its young master. Vendors called their wares. A child scrambled after a pet goat. Women carried their watering jugs upon their heads as they went to the common well. Two businessmen, momentarily pausing at an intersection, argued in Arabic. Joanna was only vaguely aware of it all. Few eyes bothered to observe her closely in the hustle of the morning traffic.

The homes of the upper-class Arabs were a maze of squarish whitewashed domes with little to distinguish them from one another, but finally she found the proper street and number.

At the door of Abdul's home the realization of what she was doing threatened to drown her resolve. Inside, she was a bird that thrashes about not knowing which way to fly when faced with danger. It was no time to be indecisive. She lifted the huge brass ring and allowed it to drop.

A servant opened the portal.

At first her voice faltered. She began again. "Is this the home of Abdul Benzanias? I'm looking for one named Chuza Benzanias."

A thought struck panic within. What if he wasn't there?

The man servant, small and bent, head covered by the thickly twisted Arabian headdress, stepped aside and motioned for her to come in. He disappeared, and she glanced about the cool entrance to the home. It was bare except for a woven mat and several pair of sandals neatly placed in one corner. The adjoining hall must lead to an atrium. She would hear a smattering of Arabic, swallowed by open air.

A man of about forty came toward her. He squinted in the darkness. His features were sharp angles etched against the light backdrop. Penetrating eyes made her a captured moth.

"I'm Joanna," she murmured.

His eyebrows shot up and the small eyes were as pebbles. "Get Chuza," he growled at the servant who had followed him back along the hall.

The servant scurried and an eternity elapsed while Joanna waited with the older man, feeling the rays of his scrutiny like the scorching sun. The image of Chuza approaching from behind his uncle brought a tremor of relief.

"Joanna! By all the gods, what are you doing here?" he demanded.

Her courage completely crumbled. *He's stricken,* she thought. *What have I done? I'm foolish in his eyes. Perhaps Father was right—Chuza doesn't really love me at all.*

❖ ❖ ❖

The hoofs of the Arabian stallion pounded the uneven trail relentlessly. Joanna's side ached. She was like a bundle of disconnected bones jostling about on the horse's back, although her arms were securely locked about Chuza's waist. The sweat of the horse was warm and damp against her bare calves. Now Chuza would have to slow down; the horse must be walked.

She sighed with relief when Chuza reined the great animal to a stop and alighted from the saddle cloth. He helped her down. At first she thought she couldn't walk. Her legs ached from the unaccustomed straddle position, and the first few halting steps brought the ground up to meet her swimming head.

"Are you all right?" Chuza asked.

"I think so. Must we go so fast?"

"Yes, if we are to get away before your father stops us."

"I didn't think it would be this way. I never thought of running away."

"What did you think would be the outcome?" Chuza's voice was harsh.

"That he would finally see how serious this is for us and how committed we are to each other."

"That he will see," Chuza said ruefully.

They were alone on the trail as they walked along beside the horse. They had seen no one for miles. The scent of horseflesh filled her nostrils. Chuza was silent and preoccupied. Joanna looked out over the rugged countryside.

"Why does your uncle hate me?" she asked.

"Abdul? He doesn't hate you."

"He treated me with little hospitality."

"He's not used to Romanlike Jewish women who take matters into their own hands."

"After Father discharged you, I didn't know what else to do."

"You could have allowed me to negotiate."

"He was pressuring me into the betrothal with Jared Bar Seth. I didn't know what you were doing."

"Did you think I was doing nothing? Abdul was understanding. After I came back to his home, he tried in every way to help. He has influential connections in Sepphoris; they might have worked in our behalf, given time. If he acted unfriendly, it was out of fear for what effect our relationship will have on me. He says that we are inflicted with Eros-madness!"

"I felt so panicky," Joanna defended herself. "If the betrothal took place, then there would be no hope. I thought that if I came to you as an unbetrothed maiden, then you could offer the bride-price and Father would have to accept it."

"That may be customary in cases of seduction, but you forget that I'm not the average Jewish 'son of the Law' from the local synagogue," Chuza reminded. "He could have taken the *mohar* and still not have given you to me."

He stopped and reached out to lift her chin. He kissed her tenderly and smoothed the disheveled hair from her face.

"You are so naive, my darling, and so full of nerve to walk from your father's home to mine. But don't worry; it will be all right.

We've made it out of Sepphoris, and we will soon be out of your father's reach. Abdul will offer the *mohar* once we are gone, and my family will welcome us in Nabatea, you'll see."

❖ ❖ ❖

The wedding dress of crimson silk was light and airy in the desert heat. Joanna felt beautiful in the vibrant garment that had been worn before by so many of the women in Chuza's family. What a contrast to the dismal black worn daily by the Bedouin women.

Dressed in elegance, she felt aloof and even more alone, yet she was surrounded by the women who had come for the ritual of dressing the bride. Chuza's mother and sisters fawned over her like she was being prepared as an offering to some god. What was marriage in the Arabian mind? Was it entered into with the same understanding and attitudes as in her Jewish culture? A Hebrew believed that the wife was the completion of the man. Certainly a Jewish bride was adorned. Perhaps her silly fears were caused by the feelings of isolation, intensified by strange language and culture.

Soon Chuza would come with his "companions" to the tent of his mother to claim her. She hadn't seen him since they arrived at the campsite of his tribe ten days ago.

Why had he deserted her? When she asked about him, the women only grinned, nodding their heads and jabbering sounds that to Joanna had no meaning. She believed that they were assuring her that they knew she belonged to Chuza.

When the wedding preparations began, the faces that were now beginning to take on names in her mind were full of joy and excitement, while Joanna's spirits plummeted. She had wanted Chuza, but now things were moving too fast. She was uncertain. What had she expected would be the outcome? Chuza had asked. Certainly nothing of what she was experiencing now!

The bridal tent stood some fifty feet away. The women had raised it this afternoon. Women did everything in this village of tents, even helping with the herds. So far she had been treated as a guest. Chuza's mother explained in labored Aramaic and many gestures that her responsibilities would begin once she became Chuza's first wife and the week of celebration was passed. The fact that she insisted on referring to Joanna by number was disconcerting. Obviously she meant it as an honor. It implied authority for her over other future wives. Chuza's mother was a first wife and exercised such authority.

Joanna's week in the tent of the women was her introduction to Bedouin family life. She learned that Chuza's father, Zanias Benzanias, had three other wives. The number of wives denoted a man's wealth. In the huge tent, they each had their own compartment, which was shared with their young children. Chuza had a host of brothers, sisters, and cousins. Joanna felt swallowed by the size of the tribe, which was beyond anything she had imagined.

At first sight of the numerous black tents pitched in a half-circle on the desert sands, she realized it was another world. The tent of the sheik was easily distinguished. His standard was displayed on a pole that extended above the entrance to his *beit shaar,* or woven goat-hair house. The sheik was Chuza's grandfather. Joanna would see him for the first time at close range when he blessed their marriage tonight under the open Arabian skies.

From beyond the rolled-up door flap, night was descending, and a panorama of stars made a canopy above the camp. Torches on poles were placed outside the bridal *beit shaar.* One by one they were set aflame, and Joanna's own heart felt torched at sight of them. *How can I feel both excitement and repulsion?* Joanna wondered. *How can I feel like running to Chuza and away from him at the same time?* She was overwhelmed. There was nowhere else to go; the choice had been made. Good or bad, it was irrevocable. For a moment she couldn't get her breath, and then she saw him coming, striding confidently toward the tent, flanked by his groomsmen.

In Galilee Chuza had looked no different to her than her Jewish countrymen, but tonight he looked thoroughly Arabian. He was dressed in a white tunic, and his multistriped mantle billowed as he strode toward her. On the wide silk girdle about his hips hung a ceremonial sword. Was it the sword that suddenly struck terror in her?

I'm marrying a stranger, a foreigner, she thought in desperation. Samuel's face sprang to her mind. *Abba—Daddy—why did you let me do it?*

The women crowded behind her to watch the groom come. There was no way but out. Chuza met her at the entrance and took her hand. He smiled at her questioningly.

"How is it that your hands are so cold in this heat?"

"I don't know."

She stiffly followed his lead back to the area for the nuptials. Members of the tribe had lined the way, and as the couple passed by they fell in behind them, noisily playing tambourines and chanting joyfully. Chuza led his bride to where his grandfather sat on camel furniture placed on the sand. Here in the desert, and when traveling, the ornate seat was used by the sheik both on and off the animal. The old man's keen, piercing eyes assessed her, as hers did him. His face was thin and leathery. His eyes were sunken and close to the bridge of his prominent, hooked nose.

Chuza placed his right hand on the old man's left shoulder and kissed his right cheek. Then he repeated the ritual on the opposite side. The patriarch raised his hand in blessing on the *beit shaar* of Chuza. Companions of the groom broke from the crowd and roughly removed Chuza's mantle. They threw it over Joanna, chanting in Arabic, over and over, a phrase she did not understand.

With Joanna still wrapped in Chuza's cloak, they were pushed to the door of the ceremonial tent. Bright tassels on the tent ropes brushed Joanna's forehead as Chuza lifted her over the threshold. Someone removed her bridal sandals. Chuza stepped out of his and onto the blue and gold carpet that floored the tent. Much laughing and jostling followed as his companions released the ties on the door flap. With a dull thump, the coarse goat-hair cloth fell into place, separating the two of them from the others.

The merrymaking went on outside while Joanna scanned the interior of the small tent. Two oil lamps gave enough light to see the stack of smaller woven carpets spread in the middle of the one room. There were too many to count at a glance, but they raised the sleeping area about a foot higher than the larger ornately designed and fringed carpet that covered the entire sandy floor. A white linen sheet was draped over the mats, and there were several plump reclining pillows on top.

"The sheet of virginity," Joanna murmured, "and there's no family of the bride to claim it."

"It's important to my family," Chuza said. "Without it they would know I had defiled you. The desert code is strict. They would refuse to defend me against your father if I had broken it."

How incredible, she thought. How much she had to learn of his people. She absorbed the rest of her new home. A wineskin hung from the central supporting pole, and on the ground below it sat a large water pitcher and basin. A dining cloth was spread beside the bed. On it was a tray of breadflaps and honey, dried fruits, and a dish of rice and herbs. Two copper wine goblets waited to be filled.

Chuza placed her on the mound of carpets and, removing his sword, sat down beside her. He reached to remove the mantle, and Joanna pulled away.

"What's wrong?" he asked.

"I haven't seen you for ten days. I didn't know what was happening. Why did you desert me?"

"Desert you? You were with my mother and sisters."

"But they're strangers."

"Not now; they're your family and you're my wife." He reached for her again.

"Your *first* wife," she accused, maneuvering out of his embrace.

"Are you jealous already?" He was amused.

"I don't think I even want to be your wife," she blurted, blinking back tears of anger.

He reached for her, and this time his arms were tight and unyielding. "Well, it's too late. You are my wife. I've gone through plenty to make it so, and your willfulness won't change that now!"

His roughness and angry tone made her heart beat erratically. She no longer pulled back, but remained stiff and silent.

"Joanna," he said in that curious accent, "don't be a child."

His accusation jarred her. *My father accused me of being a child when I told him I was a woman,* she thought. *Which am I, a woman or a child?*

"What were they chanting when they threw your robe around me?" she asked. "It was frightening."

"None shall cover thee but the cloak of Chuza," he repeated in Aramaic. "It means, you belong to me and no one else can have you. Isn't that what you wanted?"

Chuza had begun to stroke her hair and she relaxed against him, remembering the past days that had so altered her life. It had been a grueling ride through Galilee, across the Jordan into Decapolis and on into Perea. It was over one hundred miles to reach Nabatea. She had hugged his back to keep the wind from her face and to remain on the galloping horse. Many miles they had walked to rest the animal, securing fresh mounts when they could. At night she had fallen exhausted on the thin mat, never noticing the hard ground. Sometimes she would awaken briefly in the midst of star-studded darkness to find herself cradled protectively in his arms. In the morning she would be covered with his mantle and he would be up, preparing for the day's journey. Now she knew why he purposely allowed her to sleep before he lay beside her and why he arose first.

The mantle, resting now about her shoulders, evoked memories with its familiar body scent. Feelings of security stirred again. She rubbed her cheek on the rough weave of his garment. "None shall cover thee but the cloak of Chuza" repeated in her mind. *I don't want any but the cloak of Chuza,* she thought.

Together they lay back against the pillows. A smile played about his lips, and she traced it with her finger.

"Why are you smiling?" she asked.

"Did you know that you are the first wife taken by capture in this tribe for over twenty years?"

"By capture?"

"You may as well know. Our marriage could cause border problems. There's a new alliance between King Aretas IV and Herod Antipas that's in our favor. It seems that Herod is anxious to quiet border tensions right now. That and the fact that my tribe has a reputation for raiding helped."

"What do you mean?"

"You wonder what I've been doing these past ten days? I've been convincing the council of the men to accept my choice of a wife and all the uncertainty that she brings with her. They are honor-bound to defend our marriage now. Don't turn up your nose at the title of 'first wife.' If you were a woman taken by capture you would have been bedded immediately, without ceremony, and you'd be considered a concubine."

Joanna trembled, but Chuza pulled her to him gently.

"Little do they know," his whisper vibrated against her ear, striking cords of desire and excitement, "It is I who was taken by capture!"

The invisible bonds of passion were lifting her onto a plane of urgency she had never known existed and that she had no desire to deny.

Chapter 6

Joanna repeated a curse under her breath and pinched the goat-hair thread between her fingers to remove a large knot in the spool of yarn.

Once again she began to weave on the loom. If she were ever to succeed in the homey arts of these nomads and increase Chuza's tent, she must continue to work, no matter how slowly.

Actually, she was not expected to make a whole tent. The *beit shaar* of Chuza was an amount of tenting handed down from some relative who had died. Tenting was not discarded. Joanna was expected to patch its worn spots with new pieces or increase its size with additional pieces. It was a lifelong process.

She paused and looked across the expanse of sand to where the beige land met the brilliant blue sky. Heat waves were visible. She was grateful for the shade of the "women's tent," with its side flaps rolled up for air. She sighed. At least her arms and back no longer ached as they had in the beginning.

Joanna worked with no enthusiasm. At first she had stubbornly put off the learning process, for she was sure that they would soon hear from Abdul concerning her father's acceptance of the mohar. But the other women treated her with such disapproval that she found it better to put forth some effort.

Now she beat the warps upwards impatiently, giving one final thrust when they failed to line up tightly, and muttered again in disgust.

Her sister-in-law giggled.

"Keziah!" Chuza's mother reprimanded the girl. "Watch your manners." She smiled her encouragement to Joanna.

Her mother-in-law had been patient in teaching her, but there was so much to learn all at once. It was not just the weaving of goat hair and Arabian style cooking that Joanna detested, but the menial tasks of washing and grinding, which she considered servant's work. She also struggled to learn their Arabic dialect. Joanna spoke Greek, Aramaic, Hebrew, and Latin, but she was not familiar with Arabic and often felt isolated or ignorant. They were the ones who were illiterate, she consoled herself. Only the men of the camp were taught to read and write. Education was important for the sons, but a daughter's value was in homemaking and hard camp work.

Look at Chuza's mother, she thought. Her face was kindly and imprinted with the wisdom of years, but the deep lines in her tanned skin were as parched soil after days without rain. Some of her teeth were missing, and she seldom smiled. She wore no veil over her face, like those commonly worn by Arabian women of the city. She wore the black dress of the Bedouin, and her head was swathed in a white linen headdress.

Except for her own youthful beauty, Joanna knew she mirrored her mother-in-law's appearance. So did all the others. It was as if the sun bleached away all colorful hues. There was nothing to excite the eye, only black and white or camel and sand. It was a twilight of sight that matched her spirit. She longed to wear the crimson wedding dress again. The nights in Chuza's arms were all that made the days endurable. She often indulged in fantasy, or dreamed of the green hills of Galilee and the fragrant flowers of her father's garden.

There was also Monaea, moving in and out of her memory with new status. She had never been just a servant; she was almost a mother, yet Joanna had not realized until now the bond that existed between them. She yearned for the sight of Monaea's familiar face.

And Susanna. By now she would be married, living in Caesarea on the sea in a big, beautiful stone home, her days spent in luxury. Six months had passed. Maybe she had conceived the son that she and Jacob both wanted. Tears came unexpectedly. Her mother-in-law saw them and broke the silence.

"Don't become frustrated, my daughter," she said gently.

The weaving. How could she tell this woman of her homesickness? Chuza's mother had married within her own tribe. She knew no other life. Joanna was welcomed probably because she brought Chuza back to the tribe after ten years in Galilee. *She has missed her son, just as I miss Monaea and my father. Now she is trying to make a good Bedouin wife out of me, and I don't cooperate at all. I'm not even with child, as she thinks I should be.* Joanna stared off into the distance. She knew that her mother-in-law prayed daily to Al-Uzza, the fertility goddess, on her behalf.

Clouds of dust became visible on the horizon, and Joanna's heart beat quickly. The men were returning from their appointed post along the King's Highway. Whenever there was a caravan of considerable size, they imposed tribute for safe conduct along the trade route. This assured the merchants of protection from being raided by the very tribe that assessed them. Chuza found it a disagreeable business. Joanna resented the nights that she must spend in the tent of the women while he was gone.

She left her loom eagerly and went to meet him. He turned his horse over to one of the small boys who rushed to be of assistance. Together they walked toward the clumpy grass that stubbornly grew in a less sandy area.

"Did you hear any news in Medeba?" she asked, referring to their nearest border town.

"Herod is in residence at Machaerus."

"He usually visits the fortress in the summer months."

"He's preparing for his marriage to the daughter of King Aretas."

"When?"

"I don't know, but I think both sides are anxious to make a firm alliance. Until the border raids are in the past, Herod Antipas cannot convince Rome that he is capable of ruling all Palestine someday as king."

"With an Arabian queen?"

"The Herods already have Arabian blood," Chuza remarked. "Do you forget that his father, Herod the Great, had a Nabatean mother?"

"Why is it that no one frowns on exogamy for royalty?" Joanna asked.

"Expediency," Chuza summed it up. "Rome favors the unity of the land, and King Aretas wants the Nabateans to be recognized as the highly civilized people that we are. Someday I'll show you Petra. It's as magnificent a capital as Jerusalem. Even the desert tribes are becoming organized now that King Aretas has made the sheiks governors of their own localities and allowed them to levy tribute."

Joanna was impatient with their conversation. It seemed that Chuza was telling her everything but the news she wanted to know.

"Have you heard nothing from Abdul? Doesn't it seem strange that he's been silent on my father's reaction to the *mohar?*"

He didn't answer, but squinted thoughtfully out across the desert.

"What is it?" Joanna asked, watching his facial expression for a clue to his thoughts. There was a hard, set line to his jaw. She could not believe that her father would not respond to a contact from them.

"You've heard, but you haven't told me," she accused. Irrational thoughts spun through her mind. *He likes being back with his family. He's at home here, not a foreigner as he was in Palestine. He wants to stay; now it's me that's living in a land that's not my own!*

"You'd keep me here against my wishes," she screamed in frustration. "I can't stand it, Chuza." Her voice rose out of control, "I want to go back to Galilee. I'm being buried in this sand!"

Chuza had dreaded this confrontation. He had stalled as long as he could, hoping that she would adjust to Bedouin life. Perhaps she never would—not until he told her. He took her shaking shoulders in his firm grasp.

"Stop it, Joanna." Her trembling frightened him. "Yes—I've heard from Abdul. I—just couldn't tell you." He tried to be gentle. "Your father refused the *mohar.*"

"Refused!" she said incredulously.

"He said that he could not accept *mohar* for—for a daughter who was *dead.*"

"Am I a criminal to be condemned and forgotten?"

Her face became as bleached as the cloth that encircled it, and with the heaviness of sand shifting in a sack, she slipped from his grasp and crumpled at his feet.

Joanna opened her eyes against the blindingly blue sky and quickly closed them again. Her head rested on the rough weave of Chuza's mantle. Something had happened that was terrible. She didn't want to remember. The heat of the sand enveloped her body and lulled her senses. She had no desire to move. Then a cold cloth on her face shocked her to full consciousness, and she realized that her mother-in-law as well as Chuza knelt beside her.

"Perhaps she's with child," Chuza's mother said hopefully.

The older woman bathed her face with the precious, limited water from the cistern. *I'm a disappointment to her, too,* Joanna thought. She knew that her fainting spell was caused by desolation and desert heat. This arid country oppressed not only her soul, but her lungs as well. She longed for the balmy breezes of northern Palestine.

"I'm all right," she insisted, making an effort to get to her feet. Chuza helped her up and continued to hold her as they walked to their tent. His mother didn't follow, but left them alone.

Joanna leaned against Chuza gratefully. Her father's words burned in her mind. *It's time you grew up, Joanna. When have you been denied anything?*

I've been denied everything familiar, her heart screamed. *I'm working like a slave, and now I'm cut off from home and Father forever.*

As if Chuza could hear her thoughts, he spoke. "I know how hurt you are. Why do you think I put off telling you? I hoped that he would reconsider. But now he has left Palestine to go to Rome for several months, so we can no longer argue our case."

"Gone to Rome," she repeated plaintively. She turned her head so that he wouldn't see her tears. Had her father truly deserted her?

Gently he made her face him again. "I love you, Joanna, as much as my own life. Isn't that enough?"

She threw her arms about his neck. For a moment she couldn't answer. The guilt that she felt for defying her father was coupled with the guilt of being a halfhearted wife. *I'll do better,* she determined in her mind. *I'll try to learn women's work and do it well. My husband's family is my only family now, and I will have a child soon. That will make a difference. Then both the days and the nights will be worthwhile.*

❖ ❖ ❖

What Joanna failed to understand was that Chuza was equally miserable. He was caught in a daily occupation that he had never experienced and would never have chosen. Ezbai, his older brother by one year, enjoyed the authority and strength of the roving band. Chuza had been happy more than once that this brother had been born to the position of first son. It was easy to see that he sprang from the loins of Benzanias.

Although Chuza resembled his father in powerful body build, his inner being related to the intellectual mind of Abdul. Even as a child he knew that he had nothing in common with Benzanias, and the years of separation only intensified that fact. His mother was happy to welcome back her favorite son, but Chuza knew that his lack of guile and enthusiasm for tribal matters disturbed Benzanias.

And his father did not approve his choice of a wife. He encouraged Ezbai's cutting remarks about the independent, spoiled woman in their midst.

Chuza didn't want to encourage Joanna's complaints, so he didn't share his own frustrations. Yet his tension grew as the weeks became months, and once he threw her to the tent floor when she had nagged him into a fit of anger. She wasn't hurt, but both of them were shocked to find him reverting to the ways in which a nomad controlled his wife. Afterward, in remorse, he agreed to her whim of viewing the marriage caravan of Herod Antipas.

When they began the trip the weather was not threatening, but soon they were thwarted by rising winds. From his camel, Chuza looked over his shoulder to see how she and the others accompanying them fared.

From her high perch on the camel's back, Joanna huddled against the wind. The sand stung her face, and, in spite of the veil hugged close and covering most of her breathing passages, it seemed to penetrate the linen headdress, causing a grittiness in her teeth. She hardly dared to open her eyes. Once she came close to losing her balance as the camel lurched and pulled against Chuza's leading.

How could Chuza see? Stubbornly he faced into the wind and nudged the camel toward the route which led from Petra, King Aretas's capital city, to Machaerus. Were they really making progress? How could he know which way he was going?

The other camels were barely visible behind them. Some of Chuza's family had chosen to join them on this pilgrimage that would intercept the caravan near the gorge of Arnon. The marriage would have taken place in Petra. The couple would summer at Machaerus before returning to Galilee. The caravan would be a magnificent sight. Many times Joanna had viewed Herod's entourage as it entered Sepphoris with the palace guard on Arabian steeds, in perfect alignment.

The helmets and armor of the men would glint in the sun, symbolizing their strength in battle. The wedding caravan would have even more grandeur. Joanna hoped to glimpse the Arabian princess, or at least her carriage, atop a stately camel. But now she couldn't see beyond their own camel's head, and the sandstorm showed no signs of abating. Perhaps they would have to turn back without seeing the caravan at all. It was just a foolish desire!

The anticipation had excited her for weeks. It would be an event to divide one dull day from another. Now it appeared to be turning into one more disappointment.

Chuza jerked the camel impatiently.

"Don't take your anger at me out on the camel," she said to the wind. She didn't intend for him to hear her. He had thought it a silly idea from the onset. But who would have guessed that they would be caught in this storm?

"We're going to have to give up," Chuza yelled. "We'll camp and wait it out."

The others stopped their camels too. The proud-headed beasts turned away from the wind. One by one, like toppling blocks, they dropped to their knees. Joanna lurched forward precariously. She compensated by leaning back until the animal was completely down on the front legs and proceeded to drop down on the hind ones. She swung her legs over the camel seat and placed her feet on the shifting sand.

She and Chuza huddled against their camel's side, putting the animal between them and the force of the wind. *This land and the elements were in constant battle with the Bedouins,* Joanna thought as she experienced one more characteristic of her new country.

She was thirsty, but she had learned to wait for a drink. Water was limited at this season. There was so little in summer drought that they scrubbed their bodies with sand to clean themselves. Then they rubbed perfumed oils into their skin to restore softness. The leathery look of the elderly told Joanna that it was not an adequate measure against dryness.

Again she thought of Sepphoris, with its elaborate waterworks built by Herod Antipas. It supplied the city in such abundance that she had always taken it for granted. She never would again.

"Dhu-Shara be appeased!" Chuza muttered.

"What did you say?"

"Dhu-Shara, the desert god. I hope he calls off his anger soon."

"You believe in a god of the desert?"

"It's just an expression, Joanna. Some believe."

"But that's just what I was thinking! It's as if some unseen power were punishing us. Everything we try to do, or want to do, turns out wrong."

"I'm sorry to disappoint you again, Joanna," Chuza said with disgust.

"I'm not blaming you." She was irritated. Her demands weren't so great, and her sacrifices were mountainous.

"Every day you blame me," he said. "In a thousand ways you take out your unhappiness with my country and my people on me. Don't you think that I'm unhappy too? I'm a financial minister, not a herdsman. If it weren't for you, I'd still be in Galilee with a promising position."

His words slapped her. She was stunned by his honesty. That's why they had been arguing so much. He was as trapped as she was. "Eros-madness," as Abdul called it, was a web that caught you and held you until the spider of life consumed you. She had thought that passion was a blessing. It was a curse!

Did some desert god, in jealousy of their passion, enjoy pelting them with sand to spoil a joyous occasion? Joanna seldom thought about any gods. In her travels to Athens and Rome with her father, she became knowledgeable of Greek and Roman gods, and their petty, humanistic qualities of revenge. All nations had their deities. Yahweh was just the Hebrew God. People needed someone to blame for the bad times and someone to hope in for better ones, didn't they?

Her father believed that Yahweh was the Creator and King of the universe, that there was only one God and that the Hebrew people were his chosen race.

"If you *are* King of the universe," Joanna muttered quietly, "Then you could help us if you wanted to." She wasn't going to satisfy some god by begging! And since she hated this land, she certainly didn't intend to pray to Dhu-Shara!

"Come on," Chuza yelled against the wind. "We've got to get out of the path of the storm or we'll be buried! It's not abating."

He signaled to the others who scrambled to mount their camels. Joanna climbed on her beast, took the reins with one hand, and jerked the coarsely woven fabric across her face to protect herself from the relentless sand. Inside she seethed at an angry god.

Chapter 7

The bazaar flourished with activity. Colorful wares hung about the entrance of the open-aired stalls, making a gala display. When Chuza suggested this trip into town, Joanna was careful to guard her emotions. *Don't anticipate too much,* she warned herself. She determined not to be disappointed if something happened, as it always seemed to. Still fresh in her mind was the sandstorm of a month ago that had ruined their plans to view the wedding caravan of Herod Antipas.

Chuza pulled her through the narrow passageway while multiple sounds of bargaining meshed and jumbled in her mind. A miniature merchant, with pleading round, dark eyes, accosted her and dangled silver bracelets in her face. He couldn't have been more than seven years old, but his dirty face was hard and set with a kind of aging common to street urchins; and he smelled. Chuza dipped to the right to avoid a man hurrying through the street with a tray on his head laden with flat round bread, hot from the outdoor ovens. The aroma was tantalizing. He must get it to the stand, where eager hands would rush to buy it and eat greedily.

Joanna loved the bazaar. She yearned over the delicate pottery, so thin and finely painted that it was unequaled anywhere else. Made only in Nabatea, its transport to bazaars in Palestine and other parts of the world was difficult, so the pottery commanded a high price in foreign markets. Joanna stopped to look, and the woman behind the crude counter began to prattle in Arabic.

Chuza snatched her away. "This isn't what I want you to see. Today you won't think about homemaking."

He was magnanimous. She looked at him quizzically, and he flashed her his brilliant smile. How long had it been since he had smiled at her that way? She quickened her step and followed him.

Finally he found the shop he wanted. Silk materials that would make any woman's heart yearn were in rainbow profusion about the stall.

"What is your pleasure, my lady?" he asked.

"How silly, my lord; where would I wear such a beautiful garment?"

"Not garment—*garments*. How many colors please you?"

"I would be the point of laughter in the camp," Joanna insisted. "They already think me too high-minded."

"Then you shall not wear them in camp." He grinned. "You will save them for a king's palace."

She laughed. It was fun to dream. After so many dreary days and disappointments, she was happy to be matching his mood, even if it was just pretense.

"A king's palace, indeed," she said.

"Well, perhaps not a king yet, but someday he will be if I can be of any assistance."

"What are you talking about?"

Chuza dropped his voice so that others would not easily overhear him. "I'm speaking of the tetrarch, Herod Antipas. You wanted to see his marriage caravan, didn't you? Well, wouldn't his palace be better?"

"Machaerus?"

"Machaerus, Jericho, Livias, Sepphoris, or how about the one he is building at Tiberias?"

"My lord, you are mad," she laughed.

"Absolutely wild," he agreed. "You will not believe what has happened. It's like a miracle. I told you that Abdul has many influential friends; well, one of them is a colleague of Herod's, named Manaen. Herod and Manaen were school-fellows while in Rome. Herod, of course, has heard of our leaving Sepphoris. He thinks that your father was foolish to lose a good steward and a beautiful daughter because of his fanatical religious beliefs. He wants me to join his staff of financial advisors."

"Oh, Chuza—are you serious?"

His eyes caught and held hers. "It's true, my love; we are going back to Galilee."

"Galilee," she murmured thoughtfully. For a moment, her joy was suspended in uncertainty.

❖ ❖ ❖

Now that they were leaving, Joanna realized how much she would miss the older woman who so stoically bid them good-bye.

"We'll be back," she promised in Arabic.

Chuza's mother nodded. "Someday you will show me your son." She placed a hand on Joanna's arm tenderly while her words tightly twined the younger woman's heart.

Chuza bid farewell to his father, grandfather, and the council of men. Then a small number of clansmen accompanied them to the main caravan route. This time they didn't chance the dangers of traveling alone, but joined a large group of wagons moving north.

Once in Sepphoris, Joanna was too heady with delight to be concerned about living in Abdul's home. It was near the Sepphoris palace, where Chuza would work daily as part of the tetrarch's economic staff.

The only blight on her return was the thought of her father, who, though only a short distance away, considered her nonexistent. She was glad that she could not view her former home from her present one. Maybe, somehow, she could keep it from her mind. She had been Chuza's wife for almost a year. Her life as the daughter of

Samuel Bar Simeon seemed long ago, almost like a shadow of herself, never to be recaptured. If only there was a way to see Monaea . . .

One day Chuza came home with exciting news. They were invited to the royal palace.

"Praises to Gad!" he said triumphantly.

"To whom?"

"Gad, the god of good fortune."

"I didn't know you were so religious, or that you believed in so many gods."

"It's just an expression," Chuza declared. "I believe in myself. I intend to have Herod Antipas believing in me, too."

"I believe in you," Joanna laughed. "But I prayed to Yahweh when I was desperate one day. Do you suppose he had anything to do with the good things that are happening to us?"

"About as much as Gad did," Chuza answered.

Herod and his princess had arrived in Sepphoris. There would be a banquet in honor of the marriage. Chuza and Joanna were back in Roman society, where the women accompanied their men on social occasions. However, the banquet food would be acceptable according to Levitical law, since Sepphoris was predominately Jewish and was the seat of the Galilean Sanhedrin.

❖ ❖ ❖

The girl whom Abdul had assigned as her personal maiden brushed Joanna's chestnut hair until it was glossy. Then she braided it elaborately with a string of pearls and set the silken headdress in place. Joanna smoothed the aqua-green gown against her slender body and was pleased for the first time in months that she was not with child.

Watching her, Chuza chuckled. "You will outrank the princess in beauty," he predicted.

Joanna remembered her first visit to the palace when she was fourteen and how childishly she had been flattered by Herod's kind words. Now she would return to welcome his Arabian princess at the side of her own Arabian husband. How odd to think that the daughter of Aretas would occupy the palace built on the ashes of the one her father had helped to destroy.

Everyone knew that the princess's betrothal to Herod Antipas had been encouraged by Rome in recognition of her father's assistance in suppressing the uprising, and to secure the Perean and Nabatean borders. During the revolt nearly seventeen years before, Herod's palaces at Jericho and Ammatha had also been destroyed. Since then, the tetrarch had been busy rebuilding all of his palaces, and now he was building Tiberias, a completely new city of Hellenistic design. Then he would move his capital from Sepphoris to Tiberias. His land acquisitions were increasing. His staff of economic advisors was growing, too. Some said that it was Herod's aim not only to rule, but to *own* most of Palestine!

Chuza and Joanna rode their litter to the palace silently. Perhaps Chuza was as deep in thought as Joanna concerning a matter neither wanted to discuss. Returning to Sepphoris meant that the day would come when she would see her father again. Over and over in her mind she tried to anticipate how that encounter might come about. Both knew that Samuel had probably been invited to this reception. She knew that he had returned from Rome, for Abdul always supplied such information. But if her father knew of her presence and Chuza's appointment to Herod's staff, he might not come.

As they approached the palace, Joanna became tense. Chuza squeezed her hand. *He must have strong reservations himself,* she thought, but she did not ask him. Who wanted to discuss any blemish on their good fortune?

The great hall was already alive with activity, and Joanna's eyes darted from person to person as they stood talking in groups. She recognized many of her father's friends, but did not see Samuel among them.

The officer of the feast announced their arrival and a hush settled over the murmuring crowd. She and Chuza were already a topic of conversation! *Of course, we're an object of interest,* she thought. *I'm not the only one anticipating my father's reaction. He must be here.* Her eyes scanned the room again, lightly pausing on some faces in an effort to read their thoughts.

A man stepped forward. His smile was an attempt to put them at ease. He was in his thirties, Joanna guessed, and beardless, with dark curly hair cropped at the neck. He had a deep cleft in his chin and candid, dark eyes. Chuza saluted him enthusiastically.

"Joanna, this is Manaen. Remember? I told you that he is an acquaintance of my uncle."

"Oh yes, my lord." Joanna smiled with grateful pleasure to meet the man who had influenced Chuza's appointment.

A moment later trumpets sounded and all attention was drawn to the archway. Herod entered with his Arabian princess by his side. About the same age as Manaen, Herod was confident in manner and wore his regal expression to befit the occasion. He was clean-shaven, after the style of the Roman court. This seemed to bring more attention to the arched eyebrows that dipped toward the bridge of his nose, causing him to appear calculating in nature.

His princess wore a traditional Arabian blue silk gown, complete with a veil that tipped her nose and concealed her mouth. Her dark eyes were shadowed silvery white with antimony, and they were hauntingly beautiful. What was she thinking? *Would she feel as misplaced in Galilee as I felt in Nabatea?* Joanna wondered. Probably not. She was the daughter of a king, married to a tetrarch who hoped to be a king. She was moving into a society where women enjoyed more freedom, not less.

Would that be difficult for one so sheltered?

It was while she was involved in a myriad of random thoughts that her peripheral vision caught a familiar figure. She glanced aside to see her father some thirty feet away. As though on cue, he pivoted and she could not see his face. Her hand moved impulsively to her throat to smooth away the unbearable knot. She raised her head and willed herself to remain under control.

I can be as stubborn as he is, she thought.

Chapter 8

My lord," Joanna said evenly, "it seems that much has happened and I've not been informed."

She paced the common room of Abdul's home, which was a standard squarish stone dwelling of the upper class in Sepphoris. A soft breeze from the central courtyard drifted in to cool her flushed face.

She caught the frown and narrowing of Abdul's eyes as he looked at Chuza.

"We thought you'd be pleased," Abdul said.

His tone indicated that he thought her indeed hard to please and that he was tired of his nephew's efforts to do so. Joanna knew that Abdul tolerated her only for Chuza's sake. He was accustomed to Arabian women who knew their place, and having never married, he was unsympathetic toward Chuza's "Eros-madness."

"I thought you'd be happy with the prospect of a settlement with your father." Chuza was irritated too.

"How can Samuel Bar Simeon resurrect a dead daughter?" she asked sarcastically.

"Joanna," Chuza spoke, "you are letting bitterness consume you."

She turned to face Abdul and was reminded of that patriarchal grandfather in the desert who had blessed their Arabian wedding. How Abdul resembled his father! The same narrow face with close-set eyes scrutinized her now. His nose was less prominent, but nonetheless hooked. He was the youngest son of the sheik and the most highly educated. Chuza's father, the oldest, would be the next sheik.

"We are already married," she said. "How can we speak of another marriage?"

"There was no contract. Your father would consider this year as betrothal with conjugal rights and recognize a formal Israelite marriage and contract," Abdul explained. Once again his eyes shifted to Chuza.

Joanna was uneasy. "Why would my father reconsider now?"

"Herod has spoken on our behalf," Chuza said simply.

Joanna frowned. How could it be so simple? "Why would the tetrarch become involved in our petty affairs, my lord?"

Abdul shrugged. "Perhaps because Herod has an Arabian wife and the situation between a prominent man of Sepphoris and his Arabian son-in-law is embarrassing. It could appear to be discriminating at a time when it is important for the princess to be accepted."

Joanna smiled. *How ironic,* she thought, *that my father might be in a difficult position by insisting on his bigotry.* Biting her lip thoughtfully, she turned to Chuza.

"Didn't you tell me that the selection of silver and gold pieces for the new palace of Tiberias is to be made by the princess herself, my lord?"

"Yes," Chuza agreed.

"But Herod will direct her to the proper merchant."

"Your father is the best."

"But not the only one. That's why he's reconsidered," she laughed bitterly. "Herod has touched his vulnerable spot, the money pouch!"

"Joanna," Abdul spoke sharply, "there's more at stake than personal feelings."

"Oh, yes, I see."

"Put all else aside," Abdul demanded impatiently. "It's Chuza's future that needs to be considered."

Joanna had not thought of how this might affect Chuza. His accusation of her, made during the sandstorm, was imprinted vividly on her mind. "If it weren't for you, I would still be in Galilee with a promising position!" She supposed that this was crucial to his future.

"What terms has my father agreed upon?" she asked quietly.

Abdul's expression brightened. "He has agreed to a reasonable *mohar.*"

"He insists on 'marriage with manus,'" Chuza added.

"With manus?" Joanna questioned.

"It's a Roman custom," Chuza said. "Money that you inherit upon his death will remain completely in your control. I'll have no part of it. I agree. I want no part of it."

"What else?" Joanna asked. Intuitively she knew that there must be more. Both men hesitated, and Chuza avoided her eyes.

"The 'no divorce' clause will be stricken." Abdul offered.

Joanna's eyes widened. She looked to Chuza. He met her steady gaze.

Abdul continued, "It refers to the Mosaic Law where it states that a seduced maiden may never be divorced."

"And you want the option of divorce?" she asked Chuza, speaking barely above a whisper.

"Joanna, just because it's there doesn't mean that I'll use it."

"Then why? Why is it necessary?"

"Your father has made independence possible for you. Shouldn't Chuza also have some consideration?" Abdul interjected.

"If he wants it," Joanna said quietly.

"Your father is most happy to include it. I think a divorce would almost please him," Abdul said.

Would that make two of you? Joanna thought. She wondered how much longer they would have to remain in Abdul's home. Not long, she supposed, once Chuza was well established on Herod's council.

A fresh breeze from the courtyard seemed to usher in a clearing of her mind. Neither Abdul nor Samuel were important. If the contract suited them, fine. As for her and Chuza, they were drawn together and would stay together regardless of any contract. The main concern was the effect it had on Chuza's possible advancement in the affairs of the palace. Herod would someday be king. Tiberius Caesar would recognize all of his accomplishments and reward him with all of the territory once ruled by his father, Herod the Great. Roman governors in Judea were surely just a temporary solution after the deposition of Herod Antipas's brother, Archelaus. Of course there was his half-brother, Philip the tetrarch, to be considered, but the Herodians, that influential political faction, favored Herod Antipas above all the sons of Herod the Great. Chuza could be a part of bringing it all to pass.

She smiled. "Then it's settled. But the marriage must be simple, like a betrothal, with only father and ourselves present with the necessary witnesses."

On the morning of the ceremony Joanna arose early and went by litter to her father's home. Chuza was to arrive at the appointed time with Abdul. She had to see Samuel first alone. No longer a chastised child, deserted for her rebellion, she was Chuza's wife and Samuel's daughter, in that order. But she must know how he would respond to her now. Would there be any scrap of warmth left from her happy childhood?

He had named her Joanna, "The Lord is gracious." Did he think his God was ungracious to give him a thankless daughter? Was she a blight on the reputation of his name? Did he accept her back for a monarch's or for money's sake?

She alighted at the entrance to the familiar home with the help of a servant of Abdul's house. He rapped the huge brass knocker several times. The keeper of her father's portal opened the door in the gate, and he greeted her enthusiastically. Her early arrival wasn't expected, and nervous tension manifested itself in his frenzied movements. His thin, wrinkled face was a mass of small lines and there was mist in his crinkled eyes. She had known this servant since she was a child playing on the steps to the street level.

The open court was roughly floored with heavy stone and completely enclosed by the outer wall. On this level were the stables, and if Joanna had arrived on mount, the entire gate would have been opened. To her right, following the line of the outer wall, were the steps up to the main living area. She went up unaccompanied and stepped through the archway into the large public room.

It was octagonal in shape, with four intricately carved wood benches placed against every other wall. A large round polished brass table was in the center. She hesitated a moment, stung by the sight of familiar objects of art placed about the room. They were gleaming silver and gold vessels that were there more for show than for use, except on rare occasions, such as a wedding. Few would be used for her small, somber festival. Her father's wares were well represented in his own home. All were useful objects, and there was no replica of human or beast, for this was strictly forbidden in the Jewish faith.

Joanna slipped out of her sandals before walking on the elaborately patterned blue and scarlet carpet. She skirted the table and passed on through the opposite archway leading to a wide hall and then the open colonnade to the garden.

And there the beloved middle-aged servant appeared from another room and was startled by her presence.

"Monaea," Joanna cried, "how good it is to see you again."

The woman burst into tears. Advancing to Joanna, she quickly hugged her. When she had regained her composure, her eyes searched Joanna's. "Your father meditates in the garden this morning. It was wise for you to come now."

Her father did not see Joanna approach, for his head was bent almost to his chest. Samuel sat on the marble bench where she and Chuza had once huddled and confessed their love to each other. His hands were folded loosely, resting on his knees. The veins were raised like blue ridges in the age-speckled skin. Bushy brows hid his eyes, but not the pouches beneath them, nor the sagging cheeks. *He's so old!* Joanna realized. Heaviness was like a vest of mail on him. *Have I done this to him?*

He must have opened his eyes and saw her feet or skirt, for he looked up suddenly. Neither spoke. She watched his face crumple. The pouches beneath his eyes burst like plump waterskins and rivulets coursed down his face. No longer did she wonder how she would approach him. They had both been trapped in bonds of pride. Now those bonds snapped. She was his child again, kneeling beside him with both her hands in his and choking on her own tears. Their time together was like a mineral-bath, from which Joanna emerged limp and clean.

By late afternoon, when Chuza arrived with Abdul, the atmosphere of the household was giddy from relief of tension. Samuel had already drunk many glasses of wine. If part of his remorse of the morning was regret over the simplicity of the coming celebration for a marriage after-the-fact, he showed no sign of it now. The nuptial canopy was set up in the garden. Susanna's parents arrived. They would be the only witnesses besides Abdul.

Joanna was eager to hear any news of her best friend. A year was a long time, and she had missed so much of the excitement that must have surrounded Susanna's large wedding.

"The Lord God has smiled upon her marriage," Susanna's mother told Joanna. "Soon her child will be born."

Joanna became pensive. She was not superstitious, yet the thought persisted. Maybe now my marriage too will be so blessed. She had been praying diligently to both Yahweh, the Hebrew God, and Al-Uzza, the Bedouin's god of fertility, for many months.

Chapter 9

Joanna looked down at the sleeping baby with the peach-like cheeks and soft brown curls. His lower lip protruded in a baby pout. He was adorable, and she longed to hold him.

"How do you keep from squeezing him?" she asked Susanna, whose arms cradled the chubby six-month-old. He had dropped off to sleep in his mother's arms after being nursed.

"Oh, I don't; I squeeze him a lot." Susanna's dark eyes sparkled. "Would you like to hold him?"

"Yes."

Stirred by being transferred from one to the other, the baby fluttered his dark lashes, and two of the roundest black eyes looked solemnly into Joanna's soul. The small body pressure against her breast only emphasized the tightening about her heart.

The baby squirmed to sit up. Awkwardly Joanna struggled to adjust him to the position that he wanted.

Susanna laughed. "You'll get used to his constant moving. He's strong and very determined. He will be a leader some day; I just know it!"

"You mean the Messiah?" Joanna couldn't help teasing.

"Weren't we silly children?" Susanna said.

Two years and marriage had matured them both. Susanna was more round of body now, but her face was even lovelier in motherhood.

"How is Jacob?" Joanna asked.

"His joy is unspeakable now that we have Jonathan."

"And Caesarea? Do you like living near the sea?"

"It's beautiful and exciting with so many foreign ships coming into port. Won't Jonathan be delighted with all there is to see as he grows older? But it's good to be home again, visiting my parents and showing my son to everyone." Susanna caught her breath and looked away.

Joanna realized that her own thoughts must have been written in her eyes and Susanna detected them. Her friend squeezed her hand.

"Someday it will be you showing your son to everyone," she assured her.

Joanna didn't answer. Yahweh or Al-Uzza, or whoever controlled such things, hadn't seen fit to bless her.

"Tell me about Chuza and the affairs at Herod's court," Susanna said with false brightness.

The baby jabbered and they both laughed, for it sounded as though he had some opinions on Herod's court. Susanna took him again and laid him on the woven mat beside them. He began to play with his pudgy toes.

"What is it like to be involved in government?" Susanna prodded.

"Chuza is not so involved with government as he is in keeping Herod solvent as he expands his investments."

"Does he like it?"

"He's like a racehorse prancing at the gate, eager to show his potential. He believes that Herod will be king."

"There have certainly been enough governors to come and go in Caesarea," Susanna commented, referring to the Roman appointees who governed Judea from that capital city.

"Right now all efforts are being made to finish building Tiberias," Joanna said.

"We heard that it had been suspended for a time."

"It was. They uncovered a cemetery and many orthodox Jews became upset, including my father. 'It is an abomination,' he said, 'to disturb the bones of the dead in their final resting place.'"

"It does seem to be a desecration," Susanna agreed.

"Chuza says, 'What does it matter? The dead are dead, and the cemetery is so ancient that no one living has any relative of remembrance there anyway!'"

"What does Herod say?"

"He's concerned only for political implications. He doesn't want to offend the religious rulers, but then again, he has already named it Tiberias after Caesar, and a great deal of money has been spent. How can he do less than finish it now?"

"So they are going ahead?"

"Yes; most of the workman are slaves anyway. Populating the city is slow, but Chuza has suggested freeing the slaves as a reward for their diligent work, with the stipulation that they live in Tiberias. For others who will establish homes and businesses, Herod can offer tax exemptions. He liked the idea, and since he has set that policy the city is growing.'

"Once they see the economic advantages, there will be fewer religious objections," Susanna laughed. "It is the way with men."

"Chuza hopes for a promotion—perhaps to overseer of the palace at Sepphoris and financial holdings here when Herod moves his capital to Tiberias. He's brighter than all the others, and that must be obvious to Herod."

Susanna smiled. "I know how you must feel, because I also am honored to be the wife of a respected man. I want nothing more than to raise our son to be just like him."

"And my ambitions are Chuza's. I'll do everything I can to help him in every way!"

❖ ❖ ❖

In the years that followed Joanna and Chuza reveled in court life and the excitement surrounding the building of Tiberias. Finally the city was populated, and the newly finished palace at Tiberias was an arena of activity.

Furnishings were arriving by camel train after being shipped to Caesarea from Macedonian cities or from Athens and Rome. The royal couple had chosen these items on a recent trip through the Roman Empire.

Joanna and Chuza had been invited to accompany Herod and his princess on an inspection tour before the move of the capital from Sepphoris to Tiberias. It was less than a day's journey by camel. Chuza had been in Herod's service for nearly eight years now, and their contacts with the tetrarch and his wife were more and more frequent.

In expansive moments of dreaming, Joanna was sure that Herod was gleaning important opinions and recommendations from Chuza, but she also knew that the princess herself liked their company for more basic reasons. She could converse with Chuza and Joanna in her own native tongue. Although she spoke Aramaic and Greek, the Arabic dialect was more familiar and relaxing. No doubt she was happy that her husband had a Nabatean on his staff.

I just wish I enjoyed talking to her more, Joanna thought. She found it hard to concentrate on the princess. Their conversation always centered on "things" for the palace, while Chuza and Herod discussed politics and events at Rome or Judea. Joanna's ears were captured by their words.

The four of them now stood at the base of the wide marble steps. Joanna studied the massive stone sculptures of twin lions that presided on either side of the exquisitely carved doors overlaid with gold leaf. Her eyes followed the six Corinthian columns, which soared to dizzying heights in support of the upper balcony. Above stretched the golden roof, glistening in the sun. It could be seen for miles.

She felt Herod's eyes and turned to find him studying her with the same intense appreciation.

"What do you think?" he asked.

"It is beautiful beyond description." She was embarrassed by the longing in his eyes. She glanced at her husband and the princess, but they had already moved a few feet up the steps.

"Chuza," Herod's wife said. "Let me show you my 'piece of Nabatene' in Galilee. My lord has indulged me by allowing one oriental corner in this very Hellenistic palace."

Chuza followed her quick steps with long strides.

"Joanna," Herod said, as she too started up the polished marble expanse. "What do you think it would be like to live here?"

He didn't move, so she could not continue to move away from him. "Splendid, my lord," she answered, stopping in mid-step, and when he did not accompany the others, she returned to his level.

"Do you think you would like that?"

"If you are concerned about the princess, I think she is thrilled with the palace. The Greek design is majestic, and her 'piece of Nabatene' is surely just a bit of nostalgia from her homeland."

He waved away her remarks. "Of course, I know that she's pleased. What about you? Would you like to live in this palace as the wife of my steward?"

Joanna was astounded. "Of course, my lord," she murmured.

"I haven't told Chuza yet," Herod continued. "Gether is growing old, and I'm discharging him. His mistake with the building site was almost devastating. I need someone young, with good ideas. Chuza's suggestion of granting free land and tax exemptions was a brilliant solution. The population of the city is growing by the thousands. The palace is nearly ready, so it is time for Chuza's appointment."

"He will be most grateful, my lord."

"And what about you?" Herod's eyes had taken on the magnetic eyes of a man for a woman. "Will you be grateful too?"

❖ ❖ ❖

Samuel's bushy eyebrows were arched in surprise. It was the reaction that Joanna had hoped for. She laughed in delight.

"So you are now the wife of Herod's steward!" He exclaimed.

How like him, she thought, to state it in terms of her position rather than Chuza's.

Their years of reconciliation had been good ones. Often in the afternoons she visited him alone, playing knucklebones as they had done when she was a child. Samuel was no longer in his prime. His strength was declining.

Once, not long after the signing of the marriage contract, her father had again offered Chuza the job of steward in his household, but Chuza considered it a step backward. He told her that it would be better to be just one economic minister on Herod's staff with a chance of advancement than to be the highest official in the household of any wealthy merchant. Joanna agreed. She knew her father well. He would have tried to exercise control, and Chuza would not have liked it. Any subordinate position he took was carefully considered for its ultimate potential in reaching a higher goal with more influence.

Joanna didn't realize for a few moments that her father had fallen silent.

"Will you move to Tiberias?" he asked.

Joanna's joy dimmed. Was he thinking that he wouldn't see her so often? "Of course," she answered gently.

"My daughter," Samuel said gravely, "Tiberias is built on the scattered bones of Jewish people."

"That's not true," Joanna said breathlessly. "After the first caves of the dead were uncovered, the building was concentrated toward the north."

"It's defilement for a Hebrew to come in contact with the dead. It should have been abandoned."

"You know what that would have cost Herod!"

"The Lord God cannot be pleased with such disregard of his statutes. It may cost Herod God's wrath."

"It's not as if you were a Pharisee and believed in the resurrection of the dead!"

"As a Sadducee I believe it is even more important to have a sacred final rest!"

"Sometimes I don't understand you, Father."

"Sometimes I wonder if your Arabian husband has eroded your faith in the God of our Father, Abraham."

What God? Joanna screamed in her mind. *The one who answers my prayers for a son?* But she said nothing.

"Is it true that Herod has statues of animals in his palace?"

"They are impressive works of art," Joanna affirmed defensively. "Two magnificent stone lions guard the front entrance."

"You know that is strictly against our religion."

"Is it?" She wondered what he would think of the nude Greek male statues and the bust of Tiberius Caesar inside the palace.

Samuel's face became dangerously flushed while prominent veins in his neck pulsated. The shaggy eyebrows came together. "Will you defy God by living in a place of idolatry?"

"I'm married to Chuza. I will live where my husband lives."

"Then the Lord God will never bless your union with a child," Samuel shouted. "And you embark on a difficult road!"

A crawling sensation passed over Joanna's scalp. She believed her father's words were only a statement designed to work his will upon her. But she had been married for nine years; his denunciation did sound like the prophetic utterance of a patriarch.

❖ ❖ ❖

Joanna's footfalls echoed as she walked through the empty halls of the palace's east wing. These chambers were used only when guests were in residence. She was aware that Herod watched her closely once she and Chuza moved to Tiberias. He knew she was walking there alone. Did she consider becoming Herod's mistress almost as soon as he first made his intentions clear? She was severed from her father's iron-clad rules and prudish religion. How could he understand the mores at court? He was bound by such ancient laws!

She had declared to Susanna that she would do anything to help Chuza remain in Herod's favor, but she didn't fool herself. Chuza was capable of handling that himself.

She heard Herod as he caught up with her. At first, his husky voice from behind brought excitement. "You've teased me long enough, my love!"

She wheeled, pretending surprise, and he caught her in his arms. His mouth on hers was foreign and suddenly repulsive. Instinctively she squirmed to be free, regretting at once her stupidity.

He laughed and held her tightly, interpreting her honest reaction as playfulness. It fired his passion. His hands sought the softness of her body through her silken gown. It was as if she had been awakened from a dream to the reality of a nightmare. Even the smell of his perfumed body and the clean shaven face were alien.

What had possessed her to come here? She wanted Chuza. She had never wanted anyone but him. Joanna took a deep breath. Her brain felt paralyzed, but she would have to find some way out of this without angering him.

"Could the cloak of Herod cover me from the wrath of Chuza?" she asked, hoping that the mention of ancient punishment laws might cool his emotions.

He laughed. "The cloak of Herod could smother the wrath of Chuza!"

"To Herod's loss," she reminded swiftly. "Have you ever had so excellent a steward, my lord?"

This reminder of Chuza's worth helped to quiet his insistence. She stammered on. "You could cover me with your cloak, my lord, but you could not offer me a crown."

"Do *you* solicit *me!*" he asked. "You know that's impossible."

"Of course it is, my lord; that's what I hoped for you to see. We are in Palestine, not Rome. Could such . . . an arrangement as you have in mind be managed? No matter how desirable," she hastened to add, "Perhaps it should be thought through carefully."

"Women should be ruled by their hearts, not their minds," Herod declared, assuming that her desire matched his own.

"A foolish woman, perhaps," Joanna agreed. "But you wouldn't want to make love to a fool. That would be easy enough to do, if you desired it."

They were words he couldn't debate. Joanna's heart pounded as she waited for his answer. She hoped that if he detected the telltale racing of her heart, beating against his breast, that he would interpret it as passion, not fear. She walked a thin line of deception with her verbal gymnastics.

It was an agonizingly long moment before he relaxed his embrace. "I'm already married to one with proper political status who lacks your intelligence."

"Then you would not reduce me to fill her role without due honor," Joanna suggested.

"I can't place a crown on your head, Joanna."

"Nor do I expect you to, my lord."

"What do you expect?"

"That we deny ourselves." She placed her fingers on his lips when she saw that he would protest. "For this time," she added quickly, "for the good of your kingdom while Caesar considers you for the crown of Judea. Surely it won't be long."

While he stood confused by her reference to his higher goals, she slipped away from him. "Chuza must wonder where I am. You stay; I'll return first so that no one will suspect."

She walked away, leaving him baffled in her wake. Her pace quickened as she reached her own chambers. Safe. Safe—at least for now.

PART II

THE KING

At the Fullness of Time

A.D. 27

Chapter 10

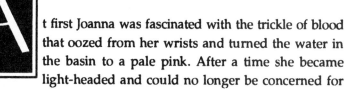

At first Joanna was fascinated with the trickle of blood that oozed from her wrists and turned the water in the basin to a pale pink. After a time she became light-headed and could no longer be concerned for messiness. She finally curled fetal fashion onto her ornate bed and experienced a floating freedom.

A voice tunneled its way into her consciousness. She thought that it was a spirit from the other realm, then she knew it couldn't be; this voice sounded upset, striving with her spirit. It must be earthly. From that moment on, Joanna fought what the voice was saying, although she really didn't make any sense of the words. She wanted to get away but no longer had the strength. Frustration filled her being. She tried to move, but her body wouldn't respond. Other voices joined the first one.

She was aware of a tight binding about her wrists, followed by a terrifying dream of captivity, before lapsing into unconsciousness.

When she awoke, Chuza was bending over her. She was lying unrestrained in her own bed.

"You're going to be all right," he said.

She nodded ever so slightly in resignation.

"Other than the physician, Emis is the only one who knows. He found you."

She didn't respond. She felt no sorrow for the slave's traumatic discovery or her husband's fears. She didn't feel anything.

"Why did you do it?" Chuza said. His voice was controlled anger. "Joanna, why did you do such a thing?"

❖ ❖ ❖

As Joanna walked out upon the palace balcony of the upper court, a gust of wind whipped her veil across her face. With a shake of her head, the wisp of blue silk dropped into place, framing her chestnut hair and allowing the sun to highlight the strands of gold. It had darkened only slightly through the years. At thirty she had a beauty intensified by maturity, with a hint of haunting preoccupation.

Lake Gennesaret came into view as she approached the marble rail. Something within her related to this sea of Galilee: the restlessness, and perhaps the relentless dashing against the rocks, as though bent on self-destruction.

The heights that bordered its eastern edge were almost invisible. They had the purple-gray cast of another world. They beckoned to her.

I'm still light-headed from the loss of blood, she thought, absentmindedly fingering the partially healed scar on her wrist. She thought she was alone when the voice of Herod Antipas came from behind.

"Joanna, how good to find you here."

Instinctively Joanna knew that he had been watching for her. Nearing fifty, he was a commanding figure whose graying hair gave him an appeal that he had not possessed in his youth.

"How was your trip, my lord?"

"Wonderful. The Greek Islands are like jewels of the sea."

"Yes," she agreed. "My father loved them best of all."

Herod adopted a condolatory mood. "I'm sorry to hear of your father's death. Chuza tells me that it happened some weeks ago."

"Soon after you left on your wedding cruise." Joanna looked away over the rising white caps of the sea. "Is Herodias well?" she asked. "Was everything satisfactory when you arrived home last night?"

"Chuza is an excellent steward. In these four years I've not known a disordered household." Herod smiled.

The strain of their conversation seemed to ease. Herod shifted his weight to lean against the marble rail. He squinted at the water.

"Joanna."

"Yes, my lord?"

"Would you do your best to make her feel at home?"

Joanna was uncomfortable and didn't know how to answer. Herodias did not seem to be the type of woman another needed to look out for.

"There's been so much talk," Herod went on. "You'd think in this day, with all the divorces and remarriages that take place in Rome . . . but Palestine is so provincial!"

"I'll do my best, my lord, but Herodias is a strong woman; perhaps you worry needlessly."

"The Baptist really upsets her. I had no choice but to get him out of sight for awhile."

"Things seem to be quieting down."

"So Chuza told me."

"I'm sure that once the people adjust . . . "

"Yes, well, she will need some guidance until she knows the people of my domain. You know the influential women of Galilee."

Joanna reflected on her new role as Herodias's advisor. She had been a condescending companion to the shallow-minded Arabian princess; perhaps this role would be more interesting. But would it be more dangerous? No one would mistake Herodias for a weak woman. Was Herod really concerned for her delicate feelings, or more for her potential blunders? He was not a monarch with unlimited powers. He was anxious to please Rome.

"Has Salome amused herself in our absence?" he inquired.

Joanna wondered how to answer that question. "Amused" was not an appropriate description for the antics of his voluptuous maiden stepdaughter. Salome's attempts to flirt with Chuza, or any other man that she fancied to be in authority, were candid enough to be embarrassing. She was bored with other activities.

"She's done some bathing in the pool," Joanna said, "and she seems to have seen the sights of the city again."

It was not Salome's first visit to Tiberias. She had spent time at the palace two years before when her father and mother had stayed for some months. Salome's father was a half-brother to Herod Antipas. He lived as a private citizen in Caesarea.

A creeping shadow overtook the balcony as the sun disappeared behind an angry cloud. Herod turned to go.

"It looks as if we are in for a storm," he remarked.

"Yes."

Joanna stayed to watch the scene below. As if on a pedestal, she could view the city as far as its outer wall, other roof tops clearly visible. Herod had built his palace above the city, into the side of the mount. Colonnades of cool marble reflected the hot sun on beautiful days, and the golden roof was dazzling. But now it looked metallic in the gloom of impending storm. How it matched her mood!

Two other buildings of size could be seen from this balcony, the newly built stadium and the synagogue. *What a waste,* Joanna thought as she considered the beauty of the seldom-used synagogue.

There was a scurrying in the marketplace some distance away. Along the shore, fishermen were quickly securing their boats. A drop of rain splattered on her arm. Dark clouds moved swiftly in from the southwest. She also heard the opening of the gate in the outer court just below. Someone was being received into the palace grounds, but it probably wouldn't concern her.

Joanna's duties at the palace demanded no more than those of the wife of any high official. Protocol required her presence only on special occasions. Otherwise she was free to come and go, treating the palace as her home, as long as Chuza served Herod favorably.

She shivered as the gusting wind again snapped the veil about her face. Retreating into the hall, she headed for her own quarters.

The silken garment wrapped itself about her slim figure and fluttered in protest behind each step. Slaves had already lit the oil lamps set into alcoves along the wall. They flickered and threatened to go out as drafts of air played about her along the corridor.

She was startled by an elongated shadow stretched above the stairway to the lower court. Emis, an Egyptian slave of unusual height, came up the steps.

"Susanna, wife of Jacob Bar Saul, is here to see you." He bowed slightly.

So the visitor was for her. Susanna. How long had it been since they had seen each other? Several years.

"Show her to my chambers." She moved quickly in her excitement. Susanna must be coming now to show her respect for the memory of Joanna's father.

She hurried through the open cypress doorway to the private suite that she and Chuza shared. Lamps had been lit and reflected a warm glow. There were eight, placed on Corinthian-style sconces about the room. In the middle of the floor was a woven rug of wine and midnight blue with a low table of inlaid pearl and gold leaf trim. Cushions lay grouped in an inviting, careless fashion.

She was at the door to greet Susanna, who was followed by her personal maiden. Embracing her, with tears and laughter, Joanna drew her into the room. The maiden melted into the shadows, crouching against the wall. The two women dropped down on the brocaded cushions.

Joanna observed her friend. She had changed little, though perhaps she was a bit more plump. *Does she notice my thinness?* Joanna wondered.

"Oh, it's good to have you come," she said, hugging Susanna again.

"You're my dearest friend. I must be here to mourn with you." In the dim light Susanna's eyes glistened with tears, but she did not look directly at Joanna.

"You were two days away, with a young son and an aging husband to care for; but you've come. I didn't think you could."

"Was it terrible for you, Joanna?"

For a moment she didn't answer. "He was ill only a short while. He refused to come to Tiberias, where he could have had the attention of Herod's physician. For all his Hellenistic ways, my father was a Jew. He remained at Sepphoris, near his friend Rabbin Kesil. Chuza didn't complain about my absence from the palace, so I was with him until the end."

"He called for you then?"

"No, he was much too stubborn. My contacts were always through his steward, Jehucal. He would not relent and speak to me personally. He's never forgiven me for moving here, Susanna. I'm just surprised that he never changed his will and disinherited me. It was as if nothing mattered to him at the end. I'm sure he knew I was there, but he didn't acknowledge my presence."

"Do you have unbearable regrets, my friend?"

"It's the doubts that haunt me."

"Doubts?"

"I don't have the faith that my father had, and for the first time I wish I did. He believed in the state of peace at death. But death was final. Some believe in the spirit surviving death. Do you believe that, Susanna?"

"A resurrection, like the Pharisees believe?"

"Yes. Remember when we were young we agreed that belief in God and an afterlife was for little children and old people?"

"Yes, I remember." Susanna's dark head was bent, eyes averted.

"I never told him. I never admitted that I didn't believe in his awesome God," Joanna said, "but I have this eerie feeling—it's—it's as if he *knows!*" The silence was awkward for a moment. "Susanna . . . " Her voice dropped to a whisper. "Sometimes I think I'm losing control of my mind. It seems that the end of life is the only peace to be found."

"You're just unnerved by his death," her friend assured her, but her voice did not convey assurance.

"No, it's more than that. I don't know what it is. I imagine myself walking into the sea. I can feel the water closing around me and I melt into nothingness."

Susanna shivered. Joanna saw her discomfort and forced a laugh. "Pay no attention to me. I'm just pessimistic with all that's happening."

"What is it, Joanna? Is there anything wrong between you and Chuza?"

"Only . . . silence between us. There are things he doesn't tell me."

"Men are secretive about the world of men's concerns. You have everything you could want. His work has provided a king's palace for you to live in!"

"For how long?"

Susanna's brows knit. "What is it?"

"What have you heard of Herod's divorce and remarriage?" Joanna asked, nervously fingering the pearls sewn on her garment.

"It's a popular topic of conversation in Caesarea. It's not often a man marries his brother's wife while his brother still lives! But there are so many divorces in Roman circles, and Herod is hardly a religious Jew, if he is a Jew at all. Most consider this one more political move. In time the sensation will die down and everyone will accept it."

"Do you know about the Baptist?"

"Who?"

"The wilderness prophet preaching down by the Jordan, near Jericho. Herod has thrown him in prison."

Susanna's eyebrows arched.

"He was denouncing the marriage," Joanna continued. "He said their adulterous union is unlawful to God."

"But why would Herold fear a desert prophet?"

"Because the people were coming by the hundreds to hear him. The Baptist has influenced public opinion just when the anger of

King Aretas is about to explode! The Arabians have been humiliated by Herod's divorce from the princess. When she fled Galilee, they say her father massed his army just beyond the Perean-Nabatean border."

"Has there been any fighting yet?"

"Not that we've heard. Chuza says that Aretas is probably waiting until the time is ripe. That's why Herod had the Baptist arrested, so that things will quiet down. He didn't want the Arabians to feel secure in an attack. He had the prophet put into the dungeon at Machaerus."

She referred to the fortress located in the craggy cliffs above the Salt Sea. It was near the Nabatean border, nearly a hundred miles south of Tiberias.

"And you're concerned about Chuza's position?"

"Yes, he *is* Arabian. It scares me, Susanna. Herod has always favored Chuza. He trusts him, but with all the treason in high places it alarms me. In Rome they smile while handing you the poison cup! Chuza will not talk about it."

"Men do not share their fears with women. But I'm glad you have shared yours with me. I too have a deep concern."

Joanna looked sharply at her friend. Susanna's eyes still avoided hers. "What is it? I have thought only of my own problems. I've not even asked you about Jacob and Jonathan. Are they all right?"

"Yes. It's me."

"Are you ill?"

"I'm going blind. I've been to the best physicians, but they aren't able to help. When the sun is high, I see forms, but I can't recognize people. When it's dark, as it is now, I can't see obstacles in my way."

"And you listened while I shared my fears!"

"I came to comfort you in your loss, but I have another reason for spending some time in Galilee. There's a healer, a Nazarene called Jesus. Have you heard of him?"

"Yes, another prophet in the hills, that's all."

"They say he performs miracles."

"Susanna, you don't believe that he can heal you!"

"I've tried everything; where else can I turn? Jacob has spent a great deal on the best medical help to be found."

"He preaches to mobs, to riffraff. You would be forced to mingle with all kinds of people."

Susanna ignored the remark. "I can't go alone, Joanna. I can't see to make my way through the crowds. I haven't told Jacob that I'm going; he would forbid it. But the thought of never seeing Jonathan's face again compels me. Go with me, Joanna; I need you."

"Me? No. I couldn't!" In the shadow of the oil lamps Joanna could see her friend's pleading expression. It unnerved her. "Chuza wouldn't understand," she added lamely. A moment later her countenance brightened. "Besides, your servants will take you right through the crowds to him on your litter."

"No, I can't go that way. It would cause too much attention."

"Your clothing will cause attention," Joanna mused.

"But clothing can be changed for something more suitable."

"You've given it a lot of thought."

"Yes, I have. I even brought garments for each of us made of the coarse wool worn by the peasants. You must go with me. I need your strength of will. No servant can give me that."

Before she could respond, Joanna heard the soft footsteps of the slave girls. Three entered in rapid succession. Each one's sleek dark hair was braided in one thick braid and coiled at the nape. They were young with flawless complexions. Herod had no unattractive servants. The first carried a tray upon her head, piled with sliced cold lamb and smoked fish. The second bore a bowl of overflowing fruit and breads; the third carried a pitcher of water. They placed the food on the low table.

Heavier footsteps announced Chuza's arrival. Joanna rose and met him as he entered. He stopped when he saw Susanna seated on the cushions by the table.

"I see we have a guest." He moved swiftly to greet her. "Susanna, how good of you to come. Joanna needs her friends right now."

Joanna watched as Susanna fixed her gaze toward Chuza's voice. She pretended well. You would not guess immediately that she was nearly blind.

Chapter 11

Joanna felt the familiar, vague apprehension as she awoke. She tried to find a more comfortable position in order to lose herself in sleep again and noticed the empty side of their couch. Chuza was gone, and she supposed she should be up. But why should she rise early? He would work until the mid-morning meal. Besides, old memories had again stolen half a night's rest. Her father's disapproval haunted her even though he was gone.

For weeks she had begun each day exhausted. The physician wouldn't give her a sleeping potion. Was he afraid that she would take too much? Would he tell Herod of the self-inflicted wounds on her wrists? Now she was fully awake. Fear crawled up beside her like an uninvited, self-appointed companion who monopolized all her time.

Chuza strode briskly into the room; he looked displeased.

"Did you forget that you have a guest?" he asked abruptly.

Joanna sat upright. "Susanna! Oh, yes, I did forget. I slept so poorly."

"I know," he answered. "Whatever troubles you controls your body and soul." He sounded resentful and unsympathetic.

I was a failure as a daughter, and now I'm a failure as a wife, Joanna thought in self-pity. *I've never had the opportunity to be a mother. Susanna has! It is Susanna who has really had everything, a handsome son, wealth, and prestige without constant fear. She's pleased her father, and her husband adores her.*

But Susanna is going *blind.*

It was like an afterthought, invading. It was as another voice speaking to her mind.

"Chuza, have you talked to Susanna this morning?"

"Yes, her servant led her out on the balcony. She seems to enjoy the sun and sea air even if she can't see Gennesaret. We talked for a short while, but I had to leave. I'm not free to entertain her." His voice intimated that she should be looking after her guest, and having come for that purpose, he turned and left their chamber.

Joanna rose quickly. She dressed in a white linen garment with a simple brocade belt. Her servant Althea brushed her hair and wound a thin gold silk ribbon loosely about the tresses from the neckline down to the middle of her back and crisscrossed it back again. In moments she was ready and joined Susanna on the balcony.

Since the palace faced east, the sun completely bathed it in sparkling marble splendor. It was approaching midsummer and would soon be too hot and stifling to enjoy this setting. When it was too humid to sleep here in Tiberias, Herod, Herodias, and his court would retreat to Machaerus.

Susanna's face was tilted toward the morning sun. She laughed. "Listen to the birds. I wish I could see them."

Joanna closed her eyes. Although the sky, the sea, the birds, and the balcony disappeared, the warmth of the sun, a slight breeze, and sounds remained. *So this is what it is like,* she thought. Yet she knew there was more to being blind than she could imagine in a few moments.

"Susanna, would you enjoy bathing in the sulphur springs at Amathus?" She was happy to think of an activity of "feeling" that her friend could enjoy. "Unless, of course, you're concerned about the burial grounds."

Amathus was two miles south of Tiberias and encompassed the ancient, much-disputed cemetery.

"Joanna, I'm not here to be entertained. You know what I've come for. Are you going with me?"

Susanna was looking almost directly at her. She could see the discoloration that was occurring and the loss of personality that had once been alive in Susanna's eyes. They no longer danced in delight or snapped in anger. Her eyes were blank and lifeless.

Joanna shuddered. Would she soon have the ugly milky white eyes of the blind beggars outside the city gates?

❖ ❖ ❖

Joanna could feel the sun beating down upon her back, penetrating the loosely woven and ill-fitting garment. It was of a lightweight wool and it itched. How could the peasants stand it? A trickle of perspiration ran down her back, and then a slight breeze brought a momentary cooling sensation.

They had reached the summit of the smaller mount. Emis stopped the donkey on which she rode, and Susanna's animal, led by her maiden, Lia, came abreast. Emis's appearance was so altered by what he wore that the only thing familiar was his unusual height. His bald head and the pierced ear with the gold ring that identified his slavery were covered with the headdress worn well over the forehead, Arabian style.

They had dressed in the common clothing once outside the walls of Tiberias. The journey was supposed to be a simple one to the baths at Amathus, but instead they turned northwest, toward where it was rumored that Jesus taught.

Joanna trusted Emis. She knew that a grapevine of gossip existed in the palace among the servants, but she felt assured that Emis would be no part of it. Susanna had the same confidence in Lia. The girl was young and had been born to the household of Jacob Bar Saul. Since she was only a few years older than Jonathan, it had been her duty as a youngster to entertain him with games. Now he attended school in Jerusalem, and Lia was devoted to his mother. Susanna treated the young girl almost as a daughter.

Emis pointed beyond the bowl-shaped valley to the opposite mount, where the hillside was a mass of moving colors against the windblown grass.

"What is it?" Susanna asked. "Why do we stop?"

"You should see the sight," Joanna said, "people coming from all directions!"

Susanna sat up straight. It was as if she willed herself to see, and Joanna regretted her remark. Coming closer, they could hear the sounds of other animals, although most people came on foot. Emis remained with the donkeys when they dismounted, while Joanna and Lia, one on each side of Susanna, helped her up the hill.

Joanna stumbled over the protruding pole of a hand-carried cot. A palsied man, as thin as a living skeleton, looked up at her. His dark eyes were like two pebbles sunk in ashen clay. She wondered how any person who looked so wretched could still breathe, and she turned away quickly. As her eyes scanned the hill, she saw that nearly half the crowd was either maimed or ill. The sight almost overwhelmed her. For the first time she thought of Susanna's blindness as a blessing.

They found a spot about one-third the distance from the top, but had to move off to the side for the people were sitting almost one upon the other. Those who tried to move in were met with curses and shoving.

"Here children, move over and let the women sit down."

The voice belonged to a young mother who sat with her children on the fringe of the crowd. The girl, about ten, and a boy, about seven, pulled in their outstretched limbs and sat cross-legged. With relief, Joanna saw that they were whole and moderately dressed, not ragged and dirty as so many others were. The woman was large-boned, with a broad forehead and handsome features.

The boy looked at Susanna curiously, and the girl smiled shyly. Joanna thanked their mother and helped to settle Susanna on the matted grass, removing some larger stones with her fingers. She became conscious of the woman watching her hands. Constant applications of creams had kept them soft and smooth. Joanna's nails were unbroken and manicured. The mother smiled.

"You must never grind the grain," she said.

"Not now, but I did once," Joanna answered and felt the warming kinship of common experience.

A swell in the murmuring of the crowd brought their attention forward. A tall, well-built man in a simple white tunic and striped cloak descended the hill and approached the crowd. His hand was raised to silence them.

"He's there, isn't he?" Susanna asked excitedly. "Tell me what he looks like."

"He's very strong looking," Joanna said, "about thirty years of age, with dark hair and beard. He's not extraordinary." She thought of the prophet locked in the dungeon at Machaerus. That one was almost wild looking, with a camel-hair skirt and leather girdle about his loins, his hair and beard a wiry mane. The Baptist yelled to command attention and then shouted God's message to repent. She was sure that people rushed to be baptized out of sheer terror of his proclaimed "wrath to come."

Rumor said that the two were kinsmen. But this one was from Nazareth, and John, the Baptist, was from Judea. They were not at all alike. Jesus had quieted the crowd with a simple raising of his hand. Now he began to speak, calmly and quietly, as if he were talking to a group of inquiring students, instead of thousands gathered on the hill. The mount made a natural amphitheater, and he had a rare quality of voice that made it possible to hear every word he spoke clearly.

A cloud of calm enveloped Joanna as he talked in parables. She experienced an unknown tranquility, yet her mind was keenly alert. He talked of the beauty of the world around them and of how God dressed the flowers of the field while they, unconcerned and trusting, danced in the sea breezes. She thought of the times that she had spent an entire day contemplating the right silk gown, the most impressive jewelry, and the most unusual hair style for an event at court.

Jesus' illustrations made her acutely aware of the natural beauty around her. Even this mother, sitting with her children, wore no lip rouge or shading for her eyes, yet the freshness of her face and the peaceful happiness reflected there were evident in shining eyes.

He talked on, of how foolish it is to place your faith in material riches, saying that it was more important to treasure spiritual things. He made it sound as if there were another, more important life, a kind of eternal destiny for which a person would sacrifice the temporal things of this world. It was confusing and mystical to Joanna. He must be a Pharisee, she thought, for he spoke of the resurrection of the dead.

Then he began a story about a man who built his house on sand. The *beit shaar* of her early marriage, raised on the Arabian desert, came quickly to mind. She followed his descriptive illustration with vivid memories of gusting sandstorms and the swelling turbulence of the wadi filled with winter rains. They could be perfectly dry and safe until a storm; then they became a flood of dangerous strength.

The story haunted her, for she grasped that she had built her own house on sand, not only physically but spiritually.

Presently he stopped talking as quietly as he had begun, and people began scrambling and stumbling and even crawling toward him. Some men, who had surrounded him while he talked, began to organize the mob into an orderly line so that all might see him in turn.

"If you want to take her to Jesus for healing, you'd better join the line," the young mother said, and then added proudly, "my husband is one of his disciples. See the tall one there near the Master?"

It was the first time Joanna had heard the prophet referred to as "The Master." She thanked the woman and turned to Susanna, who had heard and was already trying to move forward. Lia arose quickly and placed her forearm under her mistress's elbow to give her both support and direction.

The line was long, and there was great noise and confusion. Some, not wanting healing, descended the hill and dispersed, while others crowded near to gape in wonder. Still others met loved ones who had been touched by Jesus and chattered excitedly. Children darted in and out, using the moving throng as obstacles to play the games of tag or hide-and-seek.

Joanna watched Susanna's face while they waited. It was aglow with expectancy. She felt choked with fear for her friend's disappointment. Behind them, a woman held a two-year-old child who had one stunted arm. Joanna turned away and tried to focus on other things. *How awful to have your hopes raised and then crushed,* she thought.

For a moment panic took command. She wanted to break from the line and escape down the hill. She pulled the cloth of the coarse headdress close about her face.

"What's happening?" Susanna asked. "How much farther? Is someone being healed now?"

Joanna tried to peer between the people who milled about the disciples. The tall one and others lined the way to Jesus to protect him from the pressure of the crowd. In patches, she could see the man who had lain on the stretcher. He was getting to his feet and standing on those sticklike legs! She gasped.

"Tell me," Susanna demanded. But before Joanna could answer, one of the disciples asked her what her problem was.

"My friend needs her sight."

Now only she and Susanna moved through the tunnel of disciples toward Jesus. As they approached, he looked at them intently. There was no need for a spoken request. In that moment she was sure that he knew everything.

In fascination she watched as he took Susanna's face between his strong, firm hands. They were rough, workman's hands. Had she not heard somewhere that he was a carpenter? He tilted Susanna's face up, for he was much taller. When he looked at her his eyes were bright with a strange inner light that reflected the same authority as his voice.

"Woman," he commanded. "Look at me."

Susanna's eyes blinked rapidly and then a flood of tears streamed down her cheeks. Dropping to her knees she murmured, "Thank you, thank you," and kissed the hem of his robe.

He turned his attention to Joanna, but her eyes retreated from his gentle, questioning gaze.

"Oh—I have no need, my lord," she said.

"You have great need," he told her simply.

Susanna, oblivious of their exchange, arose and hugged Joanna. "Thanks be to God," she said. "Now I can see my son again."

"Your faith has established it," Jesus told her in a deep vibrating tone that echoed in Joanna's mind. Then he turned his attention to the mother and child who were next in line.

Lia had found her way to the other side, where a stream of rejoicing people made their way down the mount. She greeted them with nervous laughter. Susanna alternated between singing and tears, while Joanna moved as if in a trance. In her mind she stood on the fringe of the experience and watched like an interested bystander.

They had joined Emis and were well on the way back to Tiberias by the time Joanna could cope with the myriad of thoughts that invaded her mind.

"How will we explain this to Chuza?" she asked.

Chapter 12

"If Susanna received her sight yesterday, why do you want to go back to see the prophet again today?" Chuza asked as they dressed for the morning.

"To hear him teach," Joanna answered. "And what do you mean, '*if* Susanna received her sight?' You can see that she has."

"Perhaps she was never really blind. She said that she could see objects vaguely. Maybe there was a mist over her eyes. You mentioned her tears; maybe when he pressed her eyelids with his hands . . . "

"He didn't touch her eyes!" His skepticism bothered her, although she herself entertained doubts. *That's why I have to go to the mount again,* she thought. Her questions were more consuming than her fears. If she could find answers to the questions, perhaps her fears would not have so much control.

"I don't like it," Chuza said. "I don't want my wife mingling with the riffraff of cities like Magdala."

"There are all kinds of people who come to hear him, Chuza. Some are of average means, like the mother and her children we met on the mount yesterday. Her husband is one of his disciples."

"If you want to hear him, we could summon him to court. I'm sure that Herod would like to know what the latest prophet in his territory is teaching."

"I don't believe Jesus would come."

"What? He wouldn't be flattered with an audience before a king?"

"I don't think Jesus would be awed by Herod Antipas, or any real king—even Caesar." She wasn't sure how she knew that; perhaps it was in Jesus' manner and authority. "I think people have to come to him. He would only come to Tiberias if forced."

"That's not impossible. Remember the Baptist."

"Jesus is different. He said nothing yesterday that was political."

"Neither did the wilderness prophet, but his personal attack on Herod's morals was inadvertently political."

Joanna became momentarily silent and then spoke carefully. "Jesus is a teacher, a thought-provoking teacher. Why don't you come with us to hear him, Chuza?"

He laughed. "And be considered a fool at court? It will be embarrassing enough if Herod hears of our guest receiving her 'miraculous' sight, or of your association with the peasants on the mount!"

"Susanna wants to hear him once more before returning to Caesarea. Don't forbid me to accompany her, Chuza."

"I've never forbidden you anything," Chuza said. His eyes studied her a moment. "If I did forbid you, would it make any difference, Joanna?"

❖ ❖ ❖

The two women and their servants again took to the hills, following a trail west of the city of Magdala, which was two miles north of Tiberias. When they were in sight of the mount where Jesus had taught the day before, the crowd was dispersing. A large number made their exodus toward Capernaum, on the sea, north of Tiberias by about five miles. Moving closer, they joined the others on the road and were told that Jesus was headed there. Capernaum was now his headquarters, they said, because his own town of Nazareth did not accept him. He was too presumptuous, so the rumors went; he made himself greater than he was and alluded to being the Messiah.

Joanna didn't believe it. The townspeople were probably jealous of his popularity. The Messiah, if indeed there was one, would be a military leader. Zealot revolutionaries sometimes laid claim to the title Messiah or Deliverer, but not Jesus! His words on the mount yesterday were not those of a political fanatic. His ideas were idealistic, full of love, not hate.

The size of the crowd grew as they approached Capernaum. Like a river, it flowed into the streets of the unwalled seaport village. Sitting astride a donkey, she could see over the heads of others to where Jesus walked with the cluster of his disciples deftly screening him from the enthusiasm of the people.

"He's headed to Simon's house," someone called to another.

"Then he means to refresh himself. Let's go down to the lake."

Many diverted to rest by the waters of Galilee or left for their own homes in Capernaum and Bethsaida. The foursome from Tiberias were able to move closer. A murmur of astonishment rippled through the crowd as a delegation of city leaders with a Roman centurion, who was assigned to Capernaum, approached Jesus. Joanna watched curiously. The Roman was not detaining him in any official manner. It appeared he wanted a favor. Onlookers whispered that he wanted healing for a servant.

Now, Jesus looked about him to see if the crowd had heard. "Indeed," he commented, "I've found no greater faith in all Israel! As you have believed, so it will be done."

There it is again, Joanna thought, *the reference to faith and believing.*

❖ ❖ ❖

The three women cooled their feet at the shallow water's edge. The afternoon was hot and humid, but like so many others who had travelled to see Jesus, they stubbornly waited. It had been hours since he entered the home of Simon Bar Jona. News that Jesus had healed not only the centurion's servant, but Simon's mother-in-law, had circulated among the crowd.

Joanna was a child again, sitting on a rock, dangling her feet in the water and waiting for a special person to appear. She listened to each story in an effort to know him better. Not everyone could be everywhere he taught, so they excitedly shared the things they had seen.

"Did you see the leper that he healed at the foot of the mount?" someone asked, and when the answer was no, details of the event were told with much interruption from others who had witnessed it, too. Some insisted that he was healed immediately, others said, no, that he was sent to the priest. Still another explained that Jesus sent him to the priest merely to confirm the healing and to uphold the law.

Joanna was more concerned with the fact that a leper dared to come close to the people. Usually they kept apart and called, "unclean, unclean," to warn the healthy people to stay away from them. She cautiously looked about to see if any there had the telltale white spots of the dread disease on their hands or faces.

What am I doing here? she thought. *Chuza was right. Why am I exposing myself to such things? Not everyone was healed. Didn't the people say that he did few miracles in his own town of Nazareth because of their unbelief? I don't have faith like Susanna has!* A familiar creeping fear came over her. She didn't realize until now that the events of the day had freed her mind from such thoughts for hours.

"Perhaps we should go," she said.

"Wait, I think I see him coming," Susanna answered.

The people again crowded about the tall, broad figure as he strode purposefully toward the water. He settled himself under a large spreading oak. The sick and those helping them wormed their way closer. Those who were possessed were brought before him. Some were insane, with eyes that stared blankly. Joanna felt light-headed. Her heart pounded in her breast as though it would escape and take her with it, yet she was as petrified as the rock she sat upon.

With only a commanding word, Jesus cast out demons. Sometimes the afflicted silently sobbed as they returned to reality and responded to their loved ones. Others were not so quietly delivered, and it was a relief to see someone come, from time to time, who was not so dramatically ill.

The onlookers had swollen to a multitude, and some were rude in their attempts to press closer. Jesus was near the fishing boats of Zebedee, and when he gave the signal to depart, two brawny fisherman leaped to assist him aboard. Other disciples quickly followed, and immediately they pushed out from shore. Some people waded into the sea, others dashed for their own small boats, but the sons of Zebedee had been prepared. In moments they sailed beyond reach.

With a giant groan, the crowd began to move like a great caterpillar. It was late, and darkness would settle in before many were home. Emis helped Susanna and Joanna onto their donkeys, and he and Lia led the animals along the shoreline to Tiberias. This was the shortest route, but they would have to go by Magdala.

The crowd on the road thinned once they passed the village of Gennesaret, and Joanna became aware of a woman who walked alone. As they came alongside her, the woman spoke.

"Are you going to Dalmanutha?" she asked. "You're not from Magdala."

"No, Tiberias," Joanna answered.

"I hope you don't get wet. The storm may overtake you. You're welcome to shelter at my home." Her eyes were soft and a contradiction to the hard lines of her face. She appeared to be in her late thirties. Handsome features hinted at a onetime youthful beauty.

"Thank you," Joanna responded, "but we must return to Tiberias."

"Have you been following the Master for long?"

"We first saw him yesterday on the mount. My friend was healed of blindness."

The woman's lips formed an unspoken "ah-h." She observed Susanna on the donkey a few feet behind Joanna. They paused, and Lia brought the animal abreast.

"I too have been healed by Jesus," she told Susanna. "I had seven demons."

"Seven?" Joanna exclaimed.

"I was like seven different people. I would change like a flash of lightning." As if to illustrate her point, a brilliant jagged vein momentarily lit up the sky. "I could be as calm as the sea on a summer morning, unaware of anything around me, and just as stormy a moment later. My husband divorced me. He feared that I might harm our daughters. He was right," she added sadly. "I was unable to control my actions toward them."

"Where are they now?" Susanna asked.

"In Cana. I left and came to Magdala. Everyone shunned me in Cana."

"But you must go back and tell them of your healing," Susanna said.

She shook her head and the brightness in her eyes dimmed. "My husband has taken another wife, and my children are grown. They would not know me, nor would they want to. I had to survive. I've lived in Magdala for the past thirteen years."

Silence hung as heavy as the humid air. Joanna assessed the woman again. She wore no jewelry or make-up, nor the garments of the prostitutes of Magdala; yet was there another occupation for a single woman in such a city? Of course there was. She must not make judgments. Jesus had taught on that subject yesterday as they sat on the mount. People could change what they were. They were at a turnoff from the wider trail, which led to the right and into the commercial section of the village. The fishing community was separated by the main road and was to their left along the shore. The woman hesitated near the village trail.

Joanna could see women sitting alone on either side of the street in front of their square whitewashed stone huts. Provocatively cross-legged, they were heavily adorned with gaudy silver medallions and their faces were grotesquely painted. Men who had skirted the five travelers as they stood in the fork of the road now passed the women and were accosted in the singsong, suggestive language of their trade. Joanna shuddered. Did most of the women choose that, or were they to be pitied, knowing no other way to survive?

The woman on the trail interrupted her thoughts. "I must leave you here, but we may meet again. My name is Mary."

Joanna hoped that Mary could not read her mind. She was flustered, but she would have to share their names. "I'm Joanna, and this is Susanna," she said, dispensing with the traditional 'wife of' clarification. She almost neglected to introduce the servants, but Mary's eyes were questioning.

"And those of our household," she finished lamely, "Lia and Emis." Both servants bowed, and Joanna watched Mary's face for her reaction. Whatever her thoughts, her eyes didn't reveal them. Undoubtedly this woman had seen much of life's inconsistencies while living in Magdala.

"God be with you," Mary saluted them.

"And with you," Susanna answered.

Lightning played among the hills and thunder resounded on the lake by the time they neared the trail to Dalmanutha. They pressed on for the final mile of the trip to Tiberias, feeling the first splatters of rain. The wind whipped huge waves on the rocks along the shore. A startling crack of thunder jarred Joanna's fear. Jesus and his disciples were crossing the sea in a fishing boat. How could they possibly make it in this storm? Panic washed over her. It was like the panic that overtook her as she watched her father struggle and finally die only weeks before. Memory transported her to his couch again.

"Father, don't leave me," she had pleaded over and over again to the silent figure on the pillows. He was only a shadow of his former self, shrinking to mere bones stretched over skin. His bushy brows were a tangled accent on his sallow face, and the closed eyelids were like a transparent veil.

For days he had rambled. Some of his words she could understand. They centered on old hurts. She tried to resolve them, but she couldn't reach him. Finally he lapsed into unconsciousness. She watched him for hours, willing him to live. She was disillusioned by his mortality. He had always been so indestructible, and now his helplessness angered her.

He rallied right before his death and raised up with a strength he hadn't shown in days. At first her heart surged with hope, but his eyes stared right through her as though she weren't there. Yet it was she he spoke to in a rasping rattle.

"Don't walk on my bones, Joanna; promise me that you won't walk on my bones!"

She could hear screaming that vibrated within herself, and she thought that the professional mourners had been called to take up bewailing the death of Samuel Bar Simeon so that all might know that the end had come. It wasn't until she felt the slap on her wet face that she realized the scream had come from her own throat. She was not at her father's deathbed, but in a storm on the trail outside the walls of Tiberias, and the woolen garment that she wore hung sopping and heavy against her skin. She and Susanna were no longer seated on their donkeys; instead, Susanna cradled her shaking body.

"I'm sorry that I had to slap you, Joanna, but you were beside yourself. I was afraid that the guards of the city gates would hear you. But I think the storm muffled your cries."

Woodenly Joanna allowed them to lead her toward the gates of the city that her father hated, the pagan city Tiberias, built on the remains of the dead.

Chapter 13

I heard that we had a guest in the palace, but I decided that you must be a ghost."

The voice of Salome drifted off the shaded portico to Joanna as she approached the enclosed garden. Salome and Susanna stood in the center near the bust of Tiberius Caesar. Large, tropical shade-loving plants created a backdrop of jungle splendor. Gnarled vines snaked their way up the stone walls and displayed a leafy canopy above them.

"Have they kept you in hiding?" Herod's stepdaughter continued. Her dark eyes were large and mischievous.

Susanna smiled, and Joanna thought how good it was to see her friend's personality speaking through her eyes.

"We've been gone from the palace a good deal of the time," she answered. "I wanted to see some of the area."

Joanna reached them, and the girl turned to her. "I've just become acquainted with your friend," she said. "I do hope she will stay a while."

"I must return to Caesarea," Susanna said. "I have a son who will be home soon from temple school in Jerusalem."

"But you've only just arrived. No one travels a distance for so short a time, except the peasants."

"My husband needs me," Susanna said. "He's getting older and misses me when I'm gone."

"How touching," Salome remarked. "You're married to an older man, yet you seem devoted."

Susanna smiled. "Ours has been a good relationship."

"I'll be marrying an older man," Salome announced. "Probably my Uncle Philip, my father Herod Philip's half brother. The Herods almost always marry Herods, you know. My mother was promised to my father when she was born." She waited for their reaction and when Susanna's expression registered enough curiosity, she prattled on.

"You see, Herod the Great wasn't only my father's father, but also my mother's grandfather. My grandfather, Aristobolus, was a son born of Mariamne I. She's of the Hasmonean house," Salome bragged.

Joanna and Susanna were well aware of the complicated intermarriages of the Herods, as well as those of the Caesars, but they politely allowed Salome to go on. *The past would be enough to disturb any young girl,* Joanna thought.

Herod the Great had been married ten times and had ten sons. He had ordered the trial for treason that resulted in execution for his own son, Aristobolus, Salome's grandfather, and he had already slain the woman who bore him, Mariamne I.

Joanna remembered herself at fifteen, impressionable and caught up in the mystery of whom she would marry. For Salome it would be decided for political reasons. No wonder she flirted with every man she met. In wealthy or royal families love was not a consideration. Joanna thought of the young peasants who met at festivals and often had their choice in their marriage arrangements, but the ruling families married for position and were lightly disposed of by those in power if it was necessary.

"I've always thought that older men were interesting," Salome said. "Do you know Manaen? I think he's so handsome with that dark, curly hair. He's here in the palace, you know. He just arrived from Antioch."

This was news to Joanna, who had exchanged little conversation with Chuza since she and Susanna returned from their day in

Capernaum. She suspected that Susanna or Emis had told him of her scene outside the city gates, and he was waiting until he was sure that she was herself again before asking her about the episode.

"I like it when there are visitors in the palace," Salome continued. "It's usually so boring. Now they're all talking about the new Galilean preacher."

Joanna and Susanna exchanged glances.

"Mother thinks that he should be locked up immediately. Already they say that there are more people listening to him than followed the Baptist."

"But I understand that he doesn't do anything to cause trouble," Joanna responded.

"And he's healed so many people," Susanna added.

"I'd like to see one!" Salome replied.

Susanna started to speak, but Joanna's eyes begged her silence.

"They are probably all fakes, paid to claim a healing." Salome said.

"Perhaps it would be interesting to observe," Susanna suggested.

"Wouldn't that be exciting!" Salome agreed. "If I just knew someone who would take me. Do you think I could talk the king into sending a delegation?" She used the courtesy title for Herod Antipas, as many had begun to do these days.

"That would surely be considered official recognition of his prophet status," Joanna said.

"You're right. That would never do, but I still think it would be fun. Well, perhaps I could dress like a peasant and mingle with the others. That way no one would ever know!" she suggested mischievously.

❖ ❖ ❖

"I hope you'll settle down now that Susanna has returned to Caesarea," Chuza remarked as they ate their first dinner alone after her departure.

"What do you mean?" Joanna asked even through she was sure she already knew what he meant.

"I think your diversion of listening to hillside preachers has upset you."

"If I'm upset, as you say, it's not because I've been listening to Jesus. He calms my spirit."

"But you lost control the other night. Susanna told me; she was worried about you. You've tried to end your life. You can't find your father by killing yourself!"

"That's not what I tried to do. Twice I defied him, once to marry you and again by living in this palace. Is that what you think, that I want to be with him? I'm not sure there is a spirit world, and I'm sure Father didn't believe in one."

"I don't know why you did it. You don't talk about it. But it's clear that you want to escape from me."

Joanna pondered his remark. She had not considered that he would take it personally. *Escape? Was that what I tried to do?* She didn't think of herself as a coward, but as someone who preferred to control her own destiny, rather than have it controlled by political influences or superstition. Her thoughts were in confusion, and she didn't answer.

"Is our marriage so intolerable to you?" Pain registered in Chuza's dark eyes. "You've been the wife a man dreams of having, Joanna, supportive of my ambitions by day and a delight in my bed at night, but now you're wrapped in your own concerns and you turn to me like a concubine."

The accusation was true, and Joanna had no response except one of defense. "I've tried to talk to you, but you won't listen. You make light of my fears."

"What fears?"

"Of conditions at Rome. Sejanus acting like he's emperor instead of commander of the Pretorian Guard, while Tiberius resides at Capri. I'm afraid Herod has been involved with Sejanus. Whenever we hear from Rome someone else has been accused of treason and put to death. I hear rumors, but you hide things from me. Why, Chuza? What do you know of the flight of the princess to Nabatea?"

He didn't answer so she pressed on.

"You were involved in her escape, weren't you?"

He seemed to be considering the best answer, and so she laughed without humor. "See, you don't answer my questions."

"Yes," he said angrily. "Yes, I was involved. What would you expect me to do? She didn't deserve to be ill treated. The divorce was humiliation enough."

Knowing that the thing she feared was true didn't make Joanna less shocked by his admission. Now she knew why he hadn't told her. It was better not knowing.

"What will they do to you if they find out?"

"I don't know," Chuza said. "But I feel in my bones that Herodias is the one to watch. There's a streak of meanness in that woman. It's rumored that when she told Herod to 'get rid of her,' she wasn't suggesting divorce."

"I wish you could have had as much concern for me as for the princess," Joanna said. "Now she's safe, and we're the ones in jeopardy."

Chuza looked at her in disgust. "You have your father's inheritance. If you want safety, you can go to Sepphoris. If remaining my wife is still threatening, I'll give you a bill of divorcement."

Joanna took a deep breath. "Come with me, Chuza," she urged. "We could be ordinary citizens. With all the uncertainty at Rome and now in Palestine, let's get away from it! Susanna and Jacob live a quiet life in Caesarea. We could live quietly too."

In her enthusiasm she had taken Chuza's arm. He pulled away from her. "If I were going to run," he said, "I would have run with the princess to Nabatea. To go now would certainly make me look guilty, and to remain in Palestine would lend suspicion to treason. I was concerned for the princess's protection, but I'm not sympathetic to her father's revenge. I'll stay and trust that my past performance as the king's steward will seal my loyalty."

❖ ❖ ❖

Joanna glanced about the room at the familiar objects in her father's home in Sepphoris and wondered why she had thought that she would feel more secure here. This was no longer her home, although title and responsibility for all of Samuel's estate had passed into her hands.

If she had expected peace of mind on moving from Tiberias, she had only exchanged that uncertainty for the company of a host of bad memories. There was no escape.

She had traded her life as Samuel's daughter for that of Chuza's wife. Could she undo what was done after fourteen years? They had only been separated once before, while her father was ill. At that time her mind had been absorbed by the events surrounding his death. Now time hung heavily. Since her father had his affairs well ordered and under the management of an excellent steward, there were only the routine matters of the law to be taken care of by the scribe whom her father had depended on for years.

Only she and Chuza knew that this trip alone to Sepphoris was more than business. It would determine whether or not she would choose to remain in Sepphoris or to return to Tiberias in time to accompany Herod's court to Machaerus for the summer months. Chuza would divorce her if she wished. She should be grateful. He could refuse, and she would have no recourse. She smiled when remembering that Abdul had insisted on the divorce clause to protect Chuza. *Now it may be used to protect me,* she thought. Humiliation would be her lot. Was she ready to face that? Would it be better than living with her fears?

Her reflections were interrupted by Emis as he appeared in the archway. He bowed low. She looked at him fondly. How good it was to have one trusted servant to accompany her from Tiberias. Her father's servants were very dear, especially Monaca, but Emis—Emis had saved her life. He had been there to bind her wrists. Joanna knew Chuza sent him to protect her from herself.

"What is it?" Joanna asked. "I hope no old friend has come to call."

"No, I've heard some news among the servants that I thought might interest you, my lady."

"Oh?"

"Jesus of Nazareth is passing through the cities of Galilee. He has been to Nain and will be near Cana this afternoon on his return to Capernaum."

"Are you suggesting that we go to hear him?"

Emis hesitated.

"Speak your thoughts, Emis."

"I see you so troubled, my lady. Perhaps the words of the prophet could help you."

"He heals bodies, Emis."

"He healed the soul of the Magdalene."

"Are you saying that I have a demon?"

"I don't know what troubles you," Emis said. "But I know it will destroy you. Nothing is too hard for this prophet. It is said that he raised a widow's son from his death-bier in Nain."

Joanna's eyes widened. "A dead man can hardly express faith."

"What, my lady?"

"I thought that faith must exist to be healed."

"They say he commands nature and even the winds obey him. He is truly a man visited by God."

"If all they say is true," Joanna said skeptically, "he must *be* God.

Chapter 14

Less than two miles east of the city walls, Joanna and Emis encountered the swelling crowd. Like a ribbon of ants, they came from Sepphoris, Cana, Nazareth, and other nearby villages. The focal point was a shady grove where Jesus sat teaching all who came.

Joanna walked with Emis beside her, dressed as an equal. She was less concerned about being recognized leaving from Sepphoris than she had been when traveling from Tiberias, so she wore a simple white linen garment and woven belt. Her headdress shadowed her eyes and swathed her face as if to shield it from the sun, but it provided a measure of anonymity. Her amber eyes scanned the scene.

A cross section of humanity mingled together in the grassy meadow. Some fanned themselves and sprawled on the ground, tired from their walk. Many were jovial, sharing the latest events of Jesus' ministry, but not all were there to learn, nor did they attempt to listen. Among the people were scribes, Pharisees, and Sadducees, the various factions of Judaism arguing the law. It was easy to identify them with their robes embroidered and tasseled according to their office in the Galilean Sanhedrin. She saw Rabbin Kesil from the synagogue of Sepphoris and was careful to find a place where she could watch without being seen.

Joanna spotted the two burly fishermen who had taken Jesus aboard a boat of Zebedee's that day in Capernaum and also the one they called Simon Peter, whose wife she had met on the mount.

There were others whom she recognized as those who followed Jesus, milling about near the edge of the crowd.

A cluster of people were gathered around Jesus, waiting their turn to talk to him. He seemed to listen intently before answering their questions. Near Joanna was a group of about five people whose buzzing conversation rode roughshod over her attempts to hear what he said.

"He's just a carpenter," said one. "I know his family. I've lived in Nazareth all my life."

"I hear that he's not welcome there any more," remarked a red-faced man, wiping the perspiration from his face with his sleeve. "They nearly ran him off a cliff last time."

"Well, he got up in the synagogue and read from the scroll of Isaiah, the prophecy concerning the Messiah. Then he said that it is fulfilled today—in *him!*"

"He goes everywhere talking about the kingdom of God, as though it were *his* kingdom," accused another.

"He thinks that he is above the rest of us now that so many follow and listen to his words," a plump matron declared.

"You'd think that he had been sent to Jerusalem to sit at the feet of Rabbin Gamaliel or one of the other great teachers of the Law and the Prophets."

"Oh, no," said another sardonically, "He's God-ordained!"

They laughed, and Joanna moved away from the gossiping mouths. Followed by Emis, she worked her way toward the listening circle.

Several men, dressed in the rough, country style of the Judean wilderness, approached Jesus. He turned to them.

"Sir," said one, "We come from John, who is still in prison. He bids us ask you if you are the one we are to expect, or should we look for another?"

Jesus studied them intently. "You have watched. The blind see; the lame walk; good news is preached to the poor. Go and tell John of the things you have seen."

When the men left, Jesus spoke to the crowd. "I tell you, there is none born who is greater than John, of all the prophets, yet the least in the kingdom of God will be greater than he."

There it was again, Joanna thought, that reference to the kingdom of God. What could it mean to be part of the kingdom of God? Didn't this Hebrew, as all Hebrews, believe that he was *born* of God's chosen people and sealed by circumcision?

She was both disturbed and intrigued by his teaching. Much of it mystified her, yet she listened with fascination. When he stood up to move on, she was oblivious to others around her. She rushed to catch up with him.

"Sir," she said, and he turned to see who spoke, "I wish to know more about the kingdom of God."

"You must be born of the Spirit to see the kingdom of God," he said. "Follow me."

Joanna dropped back bewildered as other swarmed around her and plied him with questions. Emis was silent, waiting. What was hauntingly familiar about the prophet's eyes? She stood a moment more, watching the crowd part and divert around them as waters do for a twig in the stream. Others were branching off in the direction of their villages.

And then she remembered the quiet young carpenter in her own childhood garden. *Jesus Bar David? Could it be possible?*

"We'll return to Sepphoris and prepare to follow him to Capernaum," Joanna said decisively.

"And from Capernaum, will we return to Tiberias?" Emis asked.

"I don't know," she answered.

❖ ❖ ❖

Joanna relaxed in the sun, feeling the Galilean breeze brush her face. Her headdress was thrown carelessly back on her shoulders so she could take advantage of any stirring air. She was no longer concerned that she might be recognized.

Insects buzzed. Someone opened a lunch of fish and bread, but even the strong aroma of the smoked fish was pleasant. There was the gnawing of her own hunger. Emis motioned to the lunch he carried. She nodded. Servant and lady sat on the matted grass and shared a bit of goat's cheese, bread, figs, and dates. Never had she enjoyed so many simple meals.

With Sepphoris as her resting place, Joanna had followed Jesus as he ministered in the neighboring areas of Asochis and Cana. On the Sabbath he spoke in the synagogues, but daily he taught in the open countryside.

Her emotional healing was gradual. With the growth of faith, her confusion, frustration, and desire for self-destruction had melted away, as if they had belonged to someone else. Through Jesus' teachings she knew that it wasn't her father's disapproval that burdened her with guilt, but her unworthiness before her true Father, the Lord God. Death was the judgment and the ultimate fear; but the torment of the fear was worse than death itself!

"All who come unto me have eternal life," Jesus had said. "The Father sent the Son into the world to save it, not to condemn it."

Joanna's heart skipped with joy that she had made the choice to follow him the day she stood so uncertainly outside the city of Sepphoris. Squinting toward the top of the hill, she saw Jesus return from his time of prayer. This morning his countenance had been light, positive, and compassionate. Now he appeared subdued by something of great importance to share. She leaned forward and willed herself to remember all he said. Soon she was lost in his words, as if they were spoken to her alone.

"You who are rich, take warning; your consolation is in riches and you think you have no need."

The day of Susanna's healing came to mind. Those were her very words! *But I see my need now,* Joanna's heart cried to Yahweh, *and I seek the kingdom of God.*

"Give generously to those in need and to God's work, for where your treasure is, your heart will be also."

Joanna frowned. She had been seeking the kingdom of God because of what it would do for *her.* She glanced at the people sprawled on the hillside. Most were like herself; they had a need, and Jesus' kingdom promised to supply it. Thinking about what she might do *for* the kingdom was an entirely new idea.

"Whatever measure of yourself and your treasure you give unto God will be measured back to you, yes, and more, until God's blessings fill your cup to overflowing." Jesus' words painted a picture of God's delight in an obedient, trusting person.

I've been richly blessed, Joanna thought, *but where is my treasure? Is it in Herod's palace, a treasure of position for Chuza and me? Is it in Sepphoris in my father's estate? Is it in Chuza? Or is it in security and control of my own destiny?*

The last thought exploded in her mind.

My destiny, whether I live or die, is not mine to decide. My position, my husband, my father's money are all mine by the grace of God. My treasure must be in the kingdom of heaven. That is the only everlasting security. I must relinquish the control to him. The thought presented itself to Joanna as an absolute, but it stood alone with no clear directive to accompany it.

Jesus finished teaching, and the crowd began to move. Joanna stood and hesitated. It was a moment of decision. She had told Emis that they would follow Jesus to Capernaum, but Jesus might spend several days moving slowly toward his home-base. She had been returning to Sepphoris at night, but now he would be moving beyond the range where she could return daily. Capernaum and the surrounding cities were a day's journey from Sepphoris.

"Hello, Joanna." A throaty voice behind her sent a momentary alert up her spine. It was familiar. She turned and saw Mary of Magdala smiling. "Where is your friend Susanna?"

Joanna relaxed. "She was only visiting me in Tiberias. Her home is in Caesarea."

"You are going on, aren't you?" Mary asked, indicating the stream of humanity moving off behind Jesus.

"I don't know."

"Tiberias is on the way."

"I've been staying in Sepphoris."

A question appeared in Mary's eyes. "Have you met with opposition at home?" she asked.

"Opposition?"

"Some who follow find that they upset their families. It's one reason I can rejoice that there is nothing to detain me."

"There is only my husband," Joanna said, "and our problems are deeper than my involvement with Jesus. I think we are at an impasse."

"He plans to divorce you?"

Joanna hesitated. She did not know how to explain simply what faced her as Chuza's wife. This woman didn't even know that she was Chuza's wife or that she was of Herod's court.

"Actually, it's that I would have him give me a bill of divorce."

"You *want* the divorce?" Mary asked incredulously.

What could she say—that she was afraid to remain his wife? The thought came to Joanna: her treasure *was* in security!

"Have you heard Jesus' teaching on divorce?" Mary asked.

"No."

"Divorce is not the will of God. It is given for the hardness of man's heart. I had no choice, and I forgive my husband, but if it is possible—do the will of God, Joanna!"

"I'm seeking the kingdom of God. My husband is involved with other kingdoms. How can I follow Jesus if I'm not free as you are?"

"The kingdom of God is in doing the will of God. Jesus says that it is within you. Wherever you go—if you are of the kingdom, then the kingdom is there."

❖ ❖ ❖

"Why, Joanna, we thought you would never return to Tiberias."

It was the voice of Herodias, whom Joanna had encountered as soon as she entered the halls of the palace. She had hoped to go directly to her own chambers, but now she willed herself to stop and exchange courtesies with Herod's wife.

"Yes, I found more in Sepphoris to concern me than I expected," Joanna answered.

"Well, we're glad you're back. The nights are too humid; it's time we left for Machaerus." Herodias smiled.

She's trying to be friendly, Joanna thought. There had not been an opportunity for them to establish a friendship. Herodias's smile was brittle. She was an attractive woman, not beautiful in the natural sense, but she wore the latest Grecian styles well, and her personal maiden was adept at the art of make-up and elaborate hair-styling.

Herodias was in her late thirties, but she could still command the eyes of both men and women upon entering a room. Part of the mystique was in her regal and confident carriage. She had been raised in palaces with the knowledge that she was both a Herod and a Hasmonean. If the first marriage of Herod Antipas had brought stability with a neighboring nation, this second marriage united the political factions of Jewish loyalties for two opposing royal families. The Herods, most recently in power, were still threatened by those who favored the Hasmonean line, who claimed both kings and priests.

Her connections in Rome were no less impressive. Her mother was a close friend to Caesar's sister-in-law, Antonia. Joanna knew that Herodias expected to bring a good deal of influence to bear toward Herod's aspirations for the Palestinian throne.

As the wife of Herod's steward, Joanna smiled warmly. *All wives are interested in their husband's advancement,* she thought. "I'm looking forward to the cool nights and mountain air," she answered.

"You need a rest, my dear," Herodias said. "My lord told me of your father's death. I thought you looked wan before, but you look vibrant today. Perhaps getting his estate settled has eased your mind."

"Yes," Joanna agreed. "It's good to have certain decisions behind me."

"Well, I hope it won't be difficult to have your trunks ready. Our caravan leaves at the end of the week."

"I'll be prepared."

"I almost forgot to tell you." Herodias placed her well-manicured fingers on her lips delightedly, "We are planning a festival for the king's birthday. It must be special, with dignitaries from all his major cities. Chuza is already busy directing the preparations. We'll celebrate it at Machaerus near the end of summer."

Joanna was barely listening, for beyond Herodias she saw Chuza appear in the hall. Surprise was replaced with joy, and a kind of unspeakable relief was reflected in his face. Her heart contracted. She hadn't realized that he was so vulnerable, or that he loved her so much.

Herodias had turned when Joanna glanced beyond her, and seeing Chuza, she murmured awkward words of departure. Joanna walked the length of the hall into his arms and held him as desperately as she had that night, now long ago, in her father's garden. The wide sleeves and folds of his cloak completely enclosed her. Neither spoke. With their bodies pressed together and her head burrowed under his chin, words were inadequate and unnecessary.

Chapter 15

Chuza watched Joanna as she went about putting the necessary objects of their travel in convenient places in the Grecian guest room. He was delighted and mystified by the change in his wife since her return from Sepphoris. She had even gone about singing psalms as she had prepared for the trip.

The caravan was less than one day's journey from Tiberias on the trek south to Machaerus. Instead of following the Jordan valley sixty miles to the salt sea, they had crossed the river where it flowed out of Lake Gennesaret, and continued southeast to the city of Gadara. Herod had chosen to visit some of the prominent Greek cities of the Decapolis before re-entering his own territory at Perea.

With them was Agrippa, his brother-in-law, newly named administrator of Tiberias. Agrippa was a figurehead. Tiberias had operated without him and would continue to while providing him with a meaningful title. This younger brother of Herodias was a spoiled playboy who had depleted his finances in Rome and come to Palestine to appeal to his sister for help. Chuza had no patience with him.

Agrippa's young wife, Cypros, remained behind in the capital. She had recently given birth to their first child. Why do fools procreate so easily? Sometimes Chuza wondered if that was the terrible void in Joanna's life—her barrenness. She never spoke of it, yet she cradled any new infant with tenderness.

Here in the Decapolis Herod was a visiting dignitary. The federation of ten Greek cities existed as independent states under Roman rule. The western border of the area cut a swath between Galilee in the north and Perea in the south. On the southern border of the Decapolis lay Nabatea, which, rumor claimed, pawed the earth impatiently awaiting the chance to avenge its deposed princess.

Herod's trip was for diplomacy as well as for pleasure. He pursued good relations with his neighbors in case of a confrontation with King Aretas. Damascus, one of the ten cities sixty miles north in the territory of Syria, was actually under Nabatean administration.

The city of Gadara was five miles southeast of the Sea of Galilee and boasted many lovely sights to enjoy. The hot springs of el Hamme were just north of the Yarmuk between the city and the sea. There were two theaters. Several days would be spent in the leisurely pastimes of the wealthy, before moving on to another Greek city, Gerasa. The trip was like a restoration of those heady days when Chuza and Joanna had first become part of Herod's court. Chuza couldn't remember a time when Joanna appeared happier. He hoped that her fears for their safety wouldn't surface to spoil their reunion. She had not mentioned them again, even though they both knew that going to Machaerus could be dangerous. It was from this palace that Chuza had arranged the princess's escape to her father. Had any knowledge of those secret plans been leaked to the soldiers of the fortress located there? Would there be any to accuse him? This year there would be no visit to his tribe in the desert. It was too dangerous. He didn't mention this to Joanna. He didn't want to spoil the present with reminders of her fears. She had been lost to him and had now returned.

Joanna's vibrant spirit and her response to him since her return from Sepphoris reminded him of when they first discovered the pleasure of their lovemaking under the Arabian stars. Excitement stirred within him.

"What would you think of bathing at el Hamme?" He smiled a bit uncertainly. "Tonight, when others would not be there?"

She caught his mood. "And when have you taken to hot-spring bathing, my lord?" Her gentle laughter rippled a promise.

"When you came back to me—really back to me."

The hot mist of the springs as it floated mystically on the night air was as an intangible talisman. It curled and bubbled, creeping first about their ankles and swirling up their legs. They were being swallowed by something unearthly, separating them from the outside world, the court, the erratic politics of powers and kingdoms. Slipping on into the warm waters, Chuza and Joanna felt the buoyancy of the springs pull them together.

Joanna laughed as she bobbed toward him. The mist had turned her hair to wispy ringlets about her face while the bulk of it lay about her shoulders. He pulled her close and rearranged the thick locks down her back. Past months of frustration were gone. Chuza's kiss was tender. He would deny himself too much urgency, lest the pleasure of this night pass too quickly to be held forever. This was reality. This was what he lived for.

❖ ❖ ❖

The following day in the common room of the governor's mansion, the men of the delegation, including Herod, Manaen, Agrippa, and Chuza, discussed the latest events east and west of the Sea of Galilee. The women were not present. Greek custom still segregated the sexes. There were twelve men in all.

The governor of Gadara, a clean-shaven, balding man, seemed constrained in his hospitality. Chuza sensed an igniting of tension when one of the officials began to relate a story about a madman. Was it just a tale, or was it real? He wasn't sure.

A nervous outburst of laughter from Agrippa brought an embarrassing silence. Obviously it was not a tale. When Agrippa realized this, his fleshy face contorted as he fought for control.

"You find that humorous, my lord Agrippa?" asked the chief administrator in a controlled voice.

"Forgive me, sir, but two thousand swine possessed by demons dashing into the sea—the story sounds preposterous."

"It is not at all laughable to the herdsmen who lost them," another spoke evenly.

"I'm sure that Agrippa did not mean to offend." Herod rushed to recover the situation. "He thought you were jesting."

"Indeed I'm not! The loss of a herd of swine may mean nothing to a Jew, but the meat of hogs supplies a prosperous livelihood to the Gadarene herdsmen."

"And what of the man healed from demons? Is he really in his right mind?" Manaen asked in an effort to bring the conversation to safer ground.

"Well, he wears clothing now and his ravings have stopped, but his mind is that of a religious fanatic. He accosts anyone who will listen with his story of the preacher from Galilee. I would be most grateful, my lord Herod, if you would keep your wandering prophets on your own side of Lake Gennesaret!"

❖ ❖ ❖

Herod shortened his stay in Gadara, and the group moved on to the magnificent city of Gerasa, which was located on a two-thousand-foot plateau in the North Jabbok River Valley. As Herod's caravan, led by the palace guard, rounded the base of a majestic peak reaching almost four thousand feet, the city lay before them. Her circumference was two miles wide, with boundary walls ten feet thick. It was actually a fortress built across the Chrysorrhoas River. From the city gate, Joanna viewed the pomp of the slow-moving caravan stretched before and behind her carriage as it passed through the arch and moved down the wide colonnade.

The caravan passed the forum and the temples of Zeus and Artemis, which soared to a height of fifteen hundred feet. The sun was dipping behind the mountain peak and its evening rays lit the temple facade in fiery brilliance. Joanna caught her breath. It was awe-inspiring, yet she reminded herself that it was only a man-made monument to a manmade god.

The hours of travel gave plenty of time for reflection. Never had Joanna felt so whole. She smiled to herself as she thought of how mystified Chuza was by the change in her. One night as they had lain contentedly in each other's arms, he asked her what she thought had brought about the change.

"I'm no longer concerned with the 'kingdom' of Herod, or the Roman empire," she said. "Now I'm part of the kingdom of God."

He frowned as she continued. "Seek first the kingdom of God and his righteousness and all that you need will be given unto you. Yahweh *is* the only God, the King of the Universe. And Chuza," she hesitated, "I now believe that Jesus is the Messiah, the deliverer who will establish a righteous kingdom."

Chuza jerked upright, throwing her off his shoulder. "Don't speak like that!" It was a hushed command. "Whatever you think, I'm glad that it's given you peace of mind, but don't call him the Messiah again!"

Since that night she had not tried to share her faith with Chuza. It was too new. Like a tiny baby, it was too precious and fragile to be handled roughly.

Mary of Magdala, quoting Jesus, had said that the kingdom of God was within her, and Joanna was just beginning to understand the meaning of that. As the days passed in Gerasa, much as the time had always been spent in court life, Joanna realized that she was an island in a pagan sea. She was set apart. She saw everything from a new perspective. Her former existence, although glamorous, was flat. Now she viewed life from the scope of eternity.

They moved on from Gerasa, following the trail that led along a canyon above the blue waters of the gurgling Jabbok River, and pushed on toward Perea. They entered Herod's southern territory and traveled south to the palace at Livias, where they spent only one night. It was subtropical and hot. Here they were six miles north of the Salt Sea, east of Jordan, opposite Jericho on the other side. This was where John had ministered and baptized those who would repent. Jesus himself had submitted to John's baptism. It was here that John had been arrested and taken to the prison at Machaerus.

If John's disciples are allowed to visit him, then I could, too, Joanna thought.

The following day they made their way up the steep, craggy cliffs of the eastern coast of the Salt Sea. The body of water lay like a giant mineral basin, nine miles wide and nearly fifty miles long. On the western, Judean side lay a vast wilderness wasteland.

Life did not exist in the Salt Sea, and growth was sparse along its edge. The air was cooler and lighter as they climbed. Salome, who had never visited the area, was wide-eyed and breathless at the sight of glens and rushing mountain streams that plunged down into the sea from so great a height. Herodias hung back from the edge and said impatiently, "Let's go on!"

When they arrived at the palace of Machaerus, they had been traveling for two weeks and had covered more than one hundred miles.

A week passed before she was free to visit John. Joanna had never ventured near the prison. She didn't know what to expect when visiting the depths of a dungeon. From the palace on the opposite hill, the fort stood as a sinister monument to its builder, Alexander Jannaeus, the Maccabean who had reigned one hundred years before. The numerous slits in its tower walls were like all-seeing eyes watching over the main road that ran to Damascus in the north and to Nabatea in the south. The guard detail was heavier than in years past because of the current uncertainty with King Aretas. Machaerus was only about ten miles from the Gorge of Arnon, which cut the border of Perea and Nabatea.

The fort loomed above her, ever more overpowering as she neared it. Now she wondered at the strength of spirit that enabled her to walk toward it without the waves of fear that had once been a part of her life. The distaste and uncertainty were there, but the obsession to remove herself from an unpleasant experience was gone. Instead, she felt drawn toward the prophet. She missed Jesus' life-giving words.

A guard at the gate allowed her to enter. Other soldiers stared. In her discomfort she tried to ignore them. The leer of men separated from women for many months was in their eyes. In response to her request, she was led down the steep, narrow passageway to the dungeon. She had expected the fort to be cold, but it was also dark and so damp that water trickled in some places among the rocks of the cave foundation. Alexander Jannaeus had planned his dungeon first, using the natural cave formations, and then he built his fort above it.

She was shocked to find that John's cell was a hole in the cave floor with an opening only large enough for a body to pass through. It was about eight foot deep and covered with a securely locked grate. This gave him freedom of movement in little space. There was hardly any light. A putrid smell assaulted her senses.

"Is he never allowed out?" Joanna asked the guard.

He looked at her with hard, expressionless eyes. "I obey orders, my lady." He hesitated and then added. "He's there unless the king calls for him. It gives Herod entertainment to hear the prophet rave about God's judgment while bound and powerless."

"Can you bring him up for me?"

His smile indicated how foolish her question was. "No, my lady, you can speak to him as his friends do, through the opening in the top."

He walked to the opposite wall of the cave and folded his arms across his leather tunic.

Her mind pictured John on the only occasion that she had seen him. He had been preaching in Judea, and his raving had meant nothing to her then, but his strange attire of camel hair and his wild gestures had made him a creature of ridicule in her mind.

"My lord," she called into the hole, "I know that you are a prophet of God. Could I speak with you?"

John must have been insulated from her exchange with the guard, for it took him a moment to answer.

"Who are you?" His voice resounded and was distorted from the tunnel effect of the hole.

"I'm Joanna, wife of Chuza, of Herod's court. But I am a follower of the One who was sent."

"The Lamb of God?"

"The one you proclaimed as the Lamb of God. But I was there when your disciples came to ask him. Are you unsure?"

"The Messiah will deliver his people. I know that he will establish a kingdom of justice and righteousness. But I rot in this hole! Is the Messiah here or not?"

"Thousands follow him. He heals and teaches righteous ways and the love of God for man," Joanna answered quietly.

"But is he building a kingdom?"

"Yes."

"Then tell me everything you know of him."

Joanna sat as close to the opening as she could, speaking directly into his cell in conversational tones. She shared her limited experience in following Jesus and many of the stories that circulated among the crowds. John was subdued and eager to hear all she could remember. In turn, he told her of his prophetic understanding of the will of God.

She sought his company often in the summer weeks, and the two of them talked of spiritual things like thirsty people who knew the secret existence of a prized well.

❖ ❖ ❖

Joanna sat on a stone bench roughly chiseled from the natural rock and gazed at the rugged beauty surrounding the resort at Callirrhoe. While others made their way down the stone steps to the mineral baths, she remained behind, letting the sun turn her skin to a coppery brown.

Many of the guests at Herod's palace at Machaerus had never been to the thermal baths, and Joanna accompanied the group to help entertain those visiting from Galilee, Syria, Judea, and major cities of Perea. Herodias had remained at the palace because she preferred not to become mussed in front of guests. She also confided to Joanna that a period of rest from the strain of entertaining was most welcome.

Chuza remained behind, too. He had many duties to accomplish before the festival in honor of the "king's" fiftieth birthday.

Salome was like a pigeon uncaged. With her mother absent, she not only reigned as hostess but enjoyed a good deal more freedom. Herod Antipas had never made himself her disciplinarian.

Among the guests was Herod's half-brother Philip, the tetrarch of Iturea, Trachonitis, and Batanea. Salome had tripped down the steps, gaily leading the group, teasing and pulling both Philip and Manaen, one by each hand. *The girl is disgusting,* Joanna thought. But her exuberance and seductive, dancing eyes delighted the men. They followed her as the sheep follow the ewe.

Except Herod. He had announced beforehand that he would stay and relax in the sun. He looked at Joanna curiously.

"You're looking well, Joanna; the mountain air agrees with you."

"Thank you, my lord; I feel relaxed."

"But you've hardly been still," he said. "You make many trips to see the prophet."

She was not surprised that he knew, only that he had not mentioned it before, so she was prepared with her answer.

"I understand that you find him interesting as well. You call for him, to hear him talk."

"Entertainment on a sleepless night. It annoys Herodias, but his foolishness fascinates me."

"He may be a strange man, my lord, but surely not a great threat to someone of your stature. So many believe him to be a holy man; wouldn't it be better to release him for the sake of public opinion?"

"Unfortunately it's not that simple. Do you think he would stop his bellowing?"

Joanna couldn't answer.

"Of course you know he wouldn't. My wife feels secure with him locked up. That's worth something."

Her continued silence prompted him to go on. "There was a time, Joanna, when you might have asked such a favor of me." His eyes challenged her to remember.

What she had thought long buried came flooding back: a memory of that solitary walk in those seldom used halls of the palace. She had momentarily toyed with his affections. Why? As a young woman was she still flattered by a "king's" attention, as she had been at fourteen? Or did she think merely to play with his admiration? It had begun as a dangerous game and had become a battle of wits to avoid consummation. She had been worn with weariness and nervous tension. She was never sure when he finally understood, but in time she was replaced by Herodias, who *could* demand a crown and did.

For a moment they looked into each other's souls.

"You could have been my mistress," Herod reminded, "and you'd have had everything but the title. You had no aspirations greater than to be the wife of a steward. I don't think that the release of a desert prophet now would cause you to change your mind. Do you?"

Chapter 16

The drinking had progressed to the point where most of the women were happy to leave the banquet hall. Agrippa especially had become lewd and more boisterous than usual. His face was crimson and looked like a wineskin about to burst. His personality was a mass of contradictions—sullen and quiet sometimes, loud and on-stage when there were people around to impress. Herod's new "city administrator" was ambitious, but he would need to gain diplomacy.

Joanna was grateful that he would not be staying long. Agrippa would return after the festival with other officials from Galilee. The celebration marked not only Herod's fiftieth birthday, but his thirty years as tetrarch. He was commending those captains and appointees who had served him well. Spirits were high.

Chuza, on whom the success of the banquet rested, and Manaen were the only men who appeared sober. Joanna liked Manaen. He had favored Chuza's appointment to Herod's staff in the beginning, and he was a frequent visitor at court. Even though he had been a schoolmate of Herod's for a short time in Rome, as middle-aged men they were not of the same nature. Was Manaen fascinated by the antics of Salome? He seemed too intelligent, yet common sense seldom dictated to the heart. Joanna should know.

The women had dined with the men, Roman-style, in the large hall lit with torches. Only the men reclined on couches. The women had rested on giant cushions. Now they left the men to their drinking and masculine entertainment and moved to a small, intimately furnished room across the hall. Some said good night and retired. Joanna wished that she could, but her presence was needed for hospitality. She stifled a yawn.

Herodias had been nervous all evening. Was it concerning the precision of the banquet festivities? But all had gone well. Still, she sat on the edge of her bench, tracing the intricately carved arms of the seat with her fingers and talking rapidly or not at all. One ear was claimed by the other room.

Pipe music, high-pitched and unidentifiable, danced on the air. The entertainment could not be captivating, Joanna thought. Footfalls could be heard regularly leaving and returning to the hall. Chuza walked by the archway, and Herodias beckoned him. He bent to hear her whisper.

"What's wrong?"

"They're bored. Some are demanding to see the Baptist."

Oh, no, Joanna breathed to herself.

"I was afraid of that. He's always talking about how funny the fool is, ranting and raving, bound in chains," Herodias hissed.

"They want something different to remember later. Something so special it will crown the King's birthday with excitement." "Mama," Salome interrupted, unaware of the conversation. "Could I just stand in the hallway? Nothing is happening in here," she whined.

"Be quiet!" Herodias demanded. "No, wait—" The cross expression faded from her face. "Salome," she said sweetly, "how would you like to dance for the men?"

Salome's dark eyes widened and a slow smile spread over her lips. "Could I really, Mama?"

"Yes! You know that lovely number with the veils that suggest fire? That would be stunning."

"Would Herod mind? I mean, would it be all right?"

"He'll love it. I'm sure he will." Herodias smiled. "You go change, while Chuza announces a surprise." She gave Salome a little shove and added to Chuza, "Announce that Salome will honor the king with her dance of fire, and *get* those men back in the room. I want them all to see it!"

Salome was back in a matter of minutes. The scarlet silk costume she wore was as light as haze. It floated with every step she took; it would flare in the dance. Inside the torch-lit room, only her figure would show as in a wispy flame of gauze.

Of course Herod would like it. Herodias knew him well, and she gave her daughter the lesson of a lifetime. All of them would like it. Agrippa, Philip, Manaen—and even Chuza. What man wouldn't?

Joanna stood and walked out into the corridor. There was no one about, so she continued on to the balcony. Once outside, she breathed deeply of the mountain air.

There was little moonlight. The ominous fortress was a black sculpture against the midnight sky, its massive size dwarfed by the distance across the ravine. Eerie flickers of light shone from the slits of its tower. Shadows alluded to the figures of soldiers, but only because Joanna knew they were there. No forms were recognizable.

Joanna looked up at the stars. What were the thoughts of that unseen deity as he gazed down on mankind?

"Father, God," she said, "what am I doing here? I'm an alien in a foreign land. I don't belong anymore. I'm as misplaced as I was back in Nabatea."

Chuza and I love each other, she thought, *yet he doesn't even know the person within me, the new person I've become. He loves my body, but when I share my soul we become strangers.*

A blanket of sadness engulfed her, heavy and oppressive. What was wrong? Even in her periods of trouble, she had never felt such foreboding. She tried to shake the mood. *Am I to be upset by the seductive dance of a foolish girl?! I've seen enough of that many times by slave girls.* That Herodias would use her daughter in such a base way to accomplish her own ends was hardly worth shuddering over.

Salome would enjoy every minute of her performance; she was not really being exploited.

Then what is bothering me? she thought. At least it will keep John from being dragged like an animal before the drunken crowd and made to look foolish in their eyes.

With the thought came a twinge of dread and again that strange foreboding. Joanna's shoulders vibrated with a sudden chill. Perhaps she should return. She had stood on the balcony for some time.

The noise was gone as she walked down the corridor toward the banquet room. It was deathly quiet. Herodias waited opposite the archway. Salome came out of the hall, a platter held well above her head like some prized trophy. She walked directly to Herodias with a smile of triumph on her face.

Blood had formed a pool on the plate and ran over the side. At first Joanna thought it was some kind of animal sacrifice. In the space of a moment, she realized that it was a head—not the head of an animal, but the head of a man. The head of John the Baptist!

Poison-tipped arrows of repulsion found their mark in her stomach, and oblivious to anyone around, Joanna crouched and violently threw up her portion of the king's feast.

Through continuing waves of nausea she heard Herodias remark, "They wanted to see John; well, they've seen him! Now I guess none of them will forget the king's birthday."

❖ ❖ ❖

Joanna's sleep was tormented throughout the night. Hatred burned in her soul. Chuza was concerned for her, but she treated him with contempt.

"You act as if I'd done it myself," he said.

"You could have done something to stop it," she accused, knowing even while she mouthed the words that they were unfair.

"Not even Herod could stop it once he had promised to give Salome anything she asked."

"Why not? Anyone could see that it was her mother's idea. The king was duped."

"He would have lost face before his men. No man in authority can risk that!"

"No man in authority should allow a woman to rule him," Joanna said, knowing that Chuza could have no argument for those words. They were true! Herod would live to regret the climax to his birthday party, in spite of the fact that some of his guests were pleased. Many had become hardened to violence and expected a sensational ending to a drunken feast. Most would fall on their beds, not even sobered by the gruesome event!

Joanna was experienced with man's inhumanity to man. She had seen the sadistic glee in Roman eyes as they watched gladiators and called for blood. Executions of criminals were also occasions to draw a gaping crowd. She was repulsed when the victims were unknown to her, but this had been the grisly execution of a personal friend. She was trampled by grief.

John's disciples had come and taken his body for burial. In the morning, Joanna, reckless of her own safety and Chuza's peace of mind, took a horse and rode the trail to the coast. She was not used to the straddle position, but by pulling the back of her skirt between her legs and tucking it in her girdle, she could ride more comfortably. The trail was rocky, and she needed maneuverability. Chuza, busy with post-festival duties, didn't even know that she was gone.

In the confusion of her mind, she remembered little of the characteristics of the trail. This area was a large plateau between the gorge at Arnon and the one at Callirrhoe. It was cut by small glens and rushing mountain streams.

When she could see by the horizon that the earth dropped off into space, she reined in her horse and dismounted. She wrapped the reins around a scrubby twig that stubbornly grew out of the rock, and walked to the cliff. There the mountain stream that she had followed abandoned itself to the sea far below. The salty basin sparkling up at her from such a height made her dizzy.

She found a rock near the edge and sat down. How long she sat motionless, staring into the sea, she didn't know. After a while she felt a tickling sensation on her hand. An ant was traveling aimlessly up her arm. She brushed it off. It began moving again, undaunted, on its hairlike legs. This time it headed for the beads of sand that formed its home at the base of the rock. *The ant has no idea of the huge body of water so close, yet so far away,* she thought. The world was small to such a tiny insect, and its perspective was limited by the size of its own body. What value did the King of the Universe put on such a creature? If she snuffed out its life, would there be moaning among the ant kingdom?

Jesus had said that even a sparrow would not fall without God's knowledge. Finally, all Joanna's anger and frustration burst forth.

"Why, Yahweh, King of the Universe, why do you allow such a thing to happen to one who served you so well? Why are those like Herod and Herodias given life? Where *is* the justice of the kingdom of God?"

In her own ears her voice was insignificant and swallowed in space. The sun had begun its western descent. She shielded her eyes from the glare, but it was as relentless as an inquisition. As she watched, the Salt Sea turned azure. Pink fingers of the setting sun stretched across the sky as if to gather the water in its grasp.

MY WAYS ARE HIGHER THAN YOUR WAYS.

"Yes, Lord," she agreed from the depths of her soul and was subdued.

Somewhere in the recesses of her memory, Joanna recognized the message. It had been spoken before, she was sure, and was recorded in the canon of Scripture. Her father had read some of the ancient scrolls to her as a child. With excitement, she decided to ask Rabbin Kesil where that passage could be found.

Twilight was upon the cliffs as she made her way to her horse, which stamped its hoofs impatiently. Again she prepared to ride and mounted. She reached over to pat the horse's neck and smooth his mane.

"You know where home is," she said. "Take me there."

Chapter 17

It was good to be back in Galilee!

Gingerly, Joanna spread the robe across her bed in the palace at Tiberias. The muted earth tones were exactly what she had requested from the weaver before leaving for Machaerus. Instead of the usual two or three colors, he had painstakingly dyed several more. It was a handsome robe. She ran her fingers under the cloth and inspected the flawless workmanship. It was seamless, woven in one piece on a very large loom. The side warps were twisted and blind-stitched so that you could not tell where the front ended and the back began. The bottom was neatly tasseled. Anticipation for the giving of the gift sent a signal of excitement through her being.

Chuza startled her when he walked into the room. Hastily she sat on the robe. He looked at her curiously.

"What's that?" he asked.

She glanced around as though she hadn't known it was there, and wondered why she was allowing herself to act this way. She hadn't expected Chuza to walk in at this time of the day, but she acted as if she were hiding something, and she really didn't intend to be devious. It was just that she had expected to approach the subject at another time and in a way of her own choosing. So why hadn't she?

"A robe," she answered.

He looked and saw that it was indeed a robe. "A surprise for me?" He smiled at her antics.

She hesitated. "You have so many lovely cloaks, Chuza—I—I had this one made for Jesus."

"Jesus, the prophet?" He frowned. "Doesn't he have a cloak?"

"Of course, but not one so nice. This one is wool and will be warm, but at the same time it is so finely woven that it isn't heavy. He travels about so much and sometimes must sleep outside."

"You concern yourself a great deal with his well-being!"

"He's taught me so much about the kingdom of God and—" She knew that she couldn't voice what was on the edge of her thoughts. "You know how highly I regard him."

"I think I do now," Chuza said. His face was taut. "Are you . . . ?"

She read his thoughts and grasped his fear. "No, of course not. My feelings for Jesus are not those of a woman for a man. How can you even ask that when . . . ?"

"When you so obviously respond to me? The difference came when you met *him*. How do I know what makes your feelings come and go? I know that there is a part of you that I still can't reach."

"Oh, Chuza," she spoke softly, coming to him, "It's the soul part. That's where the schism is. Please come and hear Jesus, and then you will understand. He is a teacher of spiritual things."

He turned from her. "I might have known that once we returned to Galilee you would be off following him about."

"Chuza," she pleaded quietly.

He stubbornly refused to face her. "This can't go on, Joanna. What happened to the Baptist should be a warning to you. You can't keep following Jesus."

"I can't stop," Joanna murmured. "Once you told me that you *had* to do something for honor that could endanger our lives. I *have* to follow Jesus. 'No man, having put his hand to the plough, and looking back, is fit for the kingdom of God.' "

"Your 'kingdom of God' is going to come tumbling down about you and leave more rubble than the ancient walls of Jericho!"

❖ ❖ ❖

The house in Sepphoris was alive with activity. *It too has been reborn,* Joanna thought. The servants rushed about to prepare for guests. She worked along with them, directing their efforts while the melody of an ancient psalm played on her lips. Monaea joined her in the refrain.

"Unto thee, O God, do we give thanks; unto thee do we give thanks; for that thy name is near thy wondrous works declare!"

She hugged the woman whom she had loved all her life. Monaea's hair was streaked now with gray, but her face was bright, young, alive. She was Joanna's sister in the Lord, for she too had met Jesus. And it was her idea that the house in Sepphoris be used for those who followed him on his travels throughout the countryside. She would see to it that all ran smoothly. It was Joanna's answer to the question of how to use her "treasure" for the kingdom of God.

Jesus was beginning another preaching tour of Galilee, and larger numbers of his closest disciples were moving with him, both men and women. They were too large a group to be lodged in any one place, so her home in Sepphoris provided shelter for the women who were many hours from their own homes. In turn, those from the areas of Capernaum in the north and Nain in the south showed similar hospitality when Jesus' company was in their vicinity. When they were close to the sea of Galilee, Joanna always returned to Tiberias.

She was beginning to know many of the women. There was Mary, the wife of Clopas; and Salome, the wife of Zebedee, whose two sons were among the twelve specially appointed ones. Peter's mother-in-law joined the group from time to time, as well as other wives and sisters of the men. All were welcome. Mary of Magdala had emerged as the one with the most qualities of leadership among the women. Her throaty voice could always be heard, and the women respected her complete devotion to the Master.

To Joanna's joy, Susanna had come from Caesarea. She joined them now in the colonnade after a brief rest on the terrace. She regarded Joanna with a smile.

"I can't believe the change in you," she said.

"Is it so obvious?"

"You were a person tormented with your problems."

"Now I'm just a person with problems," Joanna mused.

"No longer a secret disciple?"

"Well, I haven't made a formal announcement to Herod. Chuza works hard to cover my activities. It upsets him so much that I try to be discreet, but of course it must be known in Sepphoris."

"What will Chuza do?"

"I don't know."

Susanna's questioning frown prompted Joanna to go on. "Odd, his choices are the same as mine were six months ago. He can accept the fact that I'm doing what I must do, or he can divorce me and protect his name."

"You seem so calm."

"But not without concern. I love him, Susanna." Her eyes filled with tears. "But I know that nothing must keep me from seeking the kingdom of God. He can't understand that. He's never heard Jesus preach. In fact, he's jealous of him!"

"Jealous?" Susanna smiled. "Oh yes, I suppose I can see why."

"What was Jacob's reaction?"

"Not jealousy. I guess I would say that it was eternal gratefulness. His response to my returned sight was touching. I've never seen him so moved. He seems revitalized himself and was most happy for me to travel to Sepphoris. He wants me to ask Jesus to come to Caesarea."

"And Jonathan?"

"Oh, Joanna, he's grown so tall and learned a great deal under the teaching of Rabbin Gamaliel. I had hidden the extent of my blindness from him, so he was not aware of what this healing meant to us. He's back now at the temple school in Jerusalem. At festival time, when we're all together in Jerusalem, I want Jesus to touch and bless him."

Wistfully Joanna replied, "Perhaps in Jerusalem Chuza will hear him speak."

❖ ❖ ❖

The balmy breezes of Galilee played with Joanna's loosely flowing hair. How good it was to spend the days out of doors, in meadows and groves, on the slopes of the mounts, while Jesus taught. How exciting to share in his ministry.

A half-grown boy darted behind Joanna as she spoke words of encouragement to a Galilean woman in the crowd. A moment later there was a dull thump and she turned to see a small girl sprawled on the grass, one shrunken leg doubled birdlike to her tunic, her arm reaching for a forked stick—her crutch. The tunic was badly worn and much too large. Joanna quickly retrieved the stick and helped the child to support herself again.

"Have you come for healing?" she asked, still kneeling to the child's level.

The dark eyes looked solemn and too large in the tiny face. "Yes, but it's hard to get near him."

"I know, but there are many of us to help you. Just wait; I'll get one of his strong disciples to hoist you on his shoulders and then you can see, hear, and get close to Jesus." She patted the girl's stringy hair and realized that not many months ago she would not have touched her at all.

"Are you alone?" she asked.

"No one would come with me. My parents are dead. My aunt says that it's foolish to think that he would heal me, and she has too much work to go traipsing about the countryside."

Joanna smiled. "Do *you* believe that Jesus will heal you?"

She nodded.

"Then don't worry. You will be skipping home later today." She rose and signaled to the nearest disciple, called Thomas the Twin.

He responded immediately, working his way through the milling crowd. The child laughed with delight when the stocky, sandy-haired man whisked her above the heads of thousands of people.

Joanna turned to scan the multitude for others who might need attention. Moving through the crowd was a familiar figure. Joanna had faced this moment a hundred times in her mind, but now that it came, she felt the sudden shock of the unexpected. She knew that he saw her, too, for their eyes registered mutual recognition. He stopped. It was evidently not his intention to confront her. She probed the mass of people close to him to see others from Tiberias. They were there, behind him, but they had not seen her.

She dropped down on the grass, adjusting her headdress over her eyes, and turned toward Jesus. Her heart raced. She was disgusted with her reaction, yet her desire to protect Chuza was strong.

Jesus began to teach. Like a field of wheat in the wind, the crowd sat down to listen. She became one with the host about her and didn't look for those from Tiberias again.

The clear, deep voice of the Master began a narration on the kingdom of God. It was about a farmer sowing seed in his field. The people sat listening with rapt attention. They loved his stories but she wondered how many understood them. She wasn't sure what this one meant herself. It seemed that Jesus' parables, although simplistic and placed in the setting of daily events, were at the same time perplexing in nature. The people loved them as they loved a riddle, talking among themselves of the possible meanings. Those who would understand were those who would ponder them or question Jesus about the interpretation. It was as though the kingdom of God were reserved for those who would diligently seek it! Joanna was sure that many came merely to be entertained and to see the healings.

Sometimes it angered her to see the selfishness of the crowd as she ministered among them. Each was concerned for his or her own need. *But I was like that myself,* she reflected, *never satisfied with my lot even though I lived in a king's palace. And I was ready to take my life because I was afraid of being disgraced and of losing what I had.*

She was too busy to watch the individual healings that followed Jesus' teaching, for there were always questions to answer and her own story to share with those who wanted to know more about the kingdom and what it meant to be a part of it. All of those who traveled with Jesus ministered simultaneously to those who did not need to be touched by Jesus himself. From time to time, Joanna caught Susanna's or Mary's eye and they would exchange smiles as they worked. She forgot about the men from Tiberias.

A tug on her tunic made her wheel around. The still-smudged face of the crippled child beamed up at her. Then the girl turned and purposely skipped a few feet away.

Joanna laughed. "I told you so," she called and murmured a prayer for blessing as the child waved, smiled shyly, and started down the trail to Cana.

When the people finally dispersed for the evening meal, Joanna and the other men and women disciples lingered to ask Jesus the meaning of his teaching for the day. As usual, John the son of Zebedee had positioned himself close to the Master's side. James too sat at his feet, while Peter stood beside him with arms folded across his chest. Thomas's sandy head was bent on his folded arms as they rested on his knees. Others sprawled about, relaxing after the busy day.

"Lord," John addressed him, "tell us the meaning of the parable."

Jesus smiled. "I'm happy to share the secrets of the kingdom with you, for you earnestly want to know. Many are only interested in the story, and that is all they will receive, for their spiritual ears are deaf."

"Who is the sower?" asked James.

"He is the one who shares the good news of the kingdom, which is represented by the seed. You see, it depends on the fertility of a man's soul. Some hearts are as hard as the soil in a path where the

Word cannot take root. The devil can snatch it away before it germinates, even as a bird picks up the bare seed before it has a chance to grow."

Already Joanna's mind had darted ahead, illuminated with the brief explanation. She had witnessed many whose hearts were hardened with unbelief.

"Sometimes," Jesus continued, "the Word falls on hearts that have no depth or soil in which spiritual 'water' allows roots to grow. They receive it with joy but soon fall away, withered by temptations that they cannot withstand."

Thomas raised his head and frowned thoughtfully.

"And seed that falls among thorns represents those who do not mature in faith; they are stunted or choked by the cares and pleasures of this life. And then, of course, there is the good soil." Jesus smiled and looked at each of them. "Those with hearts ready to receive hold it fast and in patience bring forth fruit in abundance, even as much as a hundredfold."

"Now that's a return!" Judas Iscariot remarked.

Joanna turned toward the tall, slim disciple who had become the treasurer of the group. At times she found him superficial. She barely knew him, yet she disliked him. Was it because he looked so much like Chuza's uncle Abdul? Or was it because he appeared to want control? The seeking of position among the twelve appointed men was not unusual. Even Salome, the mother of James the elder and John, had asked Jesus for special places in the kingdom for them. The Master had answered the request with a question: Were they willing to drink the cup of suffering that would accompany such a position?

Perhaps Joanna's gift of the robe to Jesus could be misunderstood as a desire to find favoritism. She had seen such thoughts written on the faces of some of the followers when she presented it to him. It surprised her, for she wanted only to give some tangible evidence of her love. Didn't she? Regardless, Jesus had accepted the gift graciously and then made a point to pass on the mantle he had to someone else who needed it.

"If you have two coats," he said, "you must share with someone who has none."

Joanna surveyed the band of the devoted. In many ways this circle of followers who moved with Jesus was becoming like a family, and they suffered from the natural rivalry that existed among brothers and sisters. Since she had never known natural brothers and sisters, it was a new experience for her.

Jesus' tone of voice had become gravely serious, and it brought her back to the teaching at hand. "Remember that no man lights a lamp and then covers it up. Instead, he puts it on a stand that all might see. We hide nothing that will not be revealed. So watch your own heart. If you receive well and use it, more will be given, but if not, you will lose even what you *think* you have."

Joanna was disturbed as she and the other women walked back to Sepphoris. Susanna caught her mood.

"Something troubles you," she said.

"I refused to put my light on a stand," Joanna said. "Today there were men from Tiberias in the crowd, but I hid as always."

"You're torn because of Chuza."

"I'm sure they were spying for Herod. There's been so much talk at the palace about the growing movement. I listen and remain quiet."

"There is a time to speak and a time to remain silent. Hasn't Jesus told us not to be too open about who he is yet? The time will come—remember? Perhaps silence is best for now."

Joanna remembered Jesus Bar David at thirteen, when he worked on the lattice in her father's garden. "Are you a prince then, pretending to be a carpenter?" she had asked. He had allowed her childish, even prophetic question to go unanswered. Why? Because the time was not right.

"Yes, I know that's true," Joanna replied, "but I may have no choice. Today I saw Manaen, and he saw me."

Chapter 18

In the highly polished brass disk Joanna watched the reflection of her transformation from a simply dressed and veiled Galilean woman to a silk-clad lady of Herod's court. Althea combed the long strands of chestnut hair and wound much of it into a fashionable swirl at the back of her head. Then she braided with pearls the remainder and wrapped it into a crown. An emerald ring was offered for her finger to match the vivid gown she wore.

I feel like two different people, Joanna thought. *It's as though one were on masquerade.* She liked the effect created by her reflection and had to admit that silk felt better than linen or wool. The smell of perfumed oil, which had been part of her bath, added to her sense of well-being. It was nice to be here among the familiar objects of the bedchamber that she shared with Chuza at the palace in Tiberias.

Jesus had returned to Capernaum, but not before he had commissioned the twelve apostles and sent them forth, in pairs, to go into every obscure village of Galilee and preach the coming kingdom of God. For the first time they would also manifest the power of God in Jesus' name.

Joanna and the others had witnessed the charges he gave them, then they had returned to their homes and occupations until the mission was complete. Susanna had gone back to Caesarea. Joanna had arrived at Tiberias just before a court feast celebrating the first year of marriage for Herod and Herodias. What changes one year had brought!

She put aside concerns of what she would say upon returning to court. Jesus had told his disciples not to worry about what they should say when confronted by opposition. The right words would be given them at the right time. Just as the twelve men were sent into the hamlets of Galilee, so she was sent into a king's palace, and knowing when to speak and when to be silent was her promise as well.

She was a little later than the others when entering the banquet hall. Most of the men were already reclining on benches, and the women stood in groups talking. Servants moved about filling wine goblets. Unlike the ancient dark-rock banquet hall lit by torches at Machaerus, this one was of light marble and was graced by Greek statues and carved grape-leaf cornices. Groups of flickering oil lamps lent a mystic air to the occasion.

This feast was only for family and friends, an entirely different celebration than the one that had honored captains and officers of the realm on the king's birthday.

Chuza saw her at once. Relief and gratitude passed momentarily over his face. His dark eyes assessed her hair and her emerald gown and registered approval. Desire moved quickly and unbidden within Joanna, bringing with it excitement in anticipation of their reunion. Then, as if a stone statue had taken his place, a noncommittal look came into Chuza's eyes and his jaw set as surely as though done by a sculptor's tool.

Cypros, the well-rounded wife of Agrippa, stopped her where she was and interrupted her thoughts.

"We wondered if you would be here, Joanna. Where do you go so often these days?" She tottered on her small feet, holding a wine goblet precariously. She was pregnant again and moved like a billowy cloud in her folds of silky white. Their first child, Bernice, was less than a year old.

"I've been to Sepphoris."

"Of course, Herodias mentioned that you are concerned with your father's business. Is it prospering?"

"Yes—in fact it's growing."

"Growing?" Cypros frowned, shaking her head. "I would expect you to sell and be done with it. You could invest in jewels—much less trouble."

"Actually I have become involved in a new investment, sowing seeds for an even greater return."

Her face registered confusion. "You bought some land to lease for farming?" she asked incredulously.

"Just a figure of speech," Joanna assured her.

Salome's voice rose above the jumble of talk a few feet away. "Why didn't you take me? You know that I've been wanting to see the prophet. It's the only exciting thing that is happening in all Galilee!"

A number of the Herodians had gathered in a group. Joanna noticed Salome and some of the other women on the perimeter. They had overheard the men's conversation.

"A mob is hardly the place for a woman of your rank, Salome," Agrippa reminded his niece from where he stood within the circle of men. Salome moved closer and shifted her round eyes from one to the other.

"It seems that one of you might have thought to take me. I would have been in the company of palace officials. Manaen, why didn't *you* take me?"

"We didn't go as a delegation," Manaen said. "We mixed with the crowd."

"Salome, you can find out anything you want to know by asking," her mother said impatiently.

"But I wouldn't see him! What does he look like?"

"Nothing like the Baptist," Manaen answered, "so you can relax, Herod. John's spirit hasn't taken up residence in the new prophet."

"How do you know where a man's spirit resides after death?" Herod asked. His eyes revealed the haunting fear, familiar to them all, that John's spirit was still an influence in his realm.

"Jesus was active in Galilee before John died."

"But now his following is twice the size that it was," Herod said harshly. "Isn't it? Well, isn't it?"

"Yes, but it's just the natural curiosity of the Jewish mind," one of the Herodians interjected.

"There's been no prophet for four hundred years. The people are looking for one. They see what they want to see," said another.

"Some even call him Elijah," a voice in the midst added.

"They called John that too," Herod said tersely.

"I hear that he doesn't keep the Law. What prophet breaks the Sabbath?" Herodias remarked crisply.

"That's true," Manaen agreed. "The Pharisees rebuked him for harvesting grain on the Sabbath."

"Harvesting grain?" Salome frowned.

"Oh, his disciples were hungry and they picked a few blades to eat while walking through a field." He shrugged.

"If he is a prophet, the religious leaders are the last to know," laughed one. "They hate him and try to trick him into saying the wrong thing."

"They claim he borders on blasphemy," another offered.

"Then you have nothing to worry about, Herod," Agrippa soothed. "The members of the Sanhedrin will put a stop to his activities. By the time you return from your trip to Phoenicia, all will be quiet and you won't even have to be involved."

"Nevertheless," Herodias said, "It might be well to send him a warning—a threat that if he doesn't stop inciting the crowds, his fate may be the same as the Baptist's."

"How could we convey such a message?" Agrippa asked.

"Certainly not though some known official," Manaen spoke quickly.

"It would best be passed as a rumor." His eyes moved beyond the immediate group and met Joanna's. "Perhaps a prophet has his ways of knowing without being told," he suggested. "Otherwise, he's hardly a prophet, is he?"

❖ ❖ ❖

The moment they entered their chambers Chuza spoke.

"I received a letter from Abdul. Your father's house has never seen such activity. It's rumored that you befriend the wandering followers of the Nazarene."

"But you knew that already," Joanna answered as she prepared for bed.

He watched her. "Must others know?"

"I make no proclamation."

"You don't have to. Did you know that Herod has sent spies to observe Jesus and listen to what he says?"

"Yes. I heard them talking tonight, and I saw Manaen in the crowd some days ago."

Chuza was startled. "Did he see you?"

"Yes, but we weren't close enough to speak."

His eyes darted about the room thoughtfully. "He's said nothing to Herod as far as I know. Odd, don't you think?"

"Yes, but he may not be as concerned with Jesus' influence as Herod is. Perhaps he realizes that Jesus promotes a spiritual kingdom rather than one of men."

"But people talk of making him king. That's treason!"

Joanna faced him with genuine concern in her eyes. "The rabble seem to misunderstand his kingdom. If Manaen and the others are listening to him instead of to the people, they will know that Jesus does not talk of overthrowing the government, but of changing the hearts of the men in government. Oh, Chuza." She moved close to him, "I wish you could hear him for yourself."

He didn't answer. "Would you like me to leave?" she asked. "I love you, and I don't want to be an embarrassment or to jeopardize your position."

His arms went about her, holding her too tightly. There was more possession than tenderness in his grip, and his lips sought hers demandingly. All his anger seemed vented in his passion. Like the winds of a violent storm that engulfs suddenly and levels all that lies in its path, it consumed her and, much to her dismay, swept aside her own responses. Where was the tenderness of their relationship on the trip to Machaerus? Would they ever find it again? Must she give up following Jesus to keep Chuza's love?

❖ ❖ ❖

The sound of lapping water and the gentle creak of idle fishing boats were the only accompaniment to the women's conversation. It was early morning, and Capernaum was quiet. Many had left for the Passover in Jerusalem. Those who remained went about their business, enjoying a relief from the crowds that overran the city seeking the Nazarene preacher who now resided there but was frequently away.

The sea air, mingled with the lingering smell of fish, proclaimed the village's major industry. Zebedee sat on the shore, mending nets and every so often rubbing his gray beard and peering out across the lake. Joanna guessed that he kept busy more to occupy himself rather than to think his sons, James and John, would return to the once thriving business. They now called themselves "Fishers of Men."

His wife, Salome, had begun to prepare food for the midmorning meal. Many of the women who closely followed Jesus were gathered in the common room of the substantial but plainly furnished stone home.

"I'm glad that you're with us today," Mary Magdalene remarked to Joanna. "You've kept to the palace a great deal lately."

"It pleases Chuza," Joanna answered. "Herod and Herodias are on a visit to Phoenicia, and the palace is, well, like Capernaum is today, very quiet."

"Wouldn't you think the people would let Jesus alone for once?" Mary, Clopas's wife, said. "They will hardly allow him to sleep or eat, and now that the men have returned, they all need a rest. I can see the fatigue in my son."

"Well, they won't get it," Salome, Zebedee's wife, remarked. "I wouldn't doubt that a crowd was waiting for them when they reached the other side of the lake yesterday."

"Weren't the men excited with the success of their tour!" Peter's wife exclaimed. "Can you imagine what they did by a simple command in Jesus' name?"

"I think thousands followed them back and on around the lake." Salome shook her graying head.

"When they get hungry they'll disperse," Joanna declared.

"Then the villages around Lake Gennesaret will be flooded with people seeking to buy bread," Peter's wife added.

"And there's no one at home baking it!" piped her daughter from the doorway.

They all laughed.

"They're coming!" young Simon cried excitedly. The children didn't see much of their father these days. Simon Peter's wife complained mildly from time to time, but usually she was proud of her husband's position as one of the three closest to Jesus, and she shared his excitement with the ministry.

The boat carrying Jesus and the twelve men glided slowly into port. Choppy waves through the night had now turned into light ripples in a morning breeze.

Zebedee caught the rope thrown by James and moored the boat. The women moved outside and met them at the shore. Everyone talked at once.

"What happened to the crowd?" Mary asked.

"They found us. We had no rest at all."

"The Master couldn't turn them away, so he taught and healed. He even fed them!"

"We counted five thousand men, plus women and children."

"But how—?" Joanna started.

"Andrew found a willing lad with five loaves and two fish. Jesus multiplied it as he broke it to share among them."

"We even had twelve full baskets left over!"

"They wanted to make him king right then," Judas Iscariot said. "He would have none of it—but it's only a matter of time before they do."

Joanna's anger flared as she observed the sharp-featured Judean disciple. *Listen to him,* she thought, *doesn't he know what he's saying? Would he unwittingly bring the wrath of Herod down upon Jesus? But it's not the same as it was with John,* she reminded herself. John was a prophet. He was a man with no miraculous powers, only a strong and important message. This is Jesus, the long-awaited Messiah. Who could touch him? Who had more power than he over the diseases of men and the ways of nature? She watched him as he moved slowly from the back of the boat. The other men had jumped ashore. In that moment he looked just as any man would look, clothed in exhaustion. It was a paradox that bewildered her.

Was he the Son of God, or Son of Man?

Chapter 19

The group of twenty-five men and women had barely finished the midmorning meal when boats could be seen maneuvering into port.

"They're from Tiberias," young Simon spoke up excitedly. The crest and colors of the imperial city were clearly displayed, but they were independent fishing boats, Joanna observed, not part of Herod's fleet, and they didn't carry the usual cargo of fish; they were laden with people.

"Well, the time to rest was short," Mary, Clopas's wife remarked. "Here they come!"

The small band of disciples watched as the people disembarked. A man stopped to talk to Peter's daughter, who pointed toward the house of Zebedee. Jesus rose and met the throng outside the doorway.

"When did you come here, Rabbi?" the first asked. "We didn't see you enter the boat yesterday."

"Why do you seek me?" Jesus said wearily. "Is it for bread to fill your stomachs temporarily, or do you hunger for what would sustain you eternally?"

"We would do the work of God. Tell us what to do," came a high-minded voice from the crowd.

"Believe in me," Jesus said simply. "Believe that God sent me."

"What work do you do that proves that he sent you?" asked another. "Will you continue to give us bread as we were fed yesterday, even as Moses did for our fathers in the wilderness?"

"Why do you always seek a sign? That kind of bread can only keep you alive for a while," Jesus answered, "then you will die. But if you believe that God sent me down from heaven, and accept my body as your bread and my blood as your drink to sustain you, then you will live forever!"

The crowd began to murmur. The grumbling sounded like so many disgruntled hogs in a pen, Joanna thought. Several shouted thoughts for all to hear.

"What does he mean, 'come down from heaven'?"

"Isn't this Jesus the son of Joseph of Nazareth?"

"We know his brothers and sisters; they don't make any high pretenses."

"They don't even follow him themselves."

"Are we supposed to eat him? What would he have us be—defilers of the covenant to eat human flesh?"

These men were not from Tiberias, Joanna thought. They had paid for their transport. They were hecklers from Jesus' own vicinity.

Jesus interrupted their murmurings with a forced voice to reach the fringe of the crowd. "Unless the Father draws you, you will not come to me," he said. "But I tell you the truth. The bread I give for the life of the world is my own flesh!"

Even the disciples began to discuss Jesus' words among themselves in confusion. The Master turned and walked back through the midst of those who had supported his ministry for nearly two years, leaving them to their muddled conversation.

His broad shoulders sagged, and Joanna was haunted by the sadness she saw reflected in his eyes.

❖ ❖ ❖

"Didn't I tell you that you worry for nothing?" Agrippa said. "Things have quieted down in Galilee while you've been gone."

"It's true, my lord," another spoke. "The Nazarene has lost his popularity these past two months. In fact, he doesn't seem to be preaching in Galilee at all."

"You'd convince me that my kingdom runs well without me," Herod said sarcastically. "Is it your expertise, Agrippa?"

"Well, we did manage to convey your message to Jesus," Agrippa said proudly, "by way of rumor, of course. We hinted that you meant to kill him."

"And what was his response?"

"Does it interest you?" Manaen asked.

"What did he say?" Herod demanded.

"He said, 'Tell that fox that I will continue my ministry day by day until I go to Jerusalem.' "

"He dared to call me a fox?"

"While his following was so strong, he may not have concerned himself with such threats, but now he has lost favor with so many—from thousands, he retains only a few hundred. Hardly enough for a revolt!"

Manaen glanced in Joanna's direction. The men and women gathered were a small, intimate group, dining together on the occasion of Herod's return from Phoenicia. She couldn't discern his thoughts or the reason that he had not revealed her discipleship. Was he hoping that she had been one to fall away? Perhaps he thought that her interest was a short-lived diversion of which Herod need never know. If so, his loyalty to her was touching, and she was grateful.

"Why would thousands suddenly turn away from him?" Herod asked. "Are the masses so fickle, or did he blunder in some way that you've not told me?"

"He continually displeases the religious leaders," one answered.

"I told you that the Sanhedrin would put a stop to his activities," Agrippa quipped.

"In fact, they sent some representatives from the great Sanhedrin in Jerusalem to inquire of him. Now there's a price on his head in Judea. They say he is either blasphemous or mad! They can't decide which."

Herod smiled, obviously pleased.

"Some say that he has a demon, that he casts out demons by the power of Satan himself," one of the Herodians added.

"Why would Satan cast out Satan?" Joanna asked, unable to keep silent a moment longer. She could feel the blood rush to her face. "Perhaps you should reconsider—he may be who he says he is!"

"Joanna!" Chuza was stunned.

"No." Herod motioned for him to be silent. "Let's hear what she has to say. Tell us, Joanna, who does he say that he is?"

"He has no desire for your kingdom, my lord; he has his own kingdom, the kingdom of God. He is the Messiah, the Son of God, and if there is any blasphemy, it is done unto him, not by him!"

All eyes were focused upon her, but their mouths were sealed; they were shocked speechless. Finally Herod laughed self-consciously.

"The Son of God—well, I've heard him called the Prophet, and Elijah, even John reincarnated, but never a god. You mean to tell me that the Jews are to have a godly offspring like the Greeks?" he asked.

Ripples of laughter began about the room and were joined by Herod's own.

"I think I would like to hear this Jesus," Herod said. "A madman can be quite entertaining."

Joanna was conscious of Chuza pulling at her arm, trying to remove her from the entranced circle. It was hopeless! *How do you speak to such blindness?* she thought. *How do you rise above the feeling of being as small as a mosquito and as easily squashed?* Chuza nearly dragged her from the room.

"You've acted the fool," he said as he propelled her down the hall. "And I thought that you had stopped following him; you've kept to the palace so much lately."

"I'll never stop," Joanna stated passionately. "They are right; many have quit. Their faith had no roots."

"What?" Chuza stared at her. "Sometimes you speak in riddles!"

"Jesus said that some would fall away."

"But so many, Joanna, don't you see? It's been a farce all along. Gods don't come down to live among men. He has stopped preaching in Galilee. Doesn't that tell you something?"

"I know that he's not preaching here," she said. "He is touring Phoenicia as far as the cities of Tyre and Sidon. While Herod and Herodias made their way back to Galilee, he began his tour of the very country that they visited." She laughed, for in the midst of her concern and humiliation it was ironic! "What would Herod think of that?" she asked.

❖ ❖ ❖

Machaerus. Summer again. Joanna stared out of the window of their chambers in the ugly stone palace near the Salt Sea. The imposing fortress on the other hill was tinged with the pale hues of sunrise. It looked cold, even in this season. She heard Chuza stir. He sat up and squinted toward her, trying to focus on her face. The room was in deep shadows against the early morning light.

"Didn't you sleep?" he asked.

"For a while," she answered.

"You are so restless. I thought that you would relax once we were out of Galilee."

"And Jesus too far away to think about?" she asked.

"Is it the Baptist? Are you plagued with memories of last year?"

She didn't answer. Chuza was so patronizing lately. How could he know the loss she felt? She yearned to have someone to talk to, but Chuza was like a stranger when it came to spiritual thoughts. He knew none of the people who were important to her, except Susanna and Monaea. How could he understand the isolation that she felt a hundred miles from Mary Magdalene and the other women, or the soul starvation of never hearing Jesus preach? How could a "poor" man miss the delicacies of a "rich" man's diet?

"Could we chance going to Nabatea?" she asked. "I miss your mother."

It had been their habit through the years to visit his tribe in the summer when they were residing at Machaerus. It was only one day's journey away. It had been two years since their last trip.

"We can't cross the border yet," he said. "The tension is still too great, and any attempt to do so might look suspicious."

"Do you think King Aretas will still attack? It's been two years since the divorce."

"Joanna, you don't know the Arabian mind if you can ask such a question." Chuza shook his head in mild disgust. "Aretas is waiting for Herod to become complacent, and I think he is."

"Why do you say that?"

"He isn't concerned with how the princess escaped. He's only glad that she is out of his life. The longer Aretas waits, the less reason there is for Herod to inquire into the matter. I think he's secretly glad that she's out of the country. He probably leaked the information purposely so that she would leave. It gave him a better reason for divorce. Desertion. Herod is crafty."

"You mean like a fox?" Joanna said, reminding him of Jesus' words.

"Herod does what is best for himself. If he doesn't arrest Jesus, it's because he has already pushed public opinion to the limits by executing John. But Herodias has no gift for such reasoning. She is ruthless and ambitious to a greater degree than Herod ever thought of being!"

Joanna became thoughtful. No one at court had mentioned her defense of Jesus since her declaration of faith a month ago in Galilee. It was as if she had come into court naked and no one wished to remind her of the embarrassment.

She was becoming accustomed to loneliness; she was avoided by the women of the court as if she had leprosy. With Chuza she was quiet and withdrawn, a resigned wife. He responded to her change of personality by leaving her alone and seeking greater involvement in his work. The weeks of summer at Machaerus plodded by slowly, marked by frequent court visitors and short trips to Callirrhoe.

Joanna had found a solitary spot outdoors, near the palace wall. Here she spent many hours of her day. It was uncultivated, being a small area, and wildflowers grew in the shade of the stone foundation. It gave her some feeling of the unspoiled Galilean countryside, which was so much a part of her experience with the Master.

One particularly warm day, she made her way to the shade of her refuge and sat down on a rock that jutted out of the ground. She pressed her back against the cool stone wall. Her eyes were closed as she meditated when the crack of a dead branch alerted her. She wasn't alone. Startled, she saw Manaen standing nearby.

"So this is where you hide by day," he said.

She didn't answer. Her mind raced to understand why he had followed her.

"I'm sorry if I frightened you," he apologized. "I've been wanting to talk to you—about Jesus."

"You've listened to him. You know what he preaches. He doesn't preach revolt."

"I know," Manaen agreed. "I've told Herod as much. And I didn't tell him that I saw you with Jesus' company."

"I wondered why."

"I've always respected you, Joanna—and Chuza, too—but he doesn't share your views, does he?"

"No."

Manaen sat down. Folding his hands, he rested his elbows on his knees like a young boy. Intently he looked into her eyes. "Tell me why you believe in Jesus."

Could it be possible that he really wants to know? Joanna wondered. *Or is he gathering information?*

"I thought that after your declaration to the court, you wouldn't mind my asking," he prompted.

He was right, she thought. As long as she didn't tell him that Jesus was now touring the Decapolis, what more could she say to incriminate herself than she had already said?

"You've seen his miracles, and you've heard him preach. I believe he has the truth, that he speaks of things eternal, not temporal."

"I know that he must be either mad or a liar as they say, yet he seems perfectly sane and his works are good, not evil. I can't believe he's a god, yet the question haunts me. What if he is?"

Joanna smiled.

"You have no doubts?" he asked.

"I did at first, and sometimes I still do not understand the mystery of it all," she admitted. "But I know that I've never seen anyone do the things that he does or show the compassion that he has. He delivered me from a cage of fear, and my friend Susanna from blindness. Could any Messiah deliver more completely?"

"I've seen a change in you," Manaen agreed. "That's one thing that unsettles me. While Chuza would have Herod believe that you are slightly mad, I see a return to a peaceful mind."

Joanna recoiled. "Chuza told Herod that I'm mad?"

"To protect you—to explain your belief in the prophet."

"I should have known," she muttered bitterly. "And Herod believed him!"

"Herod would prefer to believe that you are possessed than that you are disloyal. There was that episode about a year ago . . . "

"When I tried to end my life."

"Yes, the physician confirmed it."

"Perhaps Chuza thinks I really *am* mad."

"A woman is admired for her beauty," he reminded, "not her mind."

"I'm not concerned with losing Chuza's favor," Joanna answered stonily. "It's of little value under the circumstances." She didn't expect Manaen to understand. The relationship between her and Chuza had not been ordinary. Now the embalming spices of pretense would only cover up the decay of emotional ties.

❖ ❖ ❖

Joanna's laughter floated on the air. "You never run out of questions," she accused.

Manaen had been coming to her quiet place most afternoons, debating with her in an easy, friendly manner. She felt alive again! He was seriously seeking to know the truth, and she felt sure that he was on the verge of believing.

"What about the claim that no Jewish prophet, and certainly not the Messiah, will come from Galilee," he challenged.

"But Jesus was born in Bethlehem."

"Bethlehem?"

"Yes, in Judea. It's well known among the disciples. In fact, I've been studying the ancient scrolls during my times alone, and the prophet Micah foretells his birth in Bethlehem. And Isaiah predicts a perfect and just government that will last forever."

"Replacing Caesar?" Manaen frowned.

"Involving Caesar," Joanna said. "If he believes."

"Joanna, to believe in Jesus *does* hint of treason," he said soberly.

"If he is the Son of God, to put any mere man, whether king or priest, before *him* is treason!"

Manaen was silent, and Joanna waited patiently.

"I haven't taken God seriously for years," he said thoughtfully. "At school in Rome they called all faith superstition, so even we Jews seldom thought of the Lord God. Roman gods do not stimulate a man to become more than he is naturally. Ours does. Truthfully, I've wanted to believe in God but with the inferiority of Palestine to Rome, I saw no reason to believe in our Hebrew God."

"He's not just the God of the Jewish people," Joanna said. "He lives, Manaen. He's not a statue. His promises are true; the Messiah has come."

"Jesus is a remarkable man," Manaen admitted. "He never backed down to the Pharisees. He always had an answer that they couldn't dispute! I think he has no fear."

"But a great deal of sorrow."

"Why? All he commands is done in a moment, so you say."

"All but faith on the part of the people. He can't, or won't, command that. They must seek him for themselves and not for material gain. He knows whether they really believe or if they just want him for what he will give them. It breaks his heart."

"How do you know?"

"I saw it in his eyes."

"It's all right for the poor," he said after a moment of considering her words. "But no one of means would forfeit his gain in this world for what is only a promise of an ideal society and immortality."

"Unless he believed in Jesus with his whole heart," she agreed.

"I see that you do."

"But, of course, I'm mad!" she answered lightly, her eyes twinkling.

"No one could be more sane—or more beautiful."

His sincerity sobered her. As if she had been thrust into fresh spring water, Joanna breathed quickly. She couldn't deny the pleasure his admiration brought to her.

Chapter 20

Shielding her eyes against the morning sun, Joanna tried to adjust to the brilliance of its reflection off the temple only a short distance away across the Tyropoeon Valley. The imposing stark white stone structure with its golden spires and magnificent porticoes was the focal point of the most-renowned city of the East. The temple sat upon Mount Moriah and dominated Jerusalem even as the religion it represented dominated the thought and life of the people.

The day's activities had already begun. It was autumn, the first day of Succoth, the Feast of Tabernacles. Joanna and Chuza stood on a small rounded private balcony of the Hasmonean Palace that was the residence of Herod Antipas while he was in the city. Chuza leaned against the iron rail, scanning the pilgrims who gathered on the temple steps. They appeared as small as insects beside the towering facade.

"Herod the Great has certainly completed a masterpiece," he said, "and only thirty-odd years after his death."

"Is it finally finished?" Joanna asked.

"Well, I expect that they will continue to build new areas of it for years. It creates work for the populace, you know. But for the most part it's complete, and a wonder of architecture."

"I think every Jew of the diaspora has made his pilgrimage this year." She watched the continually moving scene. The plaza was a colored multi-mass of humanity.

"Perhaps they've heard what's going on in Palestine," Chuza remarked. "A new Messiah is always exciting."

"Who is to say that he's here in the city?" She was piqued by his attitude. "He didn't come to Passover last spring, and we ourselves have missed all the festivals since Herod's divorce. Not everyone comes every year."

"If he doesn't want to fade into oblivion like so many others, he must stay in the public view."

He was taunting her, she knew. Ever since Jesus began to minister in an obscure way, he had suggested subtly that it was time she rethought her discipleship. She didn't answer her husband, but gazed off across the valley. Her eyes followed the line of the Western Wall to the tower of the Fortress of Antonia. Roman guards and even Pontius Pilate himself, no doubt, watched the crowd from that vantage point.

As they watched, the people on the steps outside the temple walls began to move and form a swaying mass aligned behind the priests as they made their way south across the Hill of Ophel, through the City of David, and on to the far end, where they would fill the ceremonial jar from the Pool of Siloam. This would be the official beginning of the festival.

Even from this distance, Joanna could see the jewels sewn into the high priest's robes, reflecting the sun. Annas and Caiaphas marched at the front of the procession. Then came the priests, and finally the people, holding high their *lulabs,* the festal plumes made of myrtle, willow, and palm branches. The words of an ancient psalm lifted on the air:

> O give thanks unto the LORD; for he is good:
> Because his mercy endureth for ever!

Joanna recognized the annually repeated words of the *hallel* and her lips moved silently to join them. The chanting became a crescendo.

I will praise thee: for thou hast heard me,
And art become my salvation.
The stone which the builders refused
Is become the head stone of the corner!

Suddenly the plumes went aloft in declaration.

Save now, I beseech thee, O, LORD:
O LORD, I beseech thee,
Send now prosperity.

Chuza turned his back to the familiar scene and observed Joanna. "You and Manaen seem to share much these days."

She bit her lip. "Are you jealous of him now, as you once were of Jesus?"

"No," Chuza said matter-of-factly. Then his eyes searched hers. "Should I be?"

"Of course not. Manaen's been our friend for years."

But he seems to be a closer friend to you now."

"I'm lonely," Joanna stated. "Others of the court seem to avoid me—even you."

"If you would keep your beliefs to yourself—"

"But I can't stand by and listen to them defame him!"

"You only make matters worse for him, you know. The best that can happen is that they continue to think that Jesus is a misguided fool. If you convince them that he is to be taken seriously—well, I hate to think what you might accomplish."

Joanna stared at him. *He would put the responsibility for Jesus' safety on me?* she thought. No, it was another of his subtle ways to work his will upon her. For a moment her father's face was superimposed on Chuza's. She shook her head as if to be rid of the vision. Her long, loose hair rippled down her back. Her eyes narrowed.

"Is it difficult living with a woman who's mad, Chuza?"

"What?"

"You've let Herod believe that I've lost control of my mind, perhaps become demon-possessed." The words tumbled out of her mouth. She had never intended to say them.

"Who told you? Manaen! He told you that, didn't he?"

"Yes, and it's true, isn't it?"

"I only wanted to protect you. Herod likes you, Joanna. He wants to think that you are a faithful subject of his domain."

"We all want to think that those around us are faithful," Joanna said quietly.

❖ ❖ ❖

The pitch black of night made a startling backdrop for the four giant Menorahs that lit the temple plaza. The momentum of the dancing throng had reached a pace of abandon. Joanna, trying to move through the crowd, ducked to avoid a rotund man, his cloak swaying and his glassy eyes showing the effects of too much wine. His jowls vibrated to the the mesmeric music of the flutes. Beads of perspiration glistened on his forehead.

She turned to grab Manaen's hand. "Let's not get separated," she called above the noise. "I think there are twice as many people here as I've ever seen for Succoth. More come as the week progresses."

"I don't know how you hope to find them," Manaen said.

"It's the only way. I don't know the Jerusalem followers. Chuza and I have not attended a festival here since I became a disciple. Those from Galilee could be sheltered in almost any of the thousands of booths outside the city."

"If he came—and it looks like he didn't—wouldn't someone tell you?"

"Do you think they would come to the Hasmonean Palace with such a message? The warrants for his arrest are posted all over town."

"Then surely he isn't here."

"You said yourself that Jesus has no fear."

"He's not a fool," Manaen declared.

Joanna had reached the steps that led up to the Huldah gates of the temple. People were milling about on the two-hundred-foot-wide marble expanse, but she finally reached a height to view the bulk of the celebrating Israelites.

The seven-branched candelabras, one mounted at each of the four sides of the plaza square, were equipped with wicks fashioned of worn priestly robes. They burned like torches, illuminating the entire area. She strained to catch one familiar figure, but the maze of moving bodies, brightly robed, was like the swirl of the hues in mixing dyes.

"It's hopeless," she said.

"I told you it was impossible."

"Wait! There's Peter and his wife and children, standing at the side by the building of purification."

She darted quickly down the steps, catching Peter's family before they could disappear in the crowd.

"Did the Messiah come?" she asked excitedly.

Peter withdrew into the shadow of the building, leaving his wife and children to watch the dancing. Joanna and Manaen followed, and he eyed Manaen questioningly.

"It's all right." Joanna smiled. "He's one of us now."

"Jesus is camped outside the city," Peter answered, motioning toward the Kidron Valley. "We all came with him. Have you seen the notices threatening excommunication for all who follow him? He's wanted for arrest."

"Yes. We had no idea until we arrived that the opposition was so strong in Jerusalem."

"It all came about last spring during Passover while we stayed in Galilee. We heard of it when we returned from the Decapolis. Jesus told his brothers that he wouldn't come to this feast either, but he changed his mind and we came up quietly."

"Do they still taunt him?" Joanna asked.

"They're jealous and unbelieving. They told Jesus that he must come and do his wondrous works here if he wants acclaim. He's like a driven man. He prays through the night. He teaches us constantly and he intends to teach tomorrow in the temple."

"In the open?" Manaen asked incredulously.

"Yes, on Solomon's Porch."

"With the feast half over, maybe the authorities will have relaxed and won't be watching for him," Manaen said.

"He speaks such dark thoughts," Peter frowned. "He talks of being taken by the high priests and killed and rising again on the third day. I said, 'Oh no, Lord, that can't possibly happen to you,' and he turned on me and said that I pleased Satan, not God, for my thoughts were those of men. The others are as confused as I am. The scrolls say that the Messiah will come to reign forever. Yet Jesus speaks of terrible things."

"Surely he speaks in a parable," Manaen offered.

"We've discussed it among ourselves," Peter admitted. "Maybe he speaks of his death as symbolic of his effectiveness. We've dwindled to less than a hundred committed men because of the excommunication threat by the priests. After the feast, he is sending seventy of us into Perea to preach the Kingdom of God. Perhaps that will be the rising again that he refers to—a regrowth of his following.

Joanna sighed deeply. She hadn't realized the bonds of tension that held her body until she relaxed. "That must be it," she said. "The Messiah couldn't represent safety and deliverance to Israel if he isn't safe himself!"

Chapter 21

After leaving the grounds of the Hasmonean Palace, Joanna and Manaen became one with the swarm of pilgrims who climbed the steps to the ancient Western Gate of the temple. The sounds of bargaining merchants jumbled in her ears. Their tiny shops were squeezed into the cubbyholes of the arches that supported the bridge across the Tyropoeon Valley. From the ascent on the walkway she could see the many theaters and the stadium for athletic games. All were built on the low area of the city of Jerusalem, below the temple mount.

The archway to the Royal Stoa towered above them. It was exquisitely carved with rosettes. Once they were inside the wall, multiple columns of the porch stretched before them. These were nearly forty feet in height and culminated in domed ceilings of delicate floral and leaf design. From here they could view the entire area of the court of the Gentiles. It was a moving, noisy mass of people.

"You didn't hope to meet Susanna here, did you?" Manaen asked.

"No, we won't wait," Joanna answered. "She and Jacob are coming and bringing Jonathan, but it may be later. Jacob is getting older and moves more slowly in the press of the crowd."

They made their way along the southern portico until they reached Solomon's Porch on the east, then turned north. Jesus would be teaching near the Eastern Golden Gate, which served as the entrance from the Mount of Olives across the Kidron Valley. He could not have picked a more active spot on the three thousand feet of raised porches surrounding the courtyard. The Sheep Gate on the north was next in proximity, which added to the noise and general fairlike atmosphere. As they approached, she could see a crowd gathered near one of the massive marble columns where Jesus had already begun to minister.

Some of the people stopped for a moment at the edge of the crowd and then moved on. Others remained among the ever-widening circle. The disciples were close about, scattered on the steps, porch, and courtyard. With a tremor of excitement, Joanna saluted them and introduced Manaen to those nearby. Jesus saw her, and his eyes smiled a greeting. Joanna noticed that the lines in his forehead were more pronounced and his face was thin. *He's not getting enough rest,* she thought. *Who knows how many miles they have covered since I last saw them?*

Then Jesus began to preach, and she became absorbed in what he said. It had been four months since she and Chuza were in the vicinity of his preaching circuit. Occasionally there was a distracting remark made by someone in the crowd.

"He's a good man; why do they want to arrest him?"

"You call a man good who leads people astray? Can't you see that they worship him?" an indignant voice answered.

Joanna looked around to see the stranger who spoke, and saw that Jacob Bar Saul and his family had arrived. Jacob, at sixty-seven, was still a fine-looking man with steel gray hair and beard. He stood with only a slight roundness of the shoulders. Susanna had said that his health was greatly improved. She stood beside him, smiling. This was the first opportunity for her husband and son to see the man who had healed her blindness.

Joanna was startled at the change in Jonathan. The last time she saw him, he had been a child. Now he was a teenaged youth who towered over his mother. His thick, dark hair and eyes were Susanna's, but he was tall like Jacob. He hung back, a sullen look on his handsome face. *What's wrong?* Joanna wondered. Had what he heard in temple school from the rabbis and rulers made him fearful of Jesus?

"Isn't this the man they want to kill?" a voice muttered. "Here he is speaking openly, and no one says anything to him."

"Maybe the authorities have realized that he is the Christ," someone else offered.

"Oh, but we know where this man comes from. When the Messiah comes he will appear from nowhere!"

"Well, I doubt that he will do more signs than this man."

Joanna wished they'd be quiet. They probably only upset Jonathan more. They would know the truth if they would just listen!

Behind Jesus, Peter, James, and John—who had been relaxed—now became tense and wary.

"Don't look now," Manaen whispered, "but we've just been joined by the temple guard."

"They came so quietly," Joanna breathed.

Onlookers at the edge of the crowd became aware of the guard and dispersed, but the larger part remained. Joanna saw Jonathan tug on his father's cloak, but Jacob stayed.

"They aren't doing anything," Manaen said. "Just listening."

"Good. Maybe they will understand the message."

"I doubt it."

Joanna chanced a glance. The officers of the guard stood in rapt attention. They didn't have the blank expressions of those on a routine mission. They *were* genuinely interested in what he said. Her heart lifted.

Jesus finished teaching and stood up. He looked directly into the eyes of the temple guard one by one. The soldiers made no move. He began to walk purposely toward the Eastern Gate. His disciples quickly maneuvered their way through the crowd to follow him. Joanna and Manaen started to join them, and only the temple guard remained while the crowd dispersed.

Someone snatched at Manaen's sleeve.

"Salome!" he exclaimed, turning to discover that the daughter of Herodias had been part of the surrounding crowd. She looked from Joanna to Manaen, her round eyes suspicious.

"Are you still spying for the king, Manaen, or have you decided to join the ranks of the demented?"

❖ ❖ ❖

Joanna was surprised when Chuza joined her the following day for the midmorning meal. It was not his habit.

"Well, now I know what draws you and Manaen into such close rapport these days," he remarked.

She waited.

He tore a piece of the flat, round bread and, pinching it into an open pocket, began to spoon the rice and herbs from the large common bowl into his mouth with it. She snapped a fat grape from its stem and popped it onto her tongue. She could feel the taut skin of the fruit. She wasn't hungry, but it filled the vacancy of words. Fresh food was in abundance during this week of the harvest gathering. The peasants even used some branches still laden with fruit to make their booths of shelter on the surrounding hills of Jerusalem.

Once, as a child, Joanna had insisted that she and her father camp in a booth for the Feast of Tabernacles. Samuel had grudgingly indulged her, for he liked his comforts, and now she remembered it as part of her enchanted childhood.

"You should have been there," Chuza said when he had swallowed his food.

"Where?" For a moment she was still a little girl, in the comfort of her memories, camped on the Judean hillside. She had forgotten the unpleasant subject. It was the mind's escape, she knew, for whatever he was leading up to about Manaen was bound to come.

She squashed the grape with her teeth, and the sweet flavor burst in her mouth.

"You know what I'm speaking of, Joanna," he said irritably. "Manaen told Herod that he also follows Jesus."

"Yes, I thought that he would speak to him about it."

"Of course, Salome had already mentioned seeing you both yesterday."

"I was sure she would."

"I can't understand." He shook his head. "Manaen's no young fool. He was raised and schooled in Rome."

"He should be more intelligent, my lord," she suggested in a kind of mild sarcasm, tempered with the title of respect.

Chuza ignored her remark and went on as if speaking to himself. "He wants Herod to go to the temple to hear Jesus preach. Can you imagine such a suggestion? The man is wanted for arrest by the high priests, and Manaen thinks Herod should appear at his feet as a wandering peasant would, and listen to him!"

Joanna made no comment, and it became clear that Chuza expected none.

"Actually, I think Herod is curious. He would like to see him once, but kings don't appear before their subjects."

"Herod is really a tetrarch," Joanna reminded, "but Jesus *is* a King, and he holds court in his Father's palace, the temple."

Her words didn't anger him as she feared they might. Instead he harrumphed: "The Son of God! That's what Manaen said, but Herod reminded him that all Hebrews consider themselves sons of God. Manaen claims that Gentiles follow the prophet, too. Why would they be interested in a Jewish God?"

"He's not just Jewish. He's the King of the Universe, Chuza. My father understood that. Do you know that he opposed our marriage because your people had left the God of their father Abraham? Jesus has come to establish a universal kingdom."

"Be careful, Joanna. Your foolishness begins to sound political."

"How can you be sure that it's foolishness?" she pressed. "Manaen is a man you've always admired. He helped you acquire your position with Herod. His judgment has always been sound."

"Who knows at what age a man may become foolish?" Chuza remarked.

Joanna's patience was spent. "You've never heard Jesus for yourself! How can you judge a man you've never seen?"

❖ ❖ ❖

"It's amazing that they have made no attempt to arrest him," Manaen said, as he and Joanna, together with Chuza, approached Solomon's Porch inside the temple two days later.

"They probably intend to wait until the end of the festival and are now gathering evidence and witnesses to use against him," Chuza suggested.

"Or they are beginning to understand who he is," Joanna said hopefully.

Chuza stopped as they reached the fringe of the crowd and folded his arms objectively. Joanna remained there beside him, although she wished that they were closer. From time to time, she tried to catch his reactions. Usually he was scanning the crowd, observing the temple guard, who were again in attendance, or peering at Jesus with a scrutinizing frown. His lips were so straight that there was hardly a break in his beard.

When Chuza agreed to come, Joanna was sure that his basic reason was curiosity. He could ignore her "womanly fetishism," but not Manaen's masculine faith. For two days Jesus had taught in the Treasury, which was located in the Court of the Women. This excluded Chuza, for only Hebrews could pass through the sacred enclosure and the Gate Beautiful into the women's court. From that point, only the Jewish men could proceed through the Nicanor Gate into the Court of Israel.

At first Chuza had seemed relieved, and he had glibly remarked, "I thought that he was the God of all men. It's clear that some of us aren't welcome after all."

Today Jesus taught again in the court of the Gentiles, which surrounded the two inner courts. His nature was serious, and he spoke in an authoritative tone, including all who would accept his words.

"If you continue to follow my teaching, then you are truly my disciples, and you will know the truth and the truth will make you free."

"We are descendants of Abraham and have never been in bondage; how can *you* make us free?" a skeptic called out.

"If you commit sin, you are a slave to sin. So if the Son makes you free from sin, you will be free indeed." Jesus answered simply. "I know that you are descendants of Abraham, yet you seek to kill me. Why? I speak of what I have seen with my Father. But you do what you hear from your father, Satan, who was a murderer from the beginning."

The prophet's words jarred and infuriated the skeptics. They were quick to enter the debate. Chuza listened with interest, but Joanna's spirit was oppressed. The accusers thought that if they were Jews, born of Abraham, they automatically inherited righteousness and that all their deeds done in the name of their religion were pure!

"Which of you convicts me of sin?" Jesus asked. "If you are of God, you will recognize the truth."

"You're a demon-possessed Samaritan," someone hissed.

This was a petty taunt. "I have no demon," Jesus replied evenly. "Everything I say honors my Father, but you dishonor me. I don't seek to be glorified, but there is a Judge of these things, and I say to you, if you believe my words, you will not see death."

The people all babbled at once, but one voice rang out above the others.

"You think that you're greater than Abraham? He died!"

"So did all the prophets," shouted another.

"Who do you pretend to be?"

"Your father Abraham rejoiced at my coming," Jesus stated.

"You aren't even fifty years old. Are you trying to tell us that you *saw* Abraham?"

"I tell you as clearly as I can," Jesus spoke solemnly, "before Abraham was, I AM!"

Deafening oaths burst forth. The people knew this was an outright claim to be God. A shuffle began and soon disintegrated into bedlam. A man elbowed Joanna as he raised his arm to fling a stone the size of an orange. It struck a person near the front, who cried out in pain. Others were quick to follow the example; stones flew like angry scorpions. Chuza grabbed Joanna and wheeled her away, covering her with his cloak. Through the maze of flying arms and trampling feet, Joanna lost sight of Jesus. The palace guard, taken by surprise, moved to establish order. *What a perfect excuse for arrest!* Joanna thought. Chuza rushed her from the crush of the crowd. She caught a glimpse of the bottom fringe of the familiar seamless robe. He was already at the Eastern Gate, disappearing into the oncoming throng of pilgrims entering the temple. Like a giant wave breaking a sand castle to bits, the incoming worshippers diluted the angry mob.

When they were free of the pressing crowd, Chuza released her and began to scan the bobbing heads for sight of Manaen. In a moment he joined them.

"Where did they get all those stones?" Joanna asked, still shaken by the outburst.

"Obviously they came prepared with them hidden in their cloak sleeves!" Manaen muttered.

"Why?" Chuza asked. "What made them so angry that they would stone him on the temple grounds?"

"It was because he said, 'before Abraham was, I AM,'" Joanna answered. "When Moses asked God what his name was, he answered, 'I AM that I AM,' meaning Yahweh, the pre-existent, all powerful one. They believe he has committed blasphemy by that declaration."

"Well, didn't he?" Chuza asked.

"Not if he really is the Son of God," she answered.

Chapter 22

The majority of worshippers made their exodus from Jerusalem following the week of festivities, leaving a certain amount of debris on the hillside and an abundance of produce as gifts for the priests. Succoth would be remembered this year, for the ban placed by the Sanhedrin concerning Jesus had not been acted upon. He and his disciples left Jerusalem as quietly as they had come.

Herod prepared to leave by caravan for Tiberias. He was concerned about the city administration, and there was tension between him and Agrippa. If Agrippa would just be satisfied to remain a figurehead instead of trying to wield his influence, Herod remarked, he could cope with supporting his brother-in-law.

Manaen went back to Antioch, anxious to share Christ's teachings with his family and friends. The family of Jacob Bar Saul returned to Caesarea.

"I'm sorry," Chuza said to Joanna, "but we won't be going with Herod to Tiberias. I have some investments to negotiate for the king in Perea, and timing is important. Herod is planning to winter in Jericho, so we won't return to Tiberias until after Passover in the spring."

Did she detect a note of relief that they would not be near Jesus' headquarters? Chuza appeared to indulge her "whims" as long as they weren't threatening. Manaen had been right. A woman was loved for her beauty, not her mind. Chuza didn't really care what she thought as long as she kept it to herself and shared his bed. He had little rapport with the spirit inside the body.

She would miss Manaen. What would it be like to be married to a man who shared her excitement of a coming messianic kingdom? She sighed.

"It's only for six months," Chuza reminded.

"Oh," she said, realizing that he had misinterpreted the sigh as resignation. "I was thinking of something else. It's fine. In fact, it's wonderful! Jesus plans to minister in Perea next."

Chuza frowned. "Then it couldn't be more to your liking."

Nor further from yours, she mused, but said nothing.

The royal residence at Livias in Perea was not built like the grand palace in Tiberias, nor did it have the ancient rugged beauty of the one at Machaerus. The city itself was small, and the subtropical climate produced an abundance of flowers and groves. Both the palace here and the one at Jericho were of simple oriental design and were similar, having been rebuilt by Herod Antipas as quickly as possible after their destruction when the country was torn by revolt.

They were built around a central courtyard with multiple arched windows and open passageways. Here in the Jordan Valley, the indoor decor was almost one with the lush greenery outside. The grape arbors and the trees on the grounds formed many natural porticoes. The fragrance was intoxicating.

There was little time for them together. Chuza was deeply involved in land acquisition, which gave Joanna the freedom to minister to the disciples on tour. Jesus sent seventy-two of his men into the cities of Perea. They accepted the hospitality of those who would receive them, but when they returned, the women made provisions for a feast of rejoicing. They camped in a grove on the property of a believer only a few miles from Livias.

Mary Magdalene was the voice of organization for the wives and mothers who had followed from Galilee. Each were given a task in preparing the food for the group, which numbered well over a hundred people. Joanna sang as she ground the grain that would be used to bake bread for the following day. She smiled when she remembered how she had resented this same type of menial work in the Bedouin camp. So much of happiness depended on attitudes. *How I've changed,* she thought. *It's fun to be part of the feast preparations.* It was exciting to see the success of the mission tours into Perea. There *was* a resurrection of his popularity. What had seemed to be dying only months ago in Galilee was now pulsating with new life!

❖ ❖ ❖

The royal residence at Jericho was ten miles from the one at Livias and west of the Jordan River. This was where they spent the winter months. While she and Chuza were there, it was no longer convenient for Joanna to make frequent trips to be with Jesus' company beyond the Jordan. She looked forward to Passover, when the followers of Jesus would all be reunited in Jerusalem. Susanna would come again from Caesarea and Manaen from Antioch. Although the great Sanhedrin continued to oppose Jesus, the people themselves were rallying to him.

The reports Joanna heard made her tingle with excitement. They stood on the brink of prophetic fulfillment; she knew it! Daniel the prophet had spoken of the Messiah and predicted his coming. The time was at hand. Perhaps this was the very year that his kingdom would be recognized.

"You're in good spirits these days," Chuza remarked one evening as they relaxed in the courtyard at Jericho.

These times alone together were rare, and there was little to share but what was uppermost in her mind. Besides, Joanna always hoped that someday Chuza would come to understand, so she spoke her thoughts.

"I am. Jesus has been well received in Perea. The opposition is fading."

"Don't count on that."

"Herod appears less concerned with him than he was a year ago."

"Herod is too busy—his problems with Agrippa have delayed him in Tiberias. Besides, he expects the Sanhedrin to take care of Jesus. That way he doesn't have to cope with public opinion so soon after John the Baptist."

"Perhaps the Sanhedrin will remove the ban," Joanna suggested. "Raising Lazarus from the dead right there in Bethany near Jerusalem should satisfy their desire for a sign."

"Do you believe that tale?"

"He was dead for four days!"

Chuza raised his eyebrows and looked away.

"There were many witnesses," Joanna added. "He came out of the grave still bound in the burial cloths."

"It must have been very impressive!" Chuza said.

Frustration swelled up in Joanna. She had difficulty speaking. "Why would so many believe if it weren't true?"

"Because they want to."

The rumble in the distance was not thunder, but much like its first subtle sounds. Then the voices of children shouting in the streets commanded their attention. Joanna and Chuza quickly moved up the garden steps to the second level, where the view from the arched windows overlooked the outside court and walled enclosure.

The royal residence was set aloof from the other wealthy homes of the city and for security purposes had an excellent view of the main street all the way to the city gates. People were peering out of windows and rushing into the streets shouting to one another.

"He's coming."

"Jesus the Nazarene is here in Jericho!"

A cloud of dust raised by thousands of sandals smacking the dirt path enveloped the travelers at the city gates. Joanna saw Jesus and many of her friends leading the way. Children ran ahead, and the people of the city began to line the street. Some scrambled on top of large woven baskets or carts. They even climbed and clung to property walls to be able to see over the heads of others.

Joanna looked at Chuza. *He must be impressed,* she thought. *How could anyone watch such a display and not recognize him as the Messiah?*

But Chuza was grinning with the kind of delight she seldom saw on his face anymore. "I don't believe my eyes!" he said.

She followed his line of vision to a sycamore tree in front of the imposing residence of Zacchaeus, a Jewish man who worked for the Roman government.

"That fat little tax collector has lost his wits and just hoisted himself up that tree!" he exclaimed.

They watched as the swarm of people moved up the narrow street. Jesus walked purposefully as if he were to keep an appointment. When he reached the sycamore, he stopped. Others crowded around. All heads tilted up toward the leafy branches.

Presently that fat man's short legs could be seen dangling as he gingerly made his way down from the lowest branch. His white tunic was smudged, and uneven fringe hung from his finely woven mantle.

Once on the ground, Jesus towered above him. She and Chuza could not hear the exchange of words, but in a few moments the two men turned and walked toward Zacchaeus's home. After they passed through the gate, people pressed against the iron enclosure, trying to see as much as they could and to hear every word that was said.

"I don't believe it," Chuza said, shaking his head. "Now what will they think of him, mixing with a sinner who collects their taxes for Rome?"

"He's always mixed with sinners. His disciple Matthew used to collect taxes. We are all sinners, Chuza," Joanna spoke softly.

❖ ❖ ❖

Torches had been lit and set about the courtyard of the large brick home of Zacchaeus. People crowded into every nook of available space, and those who did not gain entrance leaned on the iron gate or climbed on the thick vines that wound their way up the stone enclosure. They clung precariously, peering over the top for any possible view of what was taking place inside.

The poor were there in ever-growing numbers. Word had spread quickly of the tax collector's vow, made the previous night after Jesus' arrival, to give half of all his wealth to those in need and to return fourfold to anyone he had ever cheated.

Chuza was more than happy to accompany Joanna this evening as they joined some of the disciples who were invited guests inside the home of Zacchaeus. Zacchaeus had gathered many of his wealthy friends. The prestigious group sat on stools, benches, woven mats, upturned earthen jars, and even cross-legged on the oriental carpet.

The fat man himself stood red-faced and beaming with pleasure at the honor of hosting so famous a man. He continually nodded and motioned for as many as could squeeze into the large common room to do so. People lined the steps to the upper level and peered over the rail from the upstairs hall, directly behind where Jesus sat. Never had so large a group sat so quietly.

The Master began one of his stories. His deep voice resounded throughout the room and into the courtyard.

The governor of a certain province was called away to the distant capital of the empire to be crowned king of his province. Before he left his estate, he called his servants to him and gave them each a sum of money to invest as stewards of his wealth while he was gone."

Joanna glanced casually at her husband. He was listening, for Jesus had chosen an illustration from Chuza's everyday experience.

"But many of his realm resented him and didn't want him to rule them. When he returned, he asked for an accounting of his money. One came showing him a return of ten times his investment, and another produced five times the original amount. Of course the king was pleased and rewarded them according to their gain. But a third one said, 'Here is your money back, lord. I kept it hidden to return to you, for I was afraid I wouldn't invest wisely and that you would be angry.' "

Chuza frowned, obviously as disgusted as the "king" with the servant's lack of ingenuity.

" 'I *am* angry,' said the king, 'because you did nothing. You could at least have put my money in the bank, where it might gain interest! Now give it to the one who increased his amount the most. For all those who have, more will be given, and those who have not will lose the little that they have. As for those who would not have me reign over them, bring them forward now, that they may be destroyed!' "

A hush settled on the room and the silence amplified the sounds of crickets outside. Joanna looked about at the faces that she could see clearly. How many understood? Did it mean anything to Chuza, who prided himself in his good stewardship of Herod's estate? He would surely equate himself with the servant who brought the largest investment, but he was really part of the group who refused to allow the king to reign over him. Would he see that?

Finally Jesus spoke again. This time it was to remind them of something he had said before.

"If you will follow me, you cannot put your love of anyone else ahead of me. No member of your family is to come before your loyalty to me. You must despise your own life and desire the kingdom of truth. It is important to count the cost. No one builds a building without first estimating what will be required to finish it; otherwise the building project may have to be abandoned before completion. Anyone who would be my disciple must take up his cross daily and follow me!"

Again the heavy silence hung about the room. Those listening seemed to be aware of the gravity of his words. He painted a strange picture, Joanna thought. The heavy crossbar that convicts struggled to drag to the place of their own execution was an extreme description of service and self-denial for the kingdom. How could it relate? Wasn't the kingdom of God meant to deliver men?

Now Joanna was not concerned with Chuza's thoughts, but with her own. *I've been delivered of paralyzing fear, yet I do carry the crossbar of disapproval and frustration. Is that what it means? And it has cost me Chuza! We aren't one anymore. There is a division between us that can't be bridged. Our loving is no more than filling a basic need. It's the bread for hunger, not the fruit for desire.*

Later, as they walked back to the royal household, Chuza spoke, "He's right, you know. The cost of following him is great. Have you really considered it, Joanna?"

"Yes," she answered, and then added quietly, "I think so."

"Well, I'm a steward. I'm used to counting the cost of any investment, and I find this one too great for the tentative return!"

Chapter 23

News of Jesus' arrival in Jerusalem for the Passover feast reached the Hasmonean Palace late in the afternoon of the first day of the week. Neither Pontius Pilate's nor Herod Antipas's caravans, complete with military escort, had created so much attention as the Galilean preacher riding on a humble donkey.

Herodians who had watched the "overwrought" display told of garments being strewn on the path and the waving of palm branches by peasants lauding his entry with shouts of "Hosanna, Son of David!"

Herod smiled. "Truly the man is suicidal," he said. "The Sanhedrin will have to act now, or they know that he will bring the wrath of the Roman empire down on the city of Jerusalem."

"That pleases you, my lord?" one asked.

"Things are peaceful in Galilee. If there's a riot in Judea, what is that to me? Perhaps the wrong person governs Judea."

"You mean that it's Pilate's problem."

"Either his or the Sanhedrin's. It's certainly not mine. Whichever way it is handled, it can be beneficial to me."

"If Pilate makes a mistake," Herodias began, her mind skipping swiftly along with the possibilities, "then it would be one more in a long list of his blunders with the Jewish people. Perhaps our trip to Rome will be perfectly timed. We can convince Caesar that with you as king, all Palestine would be well controlled."

Herod's attention was drawn beyond his wife to Joanna, who sat quietly beside her husband.

"Does our conversation bother you?" he asked.

"No, my lord."

"Do you have no fears for your friend? Don't you want to warn him? I really think you should."

"He knows of the threats on his life," she answered simply.

"You still think that he's invincible?"

"What if they discover he's a Galilean, my lord?" she asked innocently.

Chuza choked.

Herod scowled. "Rebels can originate anywhere. The question is, where do they create the rebellion?"

Joanna felt calm, even heady with the acclaim that Jesus was receiving. Nothing Herod or Chuza said could disturb her tonight. Jesus' arrival in Jerusalem had been an undisputed triumph.

The following day Manaen came to the Hasmonean Palace, but only for a brief visit. He encountered her alone in the lower hall.

"I've brought some friends from Antioch who want to meet Jesus. We're staying in the Grecian sector of the city," he said.

Joanna tried to mask her disappointment that he wouldn't be staying. "I had hoped that I wouldn't be the only believer in the palace."

"Has it been difficult?"

"No, I'm not badly treated," she admitted, "although it's clear that my views are considered ridiculous."

"Chuza hasn't changed at all?"

She shook her head. "He heard Jesus speak again in Jericho, but he said that the cost of following him was too great."

"And the cost of not following him is even greater!"

"We are like strangers; we have such different values."

He took her hand, holding it firmly, as if strength might flow from him to her.

"What will happen when Jesus comes into his kingdom?" she asked wistfully.

He frowned. "I'm not sure. But you know how I feel, Joanna." His eyes glowed with the same kind of tenderness that used to be in Chuza's. A part of her wanted to break away, yet another wanted to delay the moment's end.

"You feel it too," he said with satisfaction.

The words of denial would not come.

He pressed her hand. "Surely Jesus will want those of his kingdom . . . together."

Chuza startled them when he appeared unexpectedly. They withdrew their hands.

An odd smile twisted on Chuza's lips. "Well, Manaen, we thought you weren't coming this year."

"It's still two days until Passover," he answered.

"Well, you're here now."

"But only to greet those in the palace. I won't be staying."

"Oh?"

Manaen turned to Joanna. "Jesus is teaching in the Treasury. There are Greeks among us. How can we see him?"

"No one but the Twelve knows where he spends the nights. You know Philip of Bethsaida. Go to him and have him ask the Master for an opportunity to see him."

When he had left to speak to Herod, Chuza regarded her solemnly.

"The road you tread is becoming more complicated, Joanna, and a good deal less virtuous."

❖ ❖ ❖

Joanna waited by the Gate Beautiful to the Court of the Women for Susanna and Jacob, who were standing in line with other parents waiting for Jesus to bless their children. She had been the victim of intense feelings since the day before and was now quite immersed in her own emotions. Chuza had implied that she was mad, had stood by while Herod mocked her, and now—if she were guilty, which she certainly wasn't—would he take up stones against her as an adulteress?

She was angry, and her anger found deep pleasure in the kind of impact Jesus was making on the whole of Jerusalem. Never had she heard him speak in such strong terms. It was as if the man who had driven out the money-changers physically would verbally drive off the scribes and Pharisees too.

Susanna approached smiling. "It's done. He has blessed our son."

For a moment the remark kindled further anger in Joanna. It flared into a kind of unhealed jealousy. She was struck by desolation. Her many years of marriage had produced nothing of lasting value!

"Is something wrong?" Susanna asked.

"No." Joanna mentally shook herself loose of such thoughts.

"Shall we stay and hear them test him? Jacob and Jonathan are listening."

"What do they ask now?"

"The Sadducees want to know about marriage in heaven."

"As if they believed in heaven! I think I should like to hear that."

The two women moved back to where Jesus taught. It was clear that the question was designed to discredit him and the belief in life after death, for it had to do with a woman who had outlived seven husbands, all brothers, and produced no heir. Whose wife would she be in the resurrection?

If those of the light are separated from those of darkness, whose wife will I be? Joanna wondered.

"Why do you test me?" Jesus asked. "God is the God of the living. When they are raised from the dead, and they will be raised, there is no giving in marriage, but they will be like the angels in heaven."

She pondered that a moment. *My marriage shall be no more. All the conflicts of my life have been spawned by that marriage, and it will be completely done away with!*

❖ ❖ ❖

Passover at the Hasmonean Palace had little relationship to the sober memorial held in orthodox Jewish homes throughout the city. The feast had progressed well into the night, accompanied by festive entertainment for Herod's many guests, of which a large number were not even Hebrews.

In the early morning some men still gathered in the central courtyard, discussing the latest events in Rome or the other remote areas by sharing bits of news gleaned from relatives or acquaintances scattered throughout the empire.

Many of the women slept or kept to their chambers until after the midmorning meal, bathing and adorning themselves for the activities of the day. Joanna was already in the lower hall and heard the commotion when the doorman opened the portal. Chuza stood in the archway to the outer courtyard. Beyond him she could see the high priests conversing with Herod's guard. Chuza turned and, when he saw her, moved quickly to her side.

"They've arrested Jesus," he told her. "He was brought to Pilate, and the governor sent him to be tried by Herod."

"Oh, no!"

As they watched, Jesus was conducted through the hall, surrounded by the temple guards. He offered no resistance. His face was gaunt with weariness, and his body had the stance of resignation. Some of the scribes and Pharisees followed. Joanna and Chuza moved behind them as they entered the central courtyard. Herod and his guests turned their attention to the disturbance just inside the archway.

Annas, the high priest, moved forward alone. His elderly walk was uncertain. The elegant blue robe embroidered with pomegranates of blue, purple, and scarlet moved slightly and caused the golden bells sewn along the hem to tinkle an accompaniment. His head of wispy white hair seemed burdened by the linen turban and golden crown.

"My lord," he began in his uncertain vibrato voice, "we come to you at this hour only because the problem is one of grave concern for our nation. This man Jesus of Nazareth has been going about the countryside stirring up the people and claiming to be the Messiah. In fact, he seeks to make himself equal with almighty God!" His voice became shrill, and he turned to indicate Jesus. The twelve precious stones of his breastpiece, engraved with the names of the tribes of Israel, and the gems of the shoulder clasps on his gold-embroidered ephod sparkled in the early morning light. The words on his crown read, "Holy to Yahweh."

The scribes and Pharisees had begun to chant, "Hear O Israel: The Lord our God is one Lord."

Herod signaled for silence and motioned for the prisoner to be brought forward. Leading the procession, with a sweep of importance in his step, was Caiaphas, Annas's protégé and son-in-law. He was dressed in similar high-priestly vestments. A smoothly brushed curl hung on each side of his hawklike face, separating the beard and hair. For all his swash, he held his position only because the old priest was behind him. What Annas lacked in physical strength he possessed in political shrewdness. Caiaphas was just his representative, for the Sanhedrin was still under the control of the older man. The only threat to Annas's rule over the religious life of the people seemed to be this Nazarene.

Joanna and Chuza moved near the place where Herod sat, and mingled with others of the court. Caiaphas droned on as though fascinated with his own oratory. It seemed that after the Sanhedrin had found Jesus guilty, they had proceeded to see Pontius Pilate, who had promptly claimed that Jesus was to be tried by Herod, since he was a Galilean.

A pleased smile played on Herod's lips. *Now his curiosity about Jesus will be satisfied,* Joanna thought. He leaned forward. Herod's eyes studied Jesus' face. He was a predator with a prey, but Jesus did not flinch under his scrutiny. The words Jesus had spoken to the Pharisees, calling Herod a fox, must have been in everyone's mind.

Would Herod's pride again demand action as it had for John? Jesus' open defiance could not be ignored. Could it?

Yet Herod had said that it would be to his advantage not to be involved. Finally he spoke.

"I hear you do miracles."

Jesus did not answer, which brought a sharp slap from the chief officer of Herod's guard and a torrent of accusation from the scribes and Pharisees.

"Quiet!" Herod demanded. "I understand that you're a king." A smirk played about his lips. Jesus looked straight into his eyes and made no answer.

Herod's voice rose in frustration. "Has someone cut out your lying tongue?" This time he didn't wait for Jesus' embarrassing silence. "Our guests are waiting! Can't you give us a sign? I hear that you turn water into wine. We could use some more wine." His forced laugh was joined by a chorus of king-pleasers.

Joanna was appalled. Jesus' eyes turned to her, and she could see herself as he must see her, hair braided with pearls and her body adorned with a festive robe and expensive jewelry. She was standing with his enemies. She dropped her face into her hands.

When she looked again, she saw that the accusers had found an old white robe of Herod's with tattered gold thread embroidery and placed it on Jesus shoulders. Why did he remain silent? Where was the man who had thrown the money-changers out of the temple? Why didn't he put an end to their profanity? The guards were treating him with contempt and mocking him by bowing and then blindfolding and striking him.

"Prophesy! Who hit you?" they called. Herod would have his show! The guests would be entertained. Already they were laughing and calling out insults.

Joanna could stand it no longer; she rushed from the courtyard and her slapping sandals sounded her retreat through the stone corridor.

"What disturbs your wife, Chuza?" Herod asked.

"May I have your leave to see about her, my lord?"

"Go—go!" Herod waved him away. "We want no one here who isn't in a party mood."

Chuza found her on their small balcony overlooking the valley. The early sun's rays were diffused and scattered by gathering clouds. They plunged earthward in a dramatic crescendo. A few lights still flickered in the shadowy homes below them.

"How could you have the nerve to leave?" he demanded.

"Oh, Chuza!" She rushed to him, disregarding the tone in his voice. "Herod has such respect for you. Can't you do something?"

"Yes."

For a moment, hope flickered in her eyes.

"I can die with him. Is that what you want?"

Chapter 24

Joanna left the Hasmonean Palace on foot and joined the growing trail of people pursuing the prisoner and his guard. They moved swiftly through the streets of Jerusalem toward the palace of Herod the Great, which was the residence of Pontius Pilate while he was in the city. Joanna saw no familiar face. The crush of the crowd frightened her. Once, an overeager step from behind caught the sole of her sandal, ripping the delicate leather strap. It flapped behind her until she removed it, nearly being knocked down in the process, and then walked barefoot on the stone pavement. She extended her hands in an effort to ward off further assault.

When they reached the Praetorium, the judgment seat of Pilate, an ivory chair stood in place on the spot called The Pavement. This was a mosaic square outside the building. None of the Jewish rulers would enter the dwelling of a Roman for fear of defilement during the Passover, so Jesus' trial was in full view of the multitude who came to watch. A Roman guard surrounded the pavement, and only the high priests and a few scribes acted as accusers.

Joanna glanced around and saw that she was no longer on the fringe. The host of gawkers had deepened behind her. Faces and attire told her that many were rough highwaymen. Could they be zealots? Everywhere she looked, the temple officials moved and murmured among the people. She searched the faces. Where were the disciples? Didn't they know what was happening?

Pontius Pilate, the square-faced Roman official, was dressed meticulously in a white garment. His face was set in the authority of his position; he would not be cowed. He quieted the mob and spoke. "This man was brought to me as someone who is perverting the people. I have examined him and found him not guilty! Neither has Herod, for he sent him back to me. He's done nothing deserving of death. He will be beaten and released."

The clamor was deafening. "Away with him! Release Barabbas!"

Appalled, Joanna glanced about in disbelief. Barabbas was a murderer! He was imprisoned for starting an insurrection. Pilate wouldn't give him to them! But they could not be quieted. The governor shouted above the din.

"I find no crime deserving death."

"Crucify him," came a yell from behind her. It became a chant. Joanna placed her hands over her ears to shut out the dreaded cries.

"Why?" Pilate asked. "What has he done?"

Somewhere in the mesh of voices another cry took hold. "Barabbas, Barabbas—release to us Barabbas!"

They must be zealots, Joanna thought, and they came prepared to ask for Barabbas because of the Passover custom of releasing one prisoner each year during the feast-time.

Where were the disciples? Someone needed to plead for Jesus. The governor sent him away for scourging. She hunted desperately for the sight of anyone who would come to his defense. Not all of them were zealots or temple stooges. Some must have raised their palm branches to salute him only a few days before. Where were their cries of "Hosanna, Son of David" now?

Didn't she herself stand like a statue? Where were the words that should issue from her own dry throat? They would not come.

She tried to move through the crowd in an effort to find one friendly face. She felt the wincing pain of a heavily sandaled foot on her bare one. Ignoring it, she limped on. Few women had ventured into the mob, and without the distraction of the public trial, the men became aware of her, making her way more difficult so that she would have to press her body against them as she passed. The mingled body odors nauseated her. A leering highwayman stopped her. For the first time her fears for Jesus were temporarily taken over by fears for herself. His eyes were wild and several teeth were missing. He reached out and snatched the pearls entwined in her hair, yanking a number of hairs from her head as he pulled them loose. Tears of pain stung her eyes.

"Leave her alone!" demanded a familiar throaty voice.

The grimy man turned toward Mary Magdalene and laughed aloud. "Why? Because she's a lady?"

His mock respect gave Joanna a sudden view of how she must look. She fell gratefully into the embrace of the woman who had lived on the streets.

"Come," Mary said. "There are more of us over here. You are easy to see."

The oasis of women was a blessing. She began to cry. Other faces were already tear-stained.

"Where are the men?" she asked.

"They scattered after the arrest, afraid to be seen together because they could be easily recognized. Judas Iscariot betrayed Jesus, and the others don't know whether he will betray them or even if they can trust each other!"

"But Pilate is asking for some defense!"

"I know, but the case is set against him."

Joanna looked at her wildly. "Then *we* have to do something!'

"What good is the testimony of a woman in such matters?"

The sound of the mob was like the cry of a giant. It brought their attention back to the judgment square.

"Behold the man," Pilate said.

At first Joanna was sure it couldn't be Jesus. His broad shoulders drooped, and he was barely able to stand. The face was beaten beyond recognition. A crown of thorns had been forced down upon his scalp, and blood trickled past his eyes and streaked reddish brown against the bruised and swollen face. But the eyes—the eyes had the haunting quality of the Master's.

The mob became like a wild beast at the sight of blood. The roar of "Crucify him!" was hardly intelligible.

"Would you have me crucify your king?" Pilate shouted.

"We have no king but Caesar," came the response, met with cheers.

The sight of a weakened, defeated Christ angered them more. Joanna hated her own feelings of repulsion. Had the country been duped by another pseudo-messiah? The mob must think so. But he was the Master who had compassion for them all. Where was their compassion? Tears streamed down her face, distorting her vision.

Disgusted, Pilate grumbled, "See to it yourselves."

"We have a law that says he should die for calling himself the Son of God," Annas's wavering voice shrilled. "But you know that we can't execute him; only you can decree it."

"I don't find him guilty," Pilate insisted stubbornly.

"Then you aren't Caesar's friend!"

The accusation was a well-placed thrust of the knife. Pilate's position was precarious enough in this difficult province. His mistakes had been tallied regularly and forwarded to the emperor.

A sob escaped Joanna's lips, and she turned to Mary. "It's done," she said. She knew the reality of Roman affairs. A calm of resignation settled upon her. Her eyes were wind-blown dry, and the salt-washed skin around them felt tight. Dully Joanna watched as they removed Jesus and brought a bowl of water for Pilate to ceremoniously wash his hands of the conviction.

The throng who had called for his death would not be cheated of watching him struggle and then fall under the weight of carrying his own crossbar through the streets of Jerusalem to the hill called Calvary. Two criminals who had been awaiting execution were also set to bearing theirs. Barabbas was released, and he was met outside the Fort of Antonia by the cheers of his zealot band.

Jesus was again robed in his own cloak, which kept the cross-beam from resting directly on the raw stripes from the scourging on his back. Pain glazed his eyes. Blood began to seep through and make reddish-brown stains on the seamless robe. Joanna felt the lump of swallowed sobs. Mary disappeared and returned in a few moments with an earthen pitcher of cool water that she had wrestled from a bystander at the cistern. When Jesus fell, she rushed into the street, and Joanna after her. Both were shoved aside.

Now the soldiers seized a Cyrenian and made him lift the beam so that the procession could go on. Other women wept and followed closely.

"Joanna!" came a growl from the crowd. Chuza was suddenly beside her. "You are acting like a fool in front of all Jerusalem."

His arm went about her, and he dragged her back from the street. His grasp hurt her ribs and breasts. She tried to turn and fought to break loose, clawing at his mantle. He clapped his hand across her mouth so she would not scream.

"Joanna!" He shook her, and her chestnut hair, freed from its combs and pearls, danced wildly. He held her in an iron grip until she quieted. Then he moved her forcefully toward the Hasmonean Palace.

❖ ❖ ❖

Jesus was sentenced and sent to be executed by midmorning. When Joanna quieted down, Chuza left her alone in their room. For a while she lay there on her couch. Then she got up and methodically put on her strongest sandals and her plainest robe and left the palace by a servants' entrance. The cloudy skies of morning had become ominous. She kept her face well covered as she walked toward the northern wall and the city gate that led to Mount Calvary.

She found the group of faithful followers on a small hill, where they were watching at some distance. The dreaded "place of the skull" was shrouded in semidarkness, but three crosses and their crucified victims could be seen outlined against the sooty gray landscape.

"Joanna," Salome of Capernaum said, pulling her into her arms and rocking in anguish, "they've done it; he's dying."

"Where's Mary?" Joanna asked.

"At the foot of the cross—see there? Holding his mother."

She could see five figures huddled together. "Who are the others?"

"His aunt and Mary, the wife of Clopas, and my son John."

Behind their crumpled forms, Joanna could see the mob of tormenters, shouting insults and obscenities.

"Is there nothing more we can do?" she asked. It was the ludicrous question of a bereaved mind.

"They tried to give him the wine with gall to ease his pain, but he refused it."

Joanna had dreaded the moment of looking directly at him. She had delayed the time of acceptance and fortified herself by remembering other crosses that she had seen, with victims whom she did not know, as if that might separate her from the reality of Jesus' pain. Yet she knew it must come. She loved her Lord, even in the degradation and humiliation of his body hung so vulnerably on the ugly stake. The other two, crucified on either side, agonized aloud, one even cursing—but the Master was still.

"Is he already dead?" she asked.

"Every few moments he utters something. Sometimes his voice can be heard easily."

"What does he say?"

"They taunt him. They yell for him to prove that he is the Christ and to come down from the cross. He said, 'Father forgive them, for they don't know what they're doing.'"

Forgive them! Joanna thought, *I'll never forgive them! How can he?* She knelt, for suddenly her body began to shiver. She forced her knuckles between her teeth. She was freezing, and felt she must keep her teeth from chattering. Salome threw her mantle about Joanna.

"Are you all right?" she asked.

Joanna nodded.

"How many times he told us . . . " Salome repeated dully. "We couldn't believe that such a thing could happen."

It's senseless, Joanna thought. *The cruelty and perversion is senseless, and done in the name of religious righteousness!*

She lifted her eyes again to the cross and looked fully at the grief depicted on Jesus' face. Behind him the sky had become an ugly grayish green. Below, the soldiers were engaged in a game of chance with knucklebones.

"What are they doing?"

"They've divided the clothes among them, but the seamless robe you gave him is the best prize. They gamble for it."

Anger flared again in Joanna. Their callous collection of loot while their victims died above them filled her with hatred. Shocked, she realized that her wrath was murderous in its intensity. She bent her head to the dirt.

"Oh, God, I'm not like him. I'm not compassionate like him. I've followed him for two years, but I don't want to do what he says. I hate them! Forgive me, forgive me."

When she raised her eyes again the words of John came to her mind. The Baptist had called him "the Lamb of God." All she had been taught about Passover and the substitute sacrifice for a life unfolded in her memory.

"What does this mean, Father?" She was a little girl again at Samuel's abundantly laden table, asking the question traditionally voiced by the youngest child present at the Passover Seder. Samuel would then recount the story of how the Israelites were exempt from the condemnation of God by a blood-covering that delivered them from the bondage of sin.

She was startled by the sound of Jesus' voice: "Father, into your hands I commend my spirit. It is finished!"

For a moment they stared, watching for some movement. *He's shown us how to die,* Joanna realized. *He's taught us how to live. Now he's taught us how to die.* She began to shake, yet she was strangely calm. Then she realized that the stones and scrubby trees about them were shaking too. As if a giant hand rattled the earth, people jumped before her eyes. A crevice began to form below the hill and cracked as though a line were being drawn from the cross to the rabble below. The people cowered and screamed with fear, rushing and trampling each other.

The faithful band of men and women clung together. They were rooted to the place on which they stood. As the rumbling and shaking died away, a centurion lifted his face in awe and turned to the man on the center cross.

"Surely this man *was* the Son of God!" he declared.

They studied the limp form for some life, but the signs of death were upon him. Joanna turned away. Dazed, she turned toward Jerusalem as the mob began the wailing cries that traditionally accompany death. With no memory of her steps, she found herself back at the Hasmonean Palace. The cold stone corridors were lit with oil lamps every few feet. Her shadow rushed ahead and then fell behind her like a taunting spirit. She was lonely, yet she prayed that no one would hear her. Stealthily she walked past doorways where voices could be heard recounting the day's events. Her stomach knotted and pulsated as if her heart had slipped and was lodged there. Finally she reached her room and slumped against the wall inside the door. The brass disk, showing her own reflection, startled her. The oil lamplight only accented the despair of the red swollen eyes and disheveled hair framing a dirt-smeared face.

Chuza stepped into the room behind her. "Joanna, I thought I saw you pass by." He moved to face her squarely. "Joanna! Where have you been?"

"At Golgotha," she whispered.

His arms went about her, and Joanna gratefully allowed him to support her.

"Joanna, why?" He smoothed her wild hair and wiped her face with his sleeve. "Couldn't you see that there was nothing you could do? Oh, Joanna." Now Chuza's eyes filled with tears and he hugged her to himself as if to protect her. "I'm sorry. I'm sorry that he wasn't the one you thought he was."

Chapter 25

Joanna awoke with heaviness, with the suffocating dread of the bereaved. She went to the window and gazed at the quiet city below. Soon it would begin to move and gain momentum as the sun rose. Life would go on as usual.

"Joanna, are you awake already?" Chuza came to her and put his arms around her gently. "There's nothing you can do."

"I don't even know where they've laid him."

Chuza was silent a moment. "I can find out," he offered.

"Mary Magdalene would know."

"Is she staying in the city?"

"Yes, with Miriam and her son Mark. Chuza, I can't stay here. I have to go where they mourn him and be with those who loved him."

To her surprise Chuza nodded.

When he left, she bathed in the large brass-rimmed copper tub behind an ivory screen. Althea helped her don a white linen tunic and gird her hips with sackcloth, the traditional black woven goat-hair cloth of mourning. She hadn't worn it since her father's death.

Before she was ready, Chuza returned.

"He's buried in the new tomb of a temple ruler called Joseph of Arimathea."

"Where?"

"In the garden, near Golgotha."

She was pleased that Chuza had learned so much.

"But, Joanna, they've sealed the tomb," he warned. "There's a guard of temple police. The high priests were afraid that the disciples would steal the body and tell everyone that he rose from the dead."

"But that's ridiculous! For what reason? It would accomplish nothing if it were not true."

"They are still haunted by him even though he's dead."

"Like Herod, with John the Baptist's death. They can't destroy a good man and still have peace of mind."

Because she was fasting, she left before the midmorning meal and took a litter to the upper city. The streets were nearly deserted. Children peeked around the doorways of dwellings no larger than a carriage of one of Herod's caravans. They were built in steps, one upon another along the hill. The roof of one hovel would form the platform for a narrow ladder to another. These were the families of the cheese-makers, who were forced out of the valley when Herod the Great built his chariot stadium and amphitheater.

Soon they approached the larger homes of the upper city, and the home of Miriam came into view. Joanna alighted and sent the litter back to the palace. She walked the remaining distance on foot.

Miriam's home was one of the more palatial in Jerusalem, large enough to accommodate many overnight guests. In answer to her resounding rap of the huge brass knocker, Mark came to the door. He was about seventeen, with dark curly hair and a slight shadow of growth on his upper lip. He recognized her, but his eyes darted beyond her to the right and then the left. He motioned her inside the walled courtyard.

The home was built in the shape of a U, making a natural wall to the street on three sides. A cistern was in the center of the paved yard. Two donkeys stood nearby beneath a fig tree. Pink cistus grew near the archways to the rooms off the court. Mark led her up the steps from the gate to the large hospitality room.

"Many are here," he said. "They sit together sorrowing."

When they reached the top, Joanna could see that several of the women from Galilee were seated together on a large straw mat. Others from Jerusalem were grouped about in subdued conversation. All of Miriam's ornate chairs were filled.

Mary Magdalene saw Joanna first and came to embrace her; then Salome and Clopas's wife came. Other heads turned. She saw that they were all women.

"Where are the men?" she asked.

The faces were fearful and hesitant. *They wonder if they can trust me,* Joanna suddenly realized. "Does my coming jeopardize your safety?" she asked.

Salome hugged her. "Of course not," she said. "Everyone is on edge. It's because Judas Iscariot—"

"Betrayed him," Joanna finished, "and I'm from Herod's court. Why should you trust me either? I didn't think—I didn't realize—I just wanted to be with you."

"Hush," said Mary Magdalene. "We know you wouldn't hurt us intentionally. Besides, they will be looking for the men. They don't fear us, and as you can see the men aren't here."

Mary *did* know where they hid; Joanna was sure of it—as sure as she was that the others didn't.

"At least we no longer need to be concerned about Judas," said Miriam. "He has killed himself."

Joanna was numb. Would there be no end to the grief?

"Come, Joanna," Mary led her to join the group. "We await the end of the Sabbath so that we might prepare the spices. The Master's burial was too quick to be properly done. It is all we can do for him now."

❖ ❖ ❖

The tremor began as a low rumble, waking Joanna before the floor began to shake. It was the following morning, but still dark.

Impulsively she clutched the sides of her sleeping mat. An earthen jar pitched and broke into shards, shattering loudly. The donkeys outside were braying. The oil lamp sloshed and the faint light went out. Salome bolted upright.

"Another quake," she said. "Are you awake, Joanna?"

"Yes. Who could sleep through that?"

"Mary?"

"I'm here," the wife of Clopas answered.

"Where's Mary Magdalene?"

They all strained to see through the darkness. Her mat was empty.

"She's gone," Salome declared.

"Perhaps she's just outside," Joanna suggested.

The three women girded themselves quickly and rolled their mats for storage. Joanna stepped out into the courtyard. It was empty except for the animals. The shaking had stopped. Dawn was faint in the east. The sky seemed clear of the clouds that had hovered over Jerusalem during the two preceding days. Miriam came from across the court.

"Mary Magdalene is gone," Joanna said.

"To the tomb? The spices are still here."

"She was so eager for the Sabbath to be over—to be able to be there." Salome remarked.

"She grieves so," Miriam said.

"Perhaps because she is alone. We have our husbands, our sons, to comfort us." Clopas's wife offered.

True, Joanna thought. Even Chuza, although he didn't believe, was kind when he saw her despair.

The four women began their walk through the deserted city streets.

"What about the guard at the tomb?" Joanna asked. "Chuza said that the temple police stand watch."

"The temple guard will surely understand that he needs a proper burial!" Miriam declared. "They can watch us to make sure that we don't steal his body. At least they aren't Roman soldiers."

"Perhaps it's fortunate. We may need help to roll back the stone."

By the time they reached the city gates, the sunrise was bathing the landscape in the fresh hues of a glorious spring morning. Birds chirped loudly in the garden, and the flowers were abundant. They followed a path that circled a winepress and then descended into a small hollow. There they saw the cave and Mary Magdalene sitting alone, sobbing.

Miriam was first to reach her. Dropping to her knees, she murmured words of comfort. Mary looked up, her face desolate.

"They've taken him away, and I don't know where they've laid him."

The others looked about. The area was deserted. No temple guard was in sight.

"What are you saying?"

"When I came the place was empty."

The women looked at one another. Joanna turned toward the tomb. The gigantic flat stone disk that had closed the opening was rolled up the slight incline to expose the cave's mouth. The dark hole, which first appeared as a yawning sinister tribute to death, flared into brilliance as though the sunlight had moved inside and was shining out. She walked toward the sepulcher as if compelled by the strange sight.

All but Mary Magdalene followed. Inside, the body of Jesus was indeed gone. On the stone slab where the corpse had lain was the burial shroud and the linen headpiece. Two men stood at either end, and the robes they wore were so white that they hurt Joanna's eyes. She trembled. Finally one spoke.

"We know that you seek Jesus of Nazareth, but he isn't here. He has risen as he told you he would. There's no use seeking the living among the dead. Go and tell his disciples."

At first she was too stunned to move. Then she turned and stared at the other women crowded into the opening.

"He's risen," she breathed in awe and saw the affirmation of astonished joy reflected in their faces. They had heard it, too.

The four women spilled from the tomb. "He's not taken," Joanna declared to Mary Magdalene. "He's risen!" and she ran, stumbling in her haste, up the path, beyond the winepress, and nearly to the gate. She stopped to catch her breath, and the others caught up.

"Where's Mary Magdalene?" she asked.

"She must have gone into the tomb," Miriam answered.

"Let's wait. I have no idea how to find the disciples. I'm sure she knows where they are hiding."

"Hello." The familiar resonant voice startled the women. Jesus stood in the path just ahead of them. He was smiling. "Don't be afraid."

"Lord, is it you?" Joanna breathed. He looked like the Master, yet something was different. His robe was dazzling, but in his wrists Joanna could see the ugly scars. Slowly she moved toward him and fell on her knees. She reached out a hesitant hand and touched his feet. The flesh was warm, alive.

"Lord, it is you!" she said.

His voice was gentle, reassuring. "And now that you've seen me, you must tell the others."

In an instant he was gone. The women looked at one another. They couldn't speak, and Joanna became aware of the birds chirping ecstatically.

The birds know, she thought, *and they accept it. Why can't we? My heart does, but my mind won't grasp it.*

Footsteps on the path signaled Mary Magdalene's approach. "I've seen him," she called, "Oh, I've seen him!"

"We have, too," Miriam shouted.

Breathless, she joined them. "I saw the Lord right after you left the tomb. My eyes hurt so from crying that I thought he was the gardener, but when he spoke my name—I *knew!*

Hugging each other, they laughed and cried for joy.

"He told us to tell the others," Salome said when they had calmed down. "You know where they are, don't you, Mary?"

She nodded. "I told Peter and John already that the authorities had taken him. We must hurry to tell them the truth."

The five women dressed in the black sackcloth of mourning rushed excitedly through the streets of Jerusalem. The way was becoming congested, and maneuvering between donkey carts and women balancing the water jug on their head for the daily trip to the well was difficult.

Finally they arrived at a dwelling that had a narrow outside stairway nearly hidden by a terebinth tree. It led to an upper room. The door was securely latched. Mary pounded on the heavy cypress wood, her fist barely making a sound. But the door opened—a crack at first, and then wider as John saw the women pressed against the wall on the stairway. They hurried in, closing the door behind them.

"We've seen him!" Mary declared.

"Seen him?" Peter was bewildered.

"The Lord!" Joanna said. The others chorused her words. They all spoke at once, each giving her own version of the morning's events. When their excited chatter died away, they realized that the men were staring at them.

"You don't believe us!" Salome declared.

The men looked at one another about the room. Joanna watched them as they shared their disbelief.

"We've seen him!" Mary cried in frustration. "He told us to tell you."

❖ ❖ ❖

"Joanna?" Chuza inquired upon entering their chambers. Althea had told him of her return to the Hasmonean Palace.

"I'm here," she called from behind the ivory screen. When she emerged, the mourning clothes were gone and she was dressed in a simple pale yellow silk gown.

He frowned. "You look so different," he said.

"You disapprove?" she asked.

"You look beautiful. Aren't you mourning Jesus any longer?"

"There's no need to," she said, joy radiating from her eyes.

"He's risen," Chuza stated flatly.

"How did you know?

"Oh, Joanna!" He looked across the room, shaking his head in disbelief. "The Herodians have already brought that idle tale to Herod. He knows the rumor, and he also knows that the temple police admit to falling asleep during the night while his disciples stole the body."

"Stole the body?" Joanna remarked. "The disciples think that the temple authorities took it!"

"Then who began the rumor that he arose?"

"We told no one on our way back to Jerusalem from the grave, except the disciples, and they didn't believe us."

"I'm confused," Chuza said. "Were you at the tomb?"

"Yes, and there was no guard and the stone was rolled back. They must have already run to the high priests with the word that he was gone."

"Before you knew it?"

"And before the men knew. Mary Magdalene was the first to find the sepulcher empty, and the place was deserted when she arrived."

"Why would they try to discredit something that no one was saying?"

"He was gone. They had to have some explanation."

He stared at her.

"Chuza, why would we try to convince someone that he's alive if he's dead? What would we gain with such a pretense? The truth is, a well-guarded body is missing, and their story is the best way they can handle the embarrassment."

Chuza observed her carefully. *Why did she make so much sense?*

"The guards who admit to falling asleep on duty—have they been executed?" she asked.

He pursed his lips and stroked his cropped beard. "No," he said finally.

Joanna plunged on, "Unless they were drunken or unconscious, it would be unbelievable to think that a whole guard would sleep through such a grave robbery. That gigantic stone being rolled back would wake them instantly."

"The tale *is* preposterous," Chuza agreed. "But a man coming to life again is even more so."

"Not if he is the Son of God."

He peered at her intently, "Why are you so sure, Joanna?"

"Because I saw him!"

"Where?"

"In the garden, not far from the tomb. He talked to several of us. And he was no vision, Chuza. I touched him. He was flesh as we are. He had the holes in his wrists from being crucified."

He stared at her as though to see into the depths of her soul. "You're telling the truth," he said slowly as if he needed time to accept his own words.

"Do you finally believe me?" she asked amazed.

"You aren't just overwrought," he asked, "hoping that it's true?"

"You *saw* me after his death, Chuza. You know that I had no hope then, and that I faced the reality of his death. Do I seem overwrought to you?"

He went to the window and stared at the brilliant sunlit spires of the temple. As his mind groped for understanding, silence and peace enveloped him like a cloak. It was the kind of peace he saw in her.

"Where is he now?" he asked.

Her heart beat wildly with joy. "I hope he is appearing to the others so that they will believe it too."

PART III

THE KINGDOM

The Time of Anointing

A.D. 33

Chapter 26

Joanna awoke abruptly in the middle of night. She smelled the damp air and knew that fog must be rolling in from the Sea of Galilee. A slight breeze played across her forehead, giving her the impression of some other presence in the room besides herself and Chuza. She heard no footsteps. One oil lamp flickered faintly in its effort to dispel the dark. Everything seemed to be in place; in fact, so still that the objects made her think of coiled, rigid snakes.

There is no one here! What is this unknown thing that awakes me so often in the night and gives me such apprehension? she wondered. *An omen?*

Ever since Jesus' resurrection and the coming of the Holy Spirit, she sensed that the believers were on the brink of another overwhelming event, but foreknowledge eluded her. She tried to focus her thoughts on things at hand, pleasant things of anticipation. In the past few weeks, all the floors of the palace had exploded with activity in preparation for the grand festivities.

"You'll see him at the wedding."

The inner voice was taunting, and it created excitement. Dismayed, she turned toward Chuza and tried to take comfort in snuggling against his familiar form.

I love Chuza, Lord, Joanna insisted silently. *Why do I have this drawing toward Manaen?*

The attraction, which had sprung up in the days of lonely disillusionment that summer at Machaerus, was still a playful, uncontrolled puppy, nipping at the heels of conscience. It wasn't to be ignored, sometimes a delight, sometimes biting too hard and bringing pain, not only to her, but to Chuza who instinctively *knew.*

She kept a tight rein on her responses to Manaen. His only overture was the admiration in his eyes. Yet when she became caught up in breathless enthusiasm for all that concerned him as he told of spreading the gospel in Antioch, there was little doubt of special caring. Chuza's hurt and uncertainty would manifest itself at odd moments, silently, in his dark eyes as they captured hers. But Chuza seemed to know that they were bound in something beyond their own understanding.

She shivered and pulled the bed covers more closely about her, shaking off as superstition this feeling that a trap was set, ready to spring. She couldn't help but look forward to the court celebration, and to seeing Manaen again, with a strange mixture of fearful fascination.

❖ ❖ ❖

The palace at Tiberias was appropriately garlanded for the royal wedding of Philip the tetrarch to his niece Salome. Outside, residents of the capital city of Galilee lined the streets from the enclosure wall to the palace entrance, awaiting the pageantry of the bridegroom's appearance. Members of the Herodian family and other important wedding guests had been arriving daily. Now, the great Hellenic gathering hall became a mass of vibrant colored silks and white embroidered linen. Roman togas mingled with Palestinian mantles. Women more often wore the Grecian styles so flattering to their figures.

Joanna noted the tight little groups, partisan but apparently amicable. The father of Salome talked with Herod Antipas while they awaited their half-brother, who would seal his marriage contract and further inbreed the Herodian dynasty, should there be heirs of the union. Standing together, the two husbands of Herodias were a symbol of the confusion of relationships in Israel's leading family.

Herodias's brothers, Agrippa and Aristobolus, ignored both their uncles and carried on their own conversation with Flaccus, the Syrian governor. Joanna could tell by his mannerisms that Agrippa was once again "on stage."

Aristobolus watched his flushed-faced younger brother closely. The two were entirely different in looks as well as personality. Aristobolus, named for their father, was tall, tanned, and lean, but he too depended upon his connections. As Joanna watched, Cypros subtly signaled Agrippa to come apart.

"She's afraid he's drinking too much," Chuza mumbled into her ear.

"Oh," Joanna gasped, "you startled me."

"You shouldn't be so intent," he chided.

"What do you make of it?"

"Agrippa is looking for his next benefactor. He thinks it's Flaccus."

"And Cypros?"

"She agrees, and she doesn't want him to spoil it by making a fool of himself. She'll warn him, and if he's smart, he will heed her words."

"Where would Agrippa be now if it weren't for poor Cypros? Do you think he really would have killed himself if she hadn't talked Herodias into using her influence with Herod?"

"I doubt it. You don't hear him making those threats now that he's lost the position. Agrippa lives by his wits and by anyone willing to assist him. While his mother was alive he had Rome for a playground—but now he must find his own means of support."

Agrippa was annoyed at Cypros for drawing him away, but he followed her to a quiet place. "Why do you interrupt me?" He blinked, trying to focus on his wife's face.

She smiled sweetly. "You were speaking . . . without thought, my lord."

"Without thought?" He frowned, forcing himself to concentrate.

"Yes," she said gingerly, "about that banquet held at Tyre."

His clouded eyes seemed to clear a bit. "Did I mention Herod?"

"You were about to, I'm sure of it, my lord."

"Well, why shouldn't Flaccus know how Herod tried to make a fool of me?"

"A wise man doesn't need to defend himself against abuse. Herod discredits himself with such remarks as the one he made in Tyre. Let it be," she urged. Then smiling, "Flaccus likes you."

"Really?"

"Of course, why not? You have royal blood. You're charming and clever."

"Do you think so?" Agrippa grinned with self-satisfaction.

"And your talents are evident. Let him discover them for himself."

Cypros let her husband wander back to the other two men. She was seldom out of hearing range and was accustomed to walking a close ledge with Agrippa. Like a cat, he usually landed luckily on his feet, and she was largely responsible. With a bit of delicacy and good fortune, she thought, we will leave Galilee and take up residence in Syria soon after this wedding.

The trill of a flute rose above the murmur of the crowd. Heads spun toward the entrance, expecting that the bridegroom had finally arrived. However, the activity was not at the archway, it was in the midst of the room. Dancers, in fluttering silks, shook their tambourines above their heads, and twirled and dipped exotically. They wove their way among the guests in pursuit of the flute. It was impromptu entertainment to take their minds off of their wine-filled, empty stomachs.

Aristobolus left Flaccus and Agrippa and joined Herodias and Salome. The bride stood erect and proper, balancing her elaborate headdress. It rose six inches above her forehead and gleamed with the gems supplied to seal the marriage. The folds of her twilight blue gown modestly covered the well-rounded figure that had been so blatantly on display at Herod's birthday celebration. Without that memory you wouldn't know that such a body existed beneath the folds of material. Gold and silver threads created a rich embroidery along the edge.

"Perhaps your bridegroom changed his mind and won't be coming," Aristobolus suggested, playing on his niece's bad temper. Her soft, full, pouting mouth was easily seen behind the wispy veil of tradition. She eyed him with no loss of composure.

Sizing up his male vulnerability she remarked, "Do you hope so, Aristobolus? It would do *you* no good! Could you match such as this?" Her charcoal-shadowed eyes swept in an upward arc and returned to tantalize him. It became a duel of who would look away first. A delighted smile played about his mouth. She dropped her eyes demurely, and then looked directly into his again, playing games of promise.

"Stop," hissed Herodias. She turned to see who was watching.

"Oh, Mother—their attention is on the musicians!"

On the other side of the room, Manaen spied Joanna and Chuza among the others. He motioned for his companion to follow him through the crowd.

Joanna was no less lovely than he remembered when he allowed himself to think of her. It pleased him to see the special light of joy that sprang to her eyes now as it always did when she saw him. Would this be all he could ever hope to cherish of her? He tried not to covet the wife of Chuza, especially since he rejoiced in having heard that Chuza was now a brother in Christ.

He made his salutations and then turned to his Greek friend. "Meet Luke, who accompanied me from Syria just to meet you. He's a new believer."

"Of course," Joanna murmured. "Jesus' Spirit radiates from you."

"And from you also," Luke responded. Without hesitation he greeted Chuza with the traditional Semitic kiss of friendship, which Gentiles of "the Way" often adopted.

Instant kinsmen because of Jesus, Joanna thought. Yet Chuza made mild accusations from time to time that some of the Jewish followers did not really accept him because of his Arabian blood. What then of the Greek believers? Did they feel like lesser citizens of the new kingdom?

Luke's eyes were searching hers intently. "Manaen tells me that you were an eyewitness to many of the events in the life of our Lord, and that you were at the tomb on the morning of his resurrection."

"Yes," Joanna said. "And Chuza and I both saw him after the resurrection on the mount here in Galilee along with about five hundred followers."

"He wants to know everything," Manaen said, "from the beginning to the end."

"I intend to write an organized account," Luke explained. "Tell me all you remember, for my own knowledge and for other Gentiles."

"Oh, I don't know where to begin!" Joanna thought a moment. An idea transformed her face with enthusiasm. "You must meet his mother. She can tell you wonderful things about his birth."

"And where would I meet the mother of the Lord?"

"I can see to it," Joanna said, "but you must go to Jerusalem. All of the apostles have forsaken Galilee. They reside in Jerusalem."

"Jesus was last seen by them ascending into heaven from the Mount of Olives," Chuza explained. "Now they stay to teach in the temple and to await his return."

"The other followers have gone back to their work," Joanna said. "Chuza and I remain in Herod's court." There was a telltale ring of uncertainty in her voice.

"But your heart is in Jerusalem," Luke perceived aloud.

Chuza looked away impatiently.

"Perhaps," Joanna murmured.

"Jerusalem is close to the Jewish heart," Manaen said in an effort to smooth an obvious wrinkle in the relationship between his friends. "But wonderful things are happening at other places too, such as Antioch. The work of the Lord is not confined to Jerusalem."

"No," Chuza agreed. "Jesus was seen alive again in Galilee as often as in Judea."

"Do you share such things with Herod?" Luke asked.

"Herod finds all this talk as intriguing as the newest court magician," Manaen laughed. "His only interest is in how it's done, not who he is."

"But he listens?" Luke prodded.

"It's a favorite topic of conversation at court," Chuza commented. "It's mystical, it's exciting, but in Herod's mind there's some explanation. He strongly believes in reincarnation, you know."

"He's also too involved with keeping his balance in the political world," Manaen added. "The crucifixion of a Palestinian peasant, such as Jesus, can't compare in his mind with the execution of the commander of Caesar's Praetorian guard in Rome!"

"The fall of Sejanus from Tiberius's favor was a shock to everyone," Luke agreed.

"It has shaken Herod's confidence," Chuza added. "He hopes that Tiberius will not remember his close friendship to Sejanus. An association with one who is later put to death for treason is like dye: once set it may be impossible to remove!"

"Why do men risk their lives for a temporary glory?" Joanna mused.

"It's all they can see to hope for," Manaen answered.

A flutter of excitement behind them brought a halt to the music and shifted their attention to the archway. The bridal maidens scurried to trim their lamps and line the entrance for the groom's arrival.

Salome smiled triumphantly at Aristobolus.

In rapid step, four of Philip's royal guard passed the threshold. High leather sandals clapped the floor. Breastplates and helmets reflected the light from the flickering lamps in the maidens' hands. Copper tanned faces seemed cut from a common mold, clean-shaven, serious, with their shoulders draped in the cloth designating the Herodian dynasty. They took their places. As if controlled by a single cord, they raised long trumpets to their lips and announced the tetrarch's arrival.

Four standard bearers followed them into the hall, taking their places, two on each side to flank the royal litter as it passed under the archway. Four slaves bore the ornamented chair upon their shoulders. A slightly reclining Philip, pale in contrast to the slaves' sunburnt skin, smiled faintly and saluted the cheering crowd.

The slaves placed the litter upon the floor, and another helped Philip to his feet. He was the youngest of the Herodian brothers, but he too had reached fifty years of age. His dark hair and cropped beard were flecked with gray. A receding hairline was covered in turquoise brocade twisted into a caplike crown. The swirls of material were outlined with amethyst and crystal. His mantle was of the same rich weave as his headdress. On his finger he wore a large onyx ring with his royal seal.

Philip moved toward Salome slowly. He didn't put forth the step of an eager bridegroom. A picture of Chuza striding toward her on their wedding night stole into Joanna's mind. How he had struck both panic and excitement in her! She was sure that Salome would never know such passion. Would the jewels, the power, and the position compensate?

As though the crowd had retreated from her, suddenly Salome stood alone. The ceremony was simple, for the vows had been made months before. They faced each other. Philip removed the thin veil from her face and placed it on his shoulder. Beads of perspiration formed on Philip's nose and forehead, growing until tears of sweat rolled down his cheeks, becoming lost in his beard.

"Is he so warm in the heavy robes?" Chuza whispered.

"He's ill," Luke stated with the authority of a physician.

Chapter 27

Luke's observations were correct. Salome summoned Agur, Herod Antipas's physician, to the bridal chamber later that night. Rumor filtered down through the servants that the bridegroom was too weak to rise up from his couch. The wedding feasting continued for the traditional week, and those attending spiced their conversation with speculation. The bride, on brief appearances to join the festivities and assure them all of Philip's recovery, left little doubt that she was bored.

This amused Aristobolus. "I always knew you were too much for Philip," his deep voice vibrated seductively in her ear. "You need a younger man."

"And who could that possibly be?" she laughed.

His remark was for her alone, but her laugh played on the air of the subdued banqueting. Herodias frowned. She moved to her daughter's side.

"You're acting improperly," she warned in a low voice while maintaining a stiff smile for the benefit of those watching. Salome smiled, too, at some imaginary person across the room.

"Don't be concerned, Mother. I must be the happy bride, musn't I? Otherwise they will worry too much about Philip." Now she spun to face her mother squarely, but also gave her attention to Aristobolus just beyond. "And he will be all right. He's just fatigued from the journey."

Philip was highly regarded as an able and fair tetrarch. All were concerned, and the believers of the palace prayed for his recovery.

At the end of the week Agur decided that he was well enough to travel, so the bridal couple, with customary pomp and rejoicing, left Tiberias for Philip's capital city at Caesarea-Philippi near Mount Hermon.

In spite of her concern for Philip, Joanna enjoyed the days of celebration. Long talks with Luke, recounting her experiences with Jesus, stirred life and hope where the humdrum court existence had caused her to question why they remained a part of a pagan community when they could be part of a growing church and the excitement in Jerusalem.

Two months later, as they prepared for the trip accompanying Luke and Manaen to the Holy City, her joy bordered on giddiness. She moved gaily about their chamber selecting things for Althea to pack. This was a rare moment alone together in midday for her and Chuza.

He stroked his dark beard and watched her carefully. "Is it the anticipation of seeing Manaen or Jerusalem?" he asked.

Joanna felt the flush of excitement on her cheeks and knew that her animated spirit had conveyed her inner happiness. Now his words splashed mud on the occasion.

"Don't," she said, going to him and sliding her arms beneath his mantle to encircle his solid frame with her slender arms.

He pulled her close, regretting his words and wishing he could retract them. But she knew that. His cloak swallowed her as always. She stood, letting the mixture of feelings within her subside. *Lord, help us,* she thought. As usual she began to feel secure in the magic of his arms. *My spirit is like a bird,* she thought. *I want to fly free, my own way, yet I'm never far from the nest.*

"Oh, what a sorry bird you'd be,
If the nest fell out of the tree!"

It was a silly little rhyme that Monaea had taught her as a child. Why did she think of it now? Joanna held her husband tighter, rejoicing again that they shared the same Lord and the same hope of eternal life. How sad for those who didn't.

"Chuza," she said abruptly, "we *must* go to Arabia. I can't share our faith in Christ adequately in a letter to your mother. She doesn't understand."

"I thought you wanted to go to Jerusalem."

"Of course, Jerusalem, to introduce Luke to the apostles and to Mary, but then we must plan soon to go to Nabatea to tell your mother—and we must tell Abdul."

"In time we will go to Arabia, but we can't now. As for Abdul, I've already told him, and he certainly won't listen to you!"

"I don't even like him. I don't know why I care," Joanna commented.

"Because Jesus cares."

"Oh," she said wistfully, "do you think that sometimes I'm like the Lord?"

"Sometimes." Chuza smiled.

❖ ❖ ❖

Days later the group from Galilee was at a love feast at the home of Miriam of Jerusalem. Small groups conversed quietly in the crowded room while they waited for Peter and others. Miriam's servant Rhoda had just related a startling story to Joanna and Althea. It concerned a man and his wife who thought they could deceive the apostles and how the Holy Spirit had revealed their hypocrisy and caused their subsequent deaths.

"They wanted the praise of men." Rhoda summed it up with conviction. "Peter told them that it was their money to give or to keep, but it was a sin to lie to the Lord!" She pushed her sleek, dark hair over her shoulder. The lamplight lent a soft glow to her lovely olive complexion. Her large dark eyes brightened. "But there are wonderful things happening too. So many miracles are occurring that sick people are carried out into the street so that Peter's shadow might fall on them. And they're *healed!*"

Similar testimonies were being shared about the room. Men, women, poor or wealthy, freemen or slaves, mingled as they had when equally drawn to the Master's feet. There was no class distinction, other than that the servants, in respect for their masters, took the less desirable seats.

Joanna observed Chuza where he sat in a small circle of men. Her husband's faith in the resurrected Lord was unflinching, but otherwise there was little change in his personality or purpose. He had always been honest and loyal in his dealings for Herod, and he remained quietly firm but nonaggressive in his witness for the Messiah. She hoped he would feel the fire of the men around him as they shared the events at Jerusalem. On his face she saw the pondering expression that she had fallen in love with when he was her father's steward. A wave of tenderness touched her. What was he thinking?

Chuza was glad they had come. He was impressed with the growth of the kingdom, but he often felt on the fringes of it. Joanna must understand that he did not intend to leave Herod's employ. Believing that Jesus is the Messiah and serving as Herod's financial administrator did not create a conflict. Unless Jesus called him to another purpose, he would remain where he was. Hadn't the Lord told them to honor those in governing authority? As he sat listening to Nicolas, the Greek proselyte from Antioch who had been elected a deacon of the church, Chuza knew that Joanna would be happy if he were serving in a similar manner.

The curly-haired deacon sat leaning toward them, his elbows resting on his knees, his hands clasped loosely. Four lines were etched across his forehead. He was telling them about Peter's and John's arrests. Twice they had been imprisoned. Once they were miraculously released, only to be apprehended again when they promptly returned to preach on Solomon's Porch.

"And when they were brought before the Sanhedrin," Nicolas said, "Rabbin Gamaliel himself defended them, saying, that if the movement were of God, there would be no stopping it!"

"Do you think *he* is about to become a believer?" Luke asked.

"Perhaps. There are many of the priests who have confessed faith in Jesus, but believers are still in the minority in the Sanhedrin. The high priests had Peter and John scourged and told them not to speak again in the name of Jesus."

"Yet the number of followers increases," Luke marveled.

These last words hung on the air as a hush fell over the assembly. The tall, brawny form of Peter had entered the room, followed by the equally broad-shouldered brothers James and John, whom Jesus had called "Sons of Thunder." Joyful expectancy captured the gathering, yet the manner of the three leaders was strangely subdued.

Chuza placed his hands across his eyes. A strange premonition had come upon his spirit. He had never experienced anything like it. The face that took form in his mind for a fleeting moment was unknown to him. It was a young man, mortal yet angelic in nature. His countenance was a strange mixture of pain and glory. It was not the face of Jesus. Who?

The vision faded, and Chuza focused on Peter. The former fisherman had raised his arms above the crowd. There was no need to command their attention; it was more of a blessing.

"My brethren!" Peter's voice resounded throughout the room. "You know how the Lord God has delivered us from the hand of evil men many times, but tonight I must tell you that God has determined to receive unto himself our brother Stephen." His face worked to control the show of emotion, while those before him sat numbed to silence. Finally, one after another grasped his message, and a wave of mourning swept across the congregation.

Cries of "How? Why? Tell us," were met by Peter's signal for order.

"He was taken before the Sanhedrin, and there was a violent disruption of the council when he spoke to defend the faith. They dragged him from the city and stoned him." Peter's voice broke as he struggled to tell them what he had so recently heard himself.

Nicolas dropped his head on his arms. He and Stephen had worked together as deacons. Manaen placed a comforting hand upon his shoulder.

Chuza sat transfixed. He wanted to ask what the martyred man looked like. But he felt sure that he already knew.

❖ ❖ ❖

Ripples of persecution broke out following Stephen's death. Those in greatest danger were the Hellenistic Jews who had accepted Jesus as Messiah. Many began to leave Jerusalem and return to their homes in outlying areas. It was with fear for the safety of the others and a promise to give refuge, if needed, that Joanna and Chuza returned to Tiberias in Galilee.

Meanwhile, Philip the tetrarch had died, and Herod was faced again with planning the future of his stepdaughter, Salome.

"To think, she's a widow after less than a year of marriage!" Herodias said to her husband. "And Philip was younger than you."

Herod Antipas was shaken enough by his brother's sudden death that he didn't need his wife's reminder of his own mortality. Philip was already buried when they received the news, but members of the court at Tiberias were making quick preparations to depart for Caesarea-Philippi for the days of mourning. Herod was glad that Chuza and Joanna had returned from Jerusalem before their departure.

Ever practical, Herodias chattered on. "Surely Tiberius will assign his territory to you. We must go to Rome!"

"Do you think enough time has passed since Sejanus's execution?"

"Of course. Tiberius is getting older. Memory is short in the aging."

"It's rumored that he's even more suspicious."

Herodias sighed. "You need to remind him of your accomplishments, my lord."

Herod was not so sure and didn't answer.

"Aristobolus tells me that Agrippa and Cypros have gone to Rome. They even took little Marcus Agrippa and the girls."

"I don't doubt that Flaccus lost patience with him," Herod commented. "Perhaps Aristobolus helped things along. I'm sure he didn't like sharing his benefactor with Agrippa."

"I don't know what he hopes for; certainly he's never been a favorite of Caesar's."

"How can anyone take Agrippa seriously?"

Herodias had stopped defending her brother long ago. Now her thoughts returned to her daughter. "Poor Salome! Wife of a tetrarch and now—nothing!"

"She'll need to return to Tiberias," Herod said.

Herodias stiffened. She hadn't thought of that. Sometimes she was seized with sharp jealousy of Salome. "We need to arrange another marriage, my lord."

Her mind began to skip about on possibilities. Who could Salome marry? It can't be anyone who would seriously contend for Philip's throne. But then, who else could Caesar consider except Antipas, with Archelaus exiled and her own first husband content to be a private citizen? There was no heir, and Herod was the next of kin to Philip, both as a brother and as the bride's stepfather. Regardless, Herod Antipas did not need his stepdaughter to provide him with a strong rival.

Aristobolus!

Almost as indolent as Agrippa, Aristobolus lacked his brother's one strong quality: a burning desire for high places. Aristobolus would be perfect! Herodias smiled. She didn't think it would be difficult to persuade her brother to marry Salome, after the proper time of mourning had passed, of course.

Chapter 28

Monaea heard the stomping feet ascending the stone steps from the area of the stables. Her eyes met those of the other believers gathered in Joanna's Sepphoris home. Flickers of fear and disbelief ignited within them and reflected from the windows of their souls. Such a foul-mannered entrance could mean only one thing.

Rumors of persecution as far north as Samaria had reached them, but no one had believed that Saul of Tarsus would press into Galilee. Men and women slid to their knees in prayer. They had prayed these past months for those of Judea oppressed after Stephen's death. They had harbored those fleeing from it. Now they prayed for themselves!

In a moment the room was invaded by a detail of the temple guard. Although the believers remained calm, the soldiers created chaos by yanking them to their feet, pushing them roughly into the semblance of a line, and binding them together with such short lengths of rope that they tripped and fell against each other as they moved them out of the room. The manner of the soldiers was contrasted by the quiet apologies of the disciples to each other when they stepped on one of their own.

Monaea was transported in memory to the only other time she had experienced such fear. That was on the night Joanna was born. She had been only twenty years old herself then. Was it really so long ago? Life was no less dear now just because she was in her fifties.

"Let not your heart be troubled." The words of the Lord, as the apostles had taught them, came to comfort Monaea's heart. "Believe in God, believe also in me. In my Father's house are many mansions: if it were not so, I would have told you. I go to prepare a place for you."

A great calm had descended upon her soul.

Like common criminals, the group of believers were dragged down the steps, hurting one another as they stumbled and fell and scrambled again to their feet. Some of the women cried quietly, while one elderly man recited Isaiah fifty-three in a loud voice and began to claim this passage as a prophecy of Christ's death. The nearest guard struck him in the mouth, knocking out two of his remaining teeth. Blood trickled from his nose and mouth and dripped upon his mantle.

Monaea had led a serene life as part of the household of a respected leader in Sepphoris. It was humiliating to be dragged before the gaping eyes of the city. Many of Sepphoris's residents stood in the street watching in fear, or calling out judgmental accusations. She felt like a slave instead of the mistress of Joanna's home. Why weren't they treated with respect? The temple soldiers had already convicted them! Why couldn't their cases be heard before the Galilean Sanhedrin? Why must they be taken so far to stand trial? But she knew these were the orders issued from the high priest to the man called Saul. Prisoners from all over Palestine were dragged before the Great Sanhedrin.

In the street a caravan and mounted guard awaited them. Like the others of Judea and Samaria, they were to be transported to Jerusalem. Then Monaea saw the short, stocky man who was responsible for it all; the tyrant from Tarsus. He was giving orders. In the torch-light his beard and hair were a glowing accent, encircling a frowning face. His eyes burrowed into hers as she stared at him, as if he would examine her soul. She gazed steadily back at him with a strength that was not her own.

I must pray for him! The thought was incredibly painful. *Jesus told us to pray for our enemies,* she said to herself.

From her place near the back of the cilicium-covered vehicle, Monaea could see some people still milling in the street. She caught a glimpse of Rabbin Kesil. The sagging cheeks of the aging rabbi looked as if they were weighted by his lengthy white beard. His eyes were glazed with pain and fear.

Surely he will alert Joanna at Tiberias as to what is happening to us, Monaea thought. He had attended prayer meetings at the home many times, and it must have been providence that he was not there tonight. Jehucal too. Joanna's steward was even now in Tiberias conferring with her on some business matter. What would he think when he returned to an empty house? It was good that Rabbin Kesil could send word to Joanna.

❖ ❖ ❖

The rabbi was teaching a class in the synagogue school when Joanna arrived in Sepphoris. His attendant ushered her into his room of meditation. Ancient scrolls stood in brass holders in a large cabinet on one wall. The words of Yahweh! How awed she had been when visiting this room as a child with her father. She was comforted by the solitude and surroundings of a place that showed no outward change over the years.

"Rabbin Kesil," Joanna exclaimed as the elderly priest entered the room. *How old and frail he looks,* she thought, *and—yes, heartsick.*

"Joanna, I've been expecting you." His movements were slow and labored as he seated himself on the little bench opposite her.

Joanna took a deep breath. "As my father's dear friend and also my own, I'm hoping you can help me, Rabbin Kesil."

"I am an old man, Joanna. I have always been known as a tolerant Pharisee, but there is little tolerance these days."

"Who is this Saul of Tarsus?" Joanna implored. "How can he send his guard into my home and drag out whomever he pleases?"

Rabbin Kesil sighed heavily. "He has the written authority of the high priest at Jerusalem. No one of the Galilean Sanhedrin will oppose his actions, and some are happy to assist him."

Silence hung like a drape, separating them. A Jewish Pharisee, however tolerant, was in greater bondage to the dictates of those in power at the holy temple than he was bound by the ties of friendship to someone who had embraced a maverick sect.

His squinting eyes regarded her from his solemn face. Rabbin Kesil's hair had become as white and tangled as wool. The earlocks were no longer well-groomed, for the aging hair was stubborn and resisted care. Besides, the old rabbi had lost patience with such things. The pillar of community worship that she remembered was becoming a ruined monument to an earlier day. Perhaps she expected too much, but Joanna knew that anyone speaking on behalf of those thrown into prison from her home must be a religious leader. The temple priests had conducted their persecution without the limitation of governing authorities.

The rabbi looked away, and his mouth quivered in the silvery beard. "I did not inform on you, Joanna."

In that moment, Joanna knew that he had. She could not respond. This was the man who had indulged her as a child, enduring her presence while he discussed the interpretations of Holy Scripture with her father! But now she saw him as only a high-minded theologian with no practical religion. And the old man could see that Joanna knew he had betrayed her.

"They already knew, Joanna. I did not tell them anything they didn't already know." His face contorted in an effort to control his emotions. "You must believe that I did not go to them. They came to me. They knew I was welcome at your home. They only wanted me to confirm what they already knew."

His shifting eyes told Joanna he was lying. If he said, "already" one more time, she would scream! Her silence was worse for him than if she had succumbed to the rage of that spoiled child of long ago.

"You weren't even there, Joanna," he added. "I knew you were at Tiberias."

She could see an image of the old priest, happy to be able to oblige, especially where he felt those involved were of little importance, like servants or strangers in their midst.

"Monaea was there," she said quietly. "There were other servants and friends. Even those we had given refuge. Only Jehucal was spared because he had brought some business matters to me."

He dropped his white head and stared at his hands. Finally he made a futile gesture. The faded eyes brimmed with tears. His remorse touched her. He had betrayed her out of fear. He was not an evil man, but his religion had no power to save him from his humanity. He was to be pitied. In all his contacts with Jesus, as the Master toured near Sepphoris, and all his fellowship with the assembly of believers at Joanna's house, he had not accepted the Messiah. He acted out of fear and a desire to hold on to the scrap of life he had left. He really had no serious hope of any other!

Joanna arose and adjusted the braided belt about her waist. "I came seeking your assistance, Rabbin Kesil, but I see that any help you could have given me has already been denied."

"I'm sorry, Joanna," he murmured.

"Yes, this Saul must be a tyrant indeed, making a man of your reputation to cower. I'm surprised that he didn't invade the palace at Tiberias on his way to Damascus!"

"He hopes to make examples," Rabbin Kesil said. "This is better accomplished among the common people. Power and wealth have their own demands, but they also have their privileges."

He was always the wise philosopher, Joanna thought. But he was right. She had come in an effort to exercise power, *his* power with the leaders of the temple of Jerusalem, and now he had given her another idea, one which she was sure the temple priest could not resist. Perhaps the trip to see Rabbin Kesil wasn't wasted after all.

❖ ❖ ❖

Monaea had crawled into a corner of the huge common cell. Her body ached unmercifully. She pressed her feverish head against the coolness of the earth floor. The welts on her back from the beating throbbed, but a faint smile formed on her lips.

I did not recant!

Now a new pain began to crush her chest as if a boulder had been rolled upon her. It was confusing to her already-muddled mind. She knew that she had been returned to the prison when they had administered the lawful number of strokes for a woman of her age. The fever passed, and she was drenched in a cold sweat. Breathing was hard; her lungs were in an iron grip. Then Monaea realized the pain was from within! It was not being administered by her captors.

She had stopped praying for life days ago, or was it weeks? She had no concept of time. Now she prayed, pouring her heart out to the Lord. She prayed for death.

The stench of the jail had been overpowering at first, but she had become accustomed to it, and other things created more discomfort than the awful smell. They had arrived in Jerusalem exhausted after traveling for days, packed together in the seatless cart, jolted by every rock in the trail. They had consoled each other with their prayers and hymns.

Once in Jerusalem, they were herded into the temple prison. They were apalled to discover that the number of arrests were so large that the prison was overcrowded; the believers shared cells with common criminals, thieves, and murderers. Fears centered as much on what would happen within from moment to moment as on what would happen when they were examined by the temple authorities.

The believers from Sepphoris had banded together with those who saluted them in the name of the Lord. Together they tried to ward off the encroachment of the the thieves who plotted ways to steal their food and their cloaks.

Monaea had not been concerned with the loss of food. It had caused them dysentery soon after they arrived. She had no desire to eat, for food prolonged life. Daily a number of them were dragged forth to meet their accusers. Usually they were not returned, but a few came back, like Monaea. Was she to be an example to other prisoners of what awaited them if they did not renounce the Messiah? What happened to those who did not return? Were they released after denial of the faith? Were they stoned like Stephen if they refused to recant, or were they released after scourging as a lesson to others who might embrace the faith?

Were there believers on the outside, in hiding, who would rescue the victims and clean and pour oil into their wounds to discourage maggots?

The number of believers within the prison had begun to dwindle, and although they rejoiced that there were no more arrests, fears were increased for their safety within the cells. It was clear that the tight circle of believers was becoming a small core, unable to protect itself from the frightening threats of the hardened criminals whose ranks were replenished daily.

Monaea, almost unconscious with pain, heard the first rumblings of noise from the men's section crescendo into bedlam. There had been muted eruptions before in the night, but this time the riot was longer and louder than most.

The officer of the guard heard it, but gave no immediate signal to his men. Immer Bar Haddoz had been with the temple guard for thirty years. He was used to the sights and sounds of the inner prison populated by degenerate people. Their self-engendered problems were no more than they deserved and were to be expected. Besides, he had never seen so many incarcerated at one time. The dungeon was not built to house so many! Sending his guard in to still such a riot could only bring the wrath of the prisoners upon themselves. If they were to open the door, they would surely be overcome. Then it would be his execution for a wrongful act of duty and loss of prisoners.

No, he wouldn't chance it. Better to let them fight it out until their frustrations with the confines of prison life were spent and silence would return with exhaustion. So instead, he sent his guard with clubs to beat the grate and yell commands for order, but not to open the prison doors.

Chapter 29

"I understand that you wish to make a sizable donation to our temple treasury," Joseph Caiaphas smiled. He was pleased to meet in his private chamber the wife of Herod's administrator. The high priest tapped the tips of his fingers together in relaxed anticipation.

The two had never met, but he had seen the attractive wife of Herod's steward before. Where was it? Oh yes, in the Hasmonean Palace, when the Nazarene was brought before the Galilean tetrarch for trial.

Joanna mustered her charm and smiled warmly at the sharp-featured priest. "There is another matter of which I must implore your indulgence."

Caiaphas was not shocked by the fact that there were "favors" to be considered. Bribes were not unheard of on the temple grounds. He leaned forward. "What can we do for so lovely a lady of Herod's court?"

"See that I receive the members of my household back to their positions of service."

A puzzled look came into his dark eyes, so Joanna proceeded. "My servants and some visiting friends were taken from my Sepphoris home and brought to Jerusalem without my knowledge by temple police. I have reason to believe that even now they are imprisoned by the temple guard."

The concern on his face was genuine. "Saul of Tarsus is a very zealous man. He has filled the prisons with so many offenders that the inquisitors can't handle them quickly enough. If your people have not been found innocent and released, then they must still await examination."

With relief Joanna realized that he assumed them to be innocent. She went on boldly. "I do not want them to suffer further unpleasantness, and my home is without staff, so I am willing to gift the treasury with a sizable donation to secure their immediate release, and I want you to handle that personally."

She had spoken too quickly. Caiaphas was not a stupid man. The gift was too freely given. Now his eyes bore into hers knowingly. But without a large gift to the treasury she couldn't have expected a private meeting with him. She had to chance her own safety to secure theirs, and she depended upon his greed. She continued breathlessly and with forced confidence, "If they had any greater stature than servants, the humiliation would have caused me to consider other measures."

He need only to ask her one question and the foolish game would be over. She would not deny that they were in truth followers of the "Way," and that she herself believed Jesus to be the Messiah.

In the next fleeting moments Joanna watched Caiaphas as he thought about it. Perhaps he also weighed the embarrassment of arresting one of Herod's court.

Caiaphas decided that a wise man doesn't create greater problems for himself. Especially when the alternative could be so rewarding. He had enough blasphemers already scourged and released to make an example for the populace. But he could give Joanna a graphic lesson, one which may be as effective to this high-born woman as the scourging is to the masses.

"There is only one way to be sure that we release the right people to you," he said. He was pleased with himself to have thought of the idea. "You will have to go to the officer of the guard—I will give authorization—and identify those of your household personally."

Later that morning, in the company of Jehucal, Joanna was escorted by the guard into the large public prison. Darkness closed upon them like a damp and putrid tent. The thought occurred to her that Joseph Caiaphas may have pretended to take her money in good faith and instead planned to lock her up as well. Was it wrong to offer a bribe to secure justice? Such measures were usually equated with obscuring justice. But what better use for something as temporal as gold?

The chief officer, flanked by other guards, opened the iron grate leading to the hovel. She peered inside. It was too dark to see clearly, but the prisoners seemed in a state of exhaustion, sprawled about on the floor, asleep or unconscious, she wasn't sure. One rocked back and forth, holding his head and moaning.

"There was a riot," the chief officer said matter-of-factly. "It was uncontrollable."

As they moved among the mass of wretched humanity, many drew back in apprehension. Finally Joanna recognized one there, who scrambled to his knees. Then there was another. Two, only two of the group of twenty taken from her home?

The others had already met the inquisitors, she was told.

"Monaea? Is she gone too?"

The eyes of Hattil, her gatekeeper, were pools of desolation. "She's here, among the women. She's been flogged."

Paseah Bar Ziha took her hand. "Over there. She needs you. Thank the Lord you've come."

Joanna and Jehucal moved quickly to the women's section, and a guard unlocked the grate. A hollow-eyed woman pointed to a shadowy heap. "She rests over there."

Joanna placed her hand on the dark head with its streaks of silver. There was no response. She touched Monaea's hand and felt the cool flesh. A stab of panic, then a comforting calm surrounded her.

"I'm too late," she murmured to Jehucal. Tears made warm paths down her face.

"Are you sure?" he asked, moving closer.

Joanna nodded. "Her spirit has flown free. She is with our Lord. They could not keep her captive."

The officer of the guard still stood by the iron grate. He had not ventured inside. He watched them stoically, never moving. He wasn't even aware, and he didn't care.

Hattil and Paseah had been allowed to follow. Since Joanna had been authorized to claim twenty, she did, taking the women and elderly men among the believers and promising continued prayers for the safe release of the others.

Joanna arranged burial for Monaea before sundown in a cave outside of Jerusalem where other believers had tombs. In the morning she departed for Tiberias. Before leaving she heard reports of others of her household who had been scourged and released. They were befriended by the faithful who were in hiding in the Holy City. And amazingly, the numbers of believers still grew instead of diminishing!

❖ ❖ ❖

"Why didn't you tell me you intended to go on to Jerusalem?" Chuza asked.

"I fully expected to work through Rabbin Kesil, but when he wasn't of any assistance I felt that there wasn't a moment to lose. I had Jehucal with me, and we traveled in a caravan."

"It was dangerous to go to the high priest, Joanna. I would have gone."

"An Arabian could hardly sound plausible making a gift of gold to the Temple Treasury!"

"They could have arrested and condemned you."

She placed her fingers on his lips to still them. "But they didn't. The Lord God protected me, and for once Caiaphas' greed worked on our behalf—except that I was too late to save Monaea."

Chuza took her into his arms and cradled her head upon his shoulder. "You'll see her again," he said, "when we are all with the Lord."

She tilted her head up to look into his eyes. "Chuza, I did an unworthy thing."

"Why do you say that?"

"I used my wealth and position for preferential treatment."

"You saved some believers from scourging and maybe death," he protested.

"No! I saved them from the testing of their faith and from glorifying Christ! I see that now."

He studied her a moment, letting her words take root in his soul.

"Don't you see?" Joanna continued. "We are so accustomed to using our advantages that we do it without second thought. But I shall not do it again, and if I'm ever arrested, you must promise not to do it for me. We only encourage men's evil choices. We have to show them by example how the kingdom must operate. I am no less guilty than Caiaphas, although I thought in my own mind to do a righteous thing!"

She was so distressed that Chuza drew her more closely.

"Peace, my darling. Perhaps the persecution is past."

"Why do you say that?"

"Because Manaen has visited Tiberias while you were gone and brought some exciting news."

"What is it?"

"It is said in Damascus that Saul of Tarsus is now one of us."

"Do you believe that?" Joanna was astounded.

"It does seem impossible," he agreed.

"I've seen the havoc he caused. Oh, Chuza, maybe he just pretends so that he might discover firsthand who are the leaders in Damascus and Antioch. I hope Manaen and Nicolas and Luke are careful."

Now Chuza placed his finger on her lips to silence her. "You forget that we serve a God of miracles. Besides, what was that you were saying about showing by example how the kingdom must operate?"

It is easier to talk of doing than to do, Joanna thought. As long as Saul of Tarsus remained a nebulous figure they only spoke about, she could manage a high-minded forgiveness for Monaea's death and the pain she had witnessed in the temple prison. Chuza and the others had not seen the results of the persecution as graphically as she had! In her own mind she questioned Saul's sincerity of faith and remained suspicious of his intentions. After all, if Rabbin Kesil could betray her, why should she trust anyone? Especially the tyrant from Tarsus!

The followers had already had a few false conversions. Why were Manaen and Nicolas so willing to accept Saul?

In the weeks that followed, Saul's preaching in the synagogue at Damascus of his belief in Jesus as the Messiah filtered down to Tiberias. Joanna was never openly skeptical of the reports. In fact she seldom admitted any misgivings to Chuza. But she entertained them to herself and feared for her friends.

Besides the news circulating among believers concerning Saul, there was soon a disturbing report from Rome. Agrippa had been imprisoned by Tiberius. It was rumored that he made a remark to Caligula about how happy he would be to see him as Caesar in place of Tiberius. The foolish flattery was overheard by a carriage driver and reported to Caesar. Was there to be yet another execution—this time within Herod's family?

Chapter 30

"Did I tell you that Abdul has gone before us to Nabatea?"

"No!" Joanna responded, wondering why he spoiled her trip with such news. They had waited years for this visit.

It was the last day of their journey by caravan, which they had joined east of the Jordan as it moved south along the trade route that connected Damascus with Petra. They would depart its company in Medeba to visit his family.

"You said you wanted to tell him again of Jesus' promise of salvation," he reminded.

Oh, if he would only accept it, Joanna thought.

They had no sooner crossed the border into Nabatea when Chuza became apprehensive. Roving bands of men with angry scowls appraised them as they passed by. Twice they were stopped and diligently searched. Always, even when unseen, Chuza knew that Arabian eyes watched the caravan of travelers. He was glad that he had been careful to exclude any articles that might bear the insignia of Herod's court.

"Something is stirring," Chuza told her. "I hope I'm wrong, but it appears that King Aretas may be ready to take his revenge."

"Oh, Chuza! You've been saying that for years." She evaluated her husband's sober expression. Would he take all joy in their visit away from her?

Since Monaea's death Joanna was more acutely aware of the longing to see her mother-in-law. *How can I convince her in my limited*

Arabic that Jesus is a Messiah for all races? she prayed. The bond between the two women had grown with every visit, and Joanna felt a keen disappointment in never having a son to show the woman who prayed so earnestly and sincerely to her god.

Joanna had long ago put aside thoughts of having a child. Times were too precarious. Now she longed for the soon return of Jesus and a destiny other than motherhood. He was coming to establish his kingdom. She must tell the old woman about it before her spirit passed into the other life or Jesus came again.

From Medeba they found the wandering tribe after only one day's journey. Chuza was familiar with all their favorite locations. When the black tents raised on the sparse land came into view, Joanna remembered with poignancy her first glimpse of them before her marriage years ago. Now their strangeness was gone, but she was always grateful that they were only there for a visit.

The standard of the sheik was raised now at the rolled door flap to his father's *beit shaar.* The old patriarch, Chuza's grandfather, had been laid to rest with his ancestors several years before.

As was customary, they presented themselves first to the sheik, although they saluted members of the camp who swarmed to greet them as their camels knelt and they dismounted. They left their attendants to see to the belongings and trunks on other camels. Joanna accompanied her husband to greet his father. Chuza's father was not alone. Abdul sat on a thick stack of carpets, a goblet in his hand. How much he now resembled that austere and remote grandfather who had blessed their marriage more than twenty years ago. Abdul had shown no change in his opinion of her through the years. Instinctively she was sure that the two men had been discussing them. A telltale light flickered in Abdul's eyes as they watched Chuza give the double kiss to his father.

Joanna remained where she was, several feet behind Chuza, her head lowered in the customary stance of the Arabian woman in the presence of men. She watched carefully her father-in-law's response.

At seventy-three, Benzanias appeared to be closer to sixty. His hair and beard were only partially gray, and his muscular neck and arms gave evidence of a well-toned body beneath the loose desert garb. Had he reveled more in leading the Arabian band by mount as a younger man or by the seat of power from his tent now that he was old? He showed no emotion as he greeted this seldom seen son.

Benzanias appraised his second of many sons. This one he had given to Abdul many years before. This one was not of Arabia, but of Palestine. And he was a fool! His wife held too high a place in his thoughts. She had given him no heir. A man of the desert would have taken a second wife years ago.

The sheik had little respect for his son Chuza regardless of his accomplishments in Herod's employ. *But there may yet be a way for him to redeem himself in my sight,* he thought. *We will see whether he is made of the tough Arabian might or irreversibly softened by Jewish enterprise.*

He nodded to the daughter-in-law, who would always be a foreigner, and dismissed her.

"My son will remain," he said. "He is fortunate to have arrived in time for a tribal council."

As Joanna ducked beneath the door flap, she saw the men gathering at the tent of meeting. Some were raising the flaps on all sides of the huge oblong *beit shaar.* Others were already seated on the woven rug floor awaiting the sheik, his brother, and his sons.

Although he had never been part of a war council, Chuza recognized it instantly. Stories from his youth, shared under star-draped nights, sprinted across his memory. Past raids and wars had excited him then. Some in the camp had even participated in squelching the Jewish rebellion that had erupted in Judea after the death of Herod the Great. None of his clan had gone so far north as Sepphoris in Galilee, but there were those who had stories to tell who were only ten years older than himself. Now their sons looked forward to the same glories of battle. He could see it in their frowning faces. They had no personal desire for revenge. Their desire was for the frenzy of the fight!

Benzanias sat elevated on the camel saddle, so that he could be more easily seen. He was flanked by Ezbai, his eldest, and then his other sons in order of their age. Chuza took his place. His knees pressed into the woven rug as he rested on his heels. It was not a position he was used to anymore. He glanced at Abdul. His uncle would not be comfortable for long either.

Benzanias gave the signal for silence and spoke with the necessary projection of a leader's voice.

"Today I am honored to welcome into the arms of my bosom Chuza, my second son," he paused for emphasis, "straight from the *enemy's* camp!"

Deafening shouts of acclamation filled the tent. His father was giving him the identity of a traitor to Herod, Chuza realized. And then he wondered, *What could I expect—to return at such a time and remain neutral?* His eyes met Abdul's. His uncle had been told. He knew before leaving Galilee, Chuza was sure of it. He knew and didn't inform him! Chuza resented the subterfuge, yet he understood. Arabian blood flowed in their veins. It couldn't be denied. If war was inevitable, what would have been his position were he to remain in Galilee? Could he pretend no relationship to the opposing army? Could Herod's trust be strained to such a degree?

Ezbai, seated beside him, leaned close. "How does it feel to return a hero with no effort? Gad, our god of good fortune, smiles on one who pays him no homage!"

Startled by his brother's remark, Chuza evaluated Ezbai's envy. The one who would be the next sheik would welcome a chance at such an opportunity. Their father's high-sounding words were designed to kindle such pride in himself as well. They were meant to work a father's will upon his son.

Chuza's dilemma occupied more of his mind than the war council's strategy plans. He must make his position clear to Benzanias.

Finally the rest had been dismissed and four men alone retired to the sheik's tent to break bread.

"You asked to speak to me," Benzanias said, "but I think you can speak in the presence of Abdul and Ezbai."

"What I must say is no secret, Father," Chuza answered. "If you would have given me the opportunity, I would have spoken before the whole council."

Benzanias twisted a piece of bread, dipped it in meat juice, and placed the whole large dripping morsel into his mouth. The brown liquid trickled down and was absorbed by his thick beard. With a motion of his huge hand he encouraged Chuza to go on.

"You know that I didn't come here as a traitor to my lord Herod."

Benzanias shrugged to indicate the irrelevance of his statement.

"I do not count it honorable to be disloyal to any man."

"Your loyalty to a Jewish tetrarch makes you disloyal to your homeland's king," Benzanias returned.

"I proved my loyalty to the royal family!" Chuza declared. "I saw to the princess's escape after the divorce."

Benzanias nodded. "Her safety does not put aside the humiliation. Why is it that Jewish and Roman men must divorce their wives? It is foolishness. Herod could have taken that woman to wife and kept the peace. He brings devastation upon himself!"

"Even if the Jews practiced polygamy, Herodias would not accept second place. She would have seen to the princess's death. She may have anyway, if I had not arranged her flight from Machaerus to the gorge of Arnon, where you met her and gave her safe conduct to Petra."

"That's the trouble with women west of the Jordan," Ezbai interjected. "They want to rule equally with men!"

"Does King Aretas defend his daughter's honor, or does he seek additional fertile land in Perea?" Chuza accused.

His father's slap across his mouth split his lip. He licked it, tasting the warm blood.

"I am a governor of King Aretas," Benzanias said carefully. "You are my son. You will not dishonor me by refusing to ride with us!"

"I'm not a warrior, Father. I'm no longer a youth. I've been a Belladin most of my life, dwelling in cities, not a Bedouin as when I was a boy. I do not believe in vengeance. It is for the Almighty alone to avenge a wrong."

"Your brother is older than you, but he can lead the young in battle even as I did a short time ago. You are soft as a woman. A man who cannot act as a man is of little value." Benzanias spit the words as though they were sour to his taste.

"A man doesn't betray a trust. It is the Arabian code." Chuza insisted.

"If your allegiance is with Herod, than you are in the midst of *your* enemy!" his father warned.

"My allegiance is not with Herod, or with King Aretas, or even with you, my lord."

Benzanias's eyes became daggers.

"I serve the God of all mankind, Yahweh, and his Son, Jesus."

"You see, my brother," Abdul spoke, "It is as I have told you."

"You have become a Jew!" Benzanias roared.

"Not a Jew, my lord," Chuza said, "A follower of the Way."

"What is this 'Way'?" Ezbai's lip curled.

"The Way of truth, of righteousness, of brotherhood for all men. It is presented by the teacher Jesus, who in fact was sent by God, being his own divine Son."

Benzanias regarded Chuza in disbelief. "This Jesus is dead, and you are mad," he said. "Abdul has told me how your wife has led you into madness. I could not accept it, but now I see that I have a son who is as nothing. Not only a fool, but a child and as easily led as a woman!"

"Jesus is alive, my lord. I have seen him."

Benzanias's eyes narrowed. He shook his head. "You ask for *death!*"

❖ ❖ ❖

Joanna awoke. In the black of night she felt the empty mat beside her. Was Chuza out under the stars again, soul searching? She knew his humiliation was great. He was treated as the camp idiot; he experienced continual questioning, jibes, and the scorn of the tribesmen as they went off to the border raids, later bringing home their dead or wounded.

Chuza and Joanna tried to help with care for the suffering, but their help wasn't wanted. It was difficult to comfort Chuza in his isolation. He acted as if he didn't deserve her arms around him, as if he had failed her somehow. She prayed that she could reach him and give him the assurance of his manliness. He was torn by the old and the new man within, by multiple loyalties. Could his Arabian family really believe him a coward?

She made her way to the lowered door flap and pushed it aside to walk out into the quiet night. The moon was a tiny slice in the depths of space, but she saw Chuza's figure far beyond the outlying tents, his head raised to the sky. She joined him silently, for she knew he prayed. He looked down at her and tried to smile.

"Did I wake you?"

"Your absence woke me. I know when you aren't there."

"Joanna, I've never asked you to forgive me for letting Herod think you were mad—back before Jesus died."

"You know that I forgive you." She had not thought she harbored resentment, yet his speaking about it brought a release to her soul that was beyond her understanding.

"I've had a dream," he said.

"Did it speak to you?"

"I was riding with the tribe."

"Do you see it as a sign?"

"I've been asking the Lord. I feel sure that he would not have me deal in vengeance. Am I wanting his acceptance on a march of war because my testing is difficult?"

Joanna was silent. How could she answer him?

"I've told my father that I would not refuse to defend our homeland, but that I will not wrestle land from Herod."

"What did he say?"

"That there was little chance that I would need to prove my pledge. They are cocky in their conquests, but Herod has now moved his full army against them. King Aretas, in return, brings the tribes from the south for reinforcement. It's what he wants, a full war. No more scrimmages."

"Chuza."

"Yes?"

"Herod must think you've betrayed him."

"I'm sure he does."

"We are without a country," she said bleakly.

"No, we have the kingdom of God." He drew her close.

She clung to him, and finally Chuza held her away so that he could look into her eyes. His own were full of pain and concern.

"Perhaps it is now Yahweh's will that I go to him and that you become the wife of one who is of your own Hebrew heritage. Manaen is a good man."

She quickly placed her fingers on his mouth. "Don't punish me, Chuza. Manaen and I shared so much in those days of my spiritual isolation from you, and he took away the loneliness of being the only believer in the palace when he accepted Jesus. He is a good man, but it is *you* I love!"

Chuza had not intended to cause her distress, and certainly not guilt. In his own mind he welcomed the solution in trying to prepare them both for the inevitable. He must make her understand. Joanna didn't realize that his death was only a matter of time. His dilemma was in choosing the way he would die. What would be most honorable to God?

If he didn't ride for the major battle, Benzanias would execute him before the camp. Benzanias couldn't risk losing the other men's loyalty by allowing this bad example from his second son. The

Arabic code left no room for mercy. Benzanias would behead him if he had to, and Chuza thought that he had only waited this long hoping to escape the dishonor of having to do so.

This would leave Joanna in an alien camp with only his mother as her true friend. His father would put an end quickly to that relationship. He must speak to Abdul; he must make him promise to return Joanna to her own land. But Abdul hated Joanna. What else could he do? If Chuza chose to ride, wouldn't that be compromising his stand for Yahweh? Wouldn't this negate his testimony before Benzanias and the others?

He could not serve the interests of father, or king, or tetrarch, or even his wife and still please Christ by his actions! If only he knew the absolute will of God!

Chapter 31

Chuza decided that if it were Yahweh's will that he be executed for his loyalty to Jesus, the King over all kings, then it would come to pass. He didn't know how it would serve his Master, but he remembered that most of Jesus' followers were slow to understand how his crucifixion brought salvation or how Stephen's martyrdom furthered the cause of the kingdom. It was part of the resting in faith required of the obedient. He also had to relinquish his responsibility for Joanna, her future, and her safety, into the hands of the Lord. When he did, he realized how foolish he had been to think that he was ever in control of it!

He wanted to prepare Joanna for his beheading, but he waited, hoping to preserve some quality in the time they yet had together. On the eve of the great push into Perea, when King Aretas had called for the unity and total support of all the desert tribes to strengthen his forces, Benzanias summoned Chuza. Ezbai delivered the message and waited outside the tent to accompany him to their father's *beit shaar*.

"What is it?" Joanna asked, detecting his tension.

"He will ask for my final answer."

"But he already knows."

A softness came into his eyes and he clasped her hand. "Never forget, I love you, Joanna."

"I know." She searched his face for unexpressed thoughts. "And I love you."

"I'll be executed, probably tonight."

Her eyes widened and her lips trembled. "You've known all along." She dropped her head against his chest. There was no need to ask why he hadn't told her. She tightened her clasp of his hand.

"May the cloak of Christ cover you, my darling." His breath caught in his throat.

"May his presence comfort you." In spite of the panic within, Joanna's voice was calm. Tears formed, refusing to be controlled.

He dropped her hand abruptly and started for the tent entrance.

"Chuza—I have to tell you something."

He turned. "Yes?"

"I . . . " She hesitated seeing his strained face. She bit her lip.

"What is it, Joanna?"

She took a deep breath, faltered, and began again. "Something is happening with your mother. I think she believes."

"I'm glad you told me. I—I hope *this* won't discourage her."

"It will give her hope. How could she bear it otherwise?"

He left her with tears scorching her eyes and cheeks, wondering if she should have told him what was really on her mind.

She sat like a statue in the tent, awaiting the sounds of assembly. The execution would be public. All would be gathered to see the example of the sheik's son put to death. Should she go to his mother now? Was preparation for the dreaded event worth the horrible waiting, or was an emotional wound easier to receive if it was swift and without forewarning?

Nearly an hour passed, and still she heard no sounds of assembly.

When the door flap lifted and Chuza stood within their *beit shaar,* she dissolved into fresh tears of relief.

"What happened?"

"I've had a reprieve." He folded her into his arms.

"How? Why?"

"Don't ask, let's just be grateful."

That night they gave themselves to each other with an abandon they had not known for weeks. It was as if the forces that threatened to separate them were stilled and negated by the height of their passion and ecstasy. This was a moment that would be forever etched on their memories, unable to be stolen by evil to come, untouched and unaltered by time and circumstance.

As they had clutched each other in desperation so many years before in her father's garden, they now held each other through the night, savoring the closeness of their bodies and rejoicing in their united spirits.

Well before dawn the camp began to stir. Joanna and Chuza heard the sounds of camels and horses being prepared for the march. Chuza arose and girded himself.

"Where are you going?"

"I'm riding with the tribe."

"But—I don't understand, Chuza."

"I have to. My father has taken away my choice."

"But will it please Yahweh?"

"Yahweh provides. Be a good Arabian wife and ask me no more. Pray that I'll continue to honor the Lord."

Joanna robed herself and followed him from the tent. Other Bedouin women watched as their men gathered for the march, sheathing their swords in their girdles, cloaks billowing in the predawn breeze as they swung up on their mounts. They were a formidable mass as they left the camp. Her last view of Chuza was to see him riding the lead beside Ezbai.

Confused and heartsick, she returned to her tent and fell on her knees.

At midmorning Joanna went to her mother-in-law's tent. Keziah, Chuza's sister, was there. Her husband had also gone with the men. Only males too infirm to fight remained in camp.

The two women were grinding grain. All breadflaps had been sent with the men. There was work to be accomplished in camp. No one could sit idly wringing her hands. They would need food prepared ahead so that their time would be free to attend the wounded when the men returned to their tents.

She sat down facing them. "Chuza has left with the men."

The old woman nodded.

"I don't know how his father managed to get him to fight."

The withered-apple face regarded her solemnly. "My son Ezbai rides with his father's sword and blessing. He will fight. My son Chuza rides with *no sword* and his father's condemnation."

Joanna frowned, staring at her. She had been too upset to notice his lack of weapon.

"It's true," Keziah said. "My brother Chuza rides to battle unarmed."

"My husband will not allow him to cause the tribe dishonor," his mother said with the understanding of living her lifetime within the Arabian code.

"My father knows that King Aretas would hear of an execution, but if he dies in battle . . . " Keziah explained, her voice trailing off in the hopelessness of the situation.

Joanna remembered that Chuza had said that Yahweh provided. No wonder the burden had lifted. No wonder he called it a reprieve. Through no choice of his own he would die more honorably, yet not betray his conscience in the matter. "Pray for me," he had said. Did Benzanias yet hope to break his will? The grinding stones, the only sound, grated her nerves.

"Mother," Joanna said, "your heavy heart needs lifting."

"Yes, Joanna."

"I want to tell you that Yahweh has blessed my womb. I'm finally with child."

"Does Chuza know?"

She shook her head. "I almost told him, but something, perhaps the Lord's Spirit, stilled my voice. I'm glad I didn't. At first I waited to be sure, and then he seemed so burdened; I didn't want to increase his concern for me."

A light of hope flickered in his mother's eyes. "All these years I've prayed to Al-Uzza. Now, see, I have prayed to Yahweh!"

Keziah touched Joanna's arm. "Your God blesses you with a life to take my brother's place."

Joanna turned aside, tears developing quickly. Yahweh could give her no substitute for Chuza! She mumbled an excuse to return to her own tent.

Abdul, sitting in front of his a short distance away, watched as she left. He marveled that after so many years this woman, now in her late thirties, still held his nephew's heart. True, she had all of her teeth and her skin had been oiled and pampered. She was attractive, if women were your weakness. Yet it confounded him that Chuza's last concern was not for himself, but for this woman who had complicated his adult life almost from the beginning!

As much as he disliked Joanna, Abdul loved Chuza, as if the nephew had been born to himself instead of Benzanias. He never dreamed Chuza would be so stubborn. Clearly his God came before all else, even his wife! He *must believe* that the crucified one lived. For Chuza's sake, Abdul hoped Jesus did live. Abdul rose to his feet with the effort needed to put old, seldom-used bones in motion and walked slowly toward Joanna.

"You know that Chuza cannot return," he said.

"I know that he marched to war undefended. But he will only fall if Yahweh allows it."

"He will fall," Abdul said bluntly. "Benzanias would prefer that he die by the enemy's hand, but if he should somehow escape such a fate, my brother has instructed Ezbai to cut him down."

"And if Ezbai falls first?"

"Others will carry through."

"They can kill the body, but not his soul!"

Abdul eyed her with reluctant respect.

❖ ❖ ❖

Ezbai and Chuza rode silently for many miles, followed by their kinsmen. Other tribes joined them in the early morning pink dawn, swelling their numbers to match King Aretas's army that moved from Petra in the south. They would converge on Gabalis at the southeastern border of the Perean frontier. They knew Herod's troops waited, poised for battle. It would be the last major invasion of a six-month war. As the grandiose proportions of the coming event became a reality, a restlessness rippled among the men.

"Do you have any change of thought, brother?" Ezbai asked. "You can still take up a sword."

"Those who live by the sword will die by the sword," Chuza quoted his Master.

"But you will die by the sword regardless," Ezbai declared.

"I pray that sin will not be on your soul."

"My sin would be to shirk my command."

"If the rumor is true that Tiberius Caesar has ordered Vitelluis to bring his Roman troops to Herod's defense, then you are also a dead man and all our kinsmen with us!"

"Do you think we believe that threat to take King Aretas's head to Rome?"

"Better withdraw, Ezbai."

"Never. The Nabatean nation has waited too long for revenge."

"Revenge or additional land." Chuza shrugged. "Can either be worth the lives spent? Could you fight Rome forever? No Ezbai, we are both without hope in this life; but I have hope in another, and you could too, if you would just listen."

"Enough!"

The battlefield loomed ahead of them. Chuza sat his mount beside Ezbai and watched King Aretas's troops take their positions for the final thrust. Thousands of men stretched a line across the sparse growth of the desolate land. Behind the troops of Herod, to the west, were the fertile farmlands of southeastern Perea.

Anticipation for the fight was like lightning in the air. Even the horses stomped impatiently awaiting a forward command. Ezbai signaled his kinsmen to take their places. Less geared for battle than Aretas's troops, who were armored with helmets and shields as well as swords, the tribes were to swell numbers, create strength and density. Even so, they could never balance a backup of Vitellius's eight thousand Roman soldiers behind Herod's men.

Aretas had become self-confident after the last battle when some of the men from Philip's tetrarchy who had fought with Herod suddenly defected in sympathy with the Arabians. Now he didn't take seriously the rumored threat from Rome. Surely Tiberius Caesar was tired of sending his peace-keeping forces to remote battlefields. Only recently the Parthian conflict, east of them in the ancient land of Persia, had been settled. Aretas had declared his war on Herod during that conflict to take advantage of Roman preoccupation. He viewed this talk of back-up troops as Herod's bluff.

Chuza had spent his life in Herod's court, familiar with the network that stretched to Rome and the personal loyalties that would demand response. What he told Ezbai was true. Vitelluis would be there, for Tiberius would command it. Yes, he and his brother Ezbai were both as good as dead!

When the charge was given and the horses' hooves began to pound the land in a deafening roar, Chuza braced himself for the wild ride into conflict. Shouts arose from the tribes; swords were unsheathed and held above their heads. Horses raced headlong and meshed into one frightening, confusing maze. Stomping, whinnying animals flung men against each other to the ground. Screams of the trampled filled the air. Shouts before the thrust of a sword mingled with the cries of wounded men. Blood was everywhere that Chuza looked, and its sickening smell filled his nostrils. He wondered at the fact that he still rode his mount and was unhit.

There was a crushing pain in his leg where Ezbai's horse had been thrown against his in the conflict, and no relief as his brother's wild attempts to defend himself and strike his foe kept them pressed together.

Chuza saw the contorted face of the soldier who thrust his sword toward Ezbai's chest. At that moment the horses moved slightly apart. Chuza threw himself sideways, the top of his body across Ezbai's lap. He felt the excruciating pain of a blade that had found a mark. Head down, he watched the dirt swirl about the horse's legs and cloud up to choke him. The noise stopped as suddenly as if his head were placed under water.

For Chuza, the war was over.

Chapter 32

A cloud of dust on the horizon was the familiar signal of the returning clansmen. Joanna watched their approach and steeled herself for the coming ritual of washing her husband's dead body. The son of a sheik would be brought back if at all possible. The dreaded mass moved slowly as if it were a death vapor stalking the remnant in the camp. Then a lone rider took form and could be seen in the lead. He advanced more swiftly.

The encampment gathered, forming a pathway for the newsbearer to ride directly to the sheik's tent. Benzanias had been alerted and met him at the opening.

The horseman reined his mount abruptly. It was a triumphant arrival. Shouts arose from the crowd in anticipation of good news.

"All is well, my lord!" shouted the forerunner.

"What of Ezbai?"

"My lord, Ezbai lives."

"And my son Chuza?"

"He is fallen, my lord, yet he still breathes at this moment."

"Lives?" Confusion spread across Benzanias's face. He frowned. Why had Ezbai disobeyed? Did he now have two sons in rebellion?

"What of the battle?" he asked.

"We put them to chase after the first full thrust. The boast of Herod was false. No Roman troops appeared."

"Is it over then?"

"It is finished, my lord, Benzanias."

The watchers sent up a shout of joy. Joanna's hands clasped her mouth that her cries of relief not be audible. What would Benzanias do now? Would he yet execute a wounded son? Would he deny treatment for his wounds? She moved like a woman in a trance toward the approaching, exhausted band still making its way through the dessert sands. Others waited in camp, content to put off for a few moments more any devastating news of their own.

Chuza's entire body was swathed as protection from the relentless sun, and rested on a stretcher dragged behind a plodding horse. Ezbai rode slowly beside him. Joanna's eyes met Ezbai's, questioning, hopeful. He nodded slightly to his sister-in-law but proceeded on toward camp. She fell in stride beside the stretcher. Chuza was unconscious. A brown-red stain soaked the rough cloth wrapped around his chest. Only his nostrils and mouth could be seen under the shaded hood. The usually well-groomed beard was matted with bloody saliva and dust. His mouth twisted in pain.

She yearned to take him to their tent—to dress the wound, to see for herself the extent of his injuries. But Ezbai made his way directly to Benzanias and stopped before his scowling father.

"Why wasn't he allowed to bleed to death?" Benzanias growled.

"He saved my life," Ezbai replied. "I'm honor-bound to spare his if I can. He took the sword that was meant for me."

Noticeable relief and respect passed over Benzanias's face. His son was not a coward after all. A fool, but not a coward. Perhaps a loyalty of sorts still flowed in Chuza's veins. It could be a noble badge. Yes, if rumors reached King Aretas, they would be that he was wounded in battle. He breathed more freely.

The warriors were dismissed, and weeping could be heard as women claimed their wounded or their dead.

Joanna bathed Chuza's feverish face while Keziah and her mother prepared their tent with fresh dressings and healing oils. The war was over, but the battle for Chuza's life was still to be waged. Surely Yahweh would not allow defeat when he had brought them this far!

When she had done all she could, she curled up beside him, exhausted, yet praying continually in her spirit for some sign of recovery. In the night he stirred, and she was instantly alert. Perspiration covered Chuza's forehead, and he opened his eyes briefly. She pressed her cheek next to his damp face and praised God.

"Joanna?"

"Yes, I'm here."

"Is it over?"

"It's truly over, my darling." She held him tenderly, careful not to hurt him. "Yahweh be praised."

In the weeks that followed, she heard remnants of information about the battle that she related to an ever-improving Chuza. News traveled slowly, but finally the truth was known.

"It was the death of Tiberius Caesar that caused the shift in outcome," she told him excitedly one day. "When Vitellius heard he was dead he pulled his troops and left Herod to flounder alone."

"Retaliation for Herod's ambitions," Chuza remarked. "Vitellius didn't like him or trust him, especially when he tried to impress Caesar with information about the Parthian conflict before Vitellius had an opportunity. I wonder what will happen now."

"It's rumored that the Palestinians believe Herod's defeat is God's judgment for his adulterous union with Herodias."

"Perhaps it is."

"Regardless, your Nabatean brethren feel confident in being accepted in the areas of occupation this side of the Jordan."

"Herod's land shrinks in spite of my efforts on his behalf!"

"Perhaps you will expand on your own behalf," she said mysteriously.

"In Galilee or Nabatea?"

"Hopefully Galilee, although your investment definitely has its beginnings in Nabatea."

He frowned. "What are you talking about, Joanna?"

"Your heir, my lord. The seed of your own body grows in mine. An 'investment' I could not tell you about until now that you are almost well."

Her eyes were bright with the game and the pleasure of his amazement. He sat up quickly, wincing slightly, and reached for her.

"Be careful, my lord," she laughed. "Our child must have a father who is strong again." But she snuggled gingerly into his arms and pressed her head close against his neck. "Do you think we can ever go back to Galilee?" she asked wistfully.

"If God wills it, darling. As we know, he can do anything—and what he does is often beyond our imagination."

Epilogue

Immediately preceding or following the war between Herod and Aretas, Pontius Pilate was replaced with Marcellus and Caiaphas was deposed as high priest and replaced with a priest named Jonathan.

In Rome, after the death of Tiberius, Caligula became Caesar. He released Agrippa I from prison and gave him both Philip's territory and Herod Antipas's territory after stripping Herod of his wealth and sending him into exile in Gaul. Agrippa then took the dynastic name of Herod as well as being named king, the title much coveted by Herod Antipas.

Salome married Aristobolus, who was later named king of Chalcis.

Tradition claims that Chuza became a seer of the early church.

Author's Notes

Facts within the Fiction

Joanna spans a forty-year period of history, beginning in 3 B.C. and ending in A.D. 37.

Chapter 1

Sepphoris was the capitol of Galilee in 3 B.C. Judas Bar Hezekias torched the palace during the insurrection that took place after the death of Herod the Great in 4 B.C. Rome secured Syrian forces with Nabatean (Arabian) assistance to liberate it from his control. Jesus had been born shortly before the death of Herod the Great. After escaping the slaughter of the Bethlehem infants, Mary, Joseph, and Jesus were safe in Egypt during the uprising.

Chapter 2

In 3 B.C. the kingdom was divided between three of Herod's sons: Archelaus, Herod Antipas, and Philip. Herod Antipas was about twenty years old. He rebuilt Sepphoris as a garden city with a superb waterworks. It was located four miles southwest of Nazareth. So many workers were employed in the rebuilding of Sepphoris over a number of years that Joseph and Jesus were undoubtedly involved. Sepphoris was the seat of the Galilean Sanhedrin, which ruled the religious community of that area, but it was subject to the Great Sanhedrin of Jerusalem in matters of national religious importance.

Archelaus, Herod Antipas's full blood brother, was deposed in A.D. 6. The Jews disliked him, and he was removed by Rome in a peace-keeping measure. Rather than giving greater strength and territory to Herod Antipas, who longed to be named king over all Palestine, Rome appointed a Roman governor .

The name Jesus Bar David, meaning "son of David," was how the blind man Bartimaeus addressed Jesus in Mark 10:47. This was a known legal title. Jesus was in direct line to the throne of David, although it no longer existed in reality, because he was the first son (as was supposed) of Joseph who was in direct line to the throne, (Matthew 1:16). He was also in direct line to David the king through his mother Mary's lineage (Luke 3:23). A careful check of both genealogies show that they are not the same. Because women were not considered in genealogies, Luke's account sounds like it also traces Joseph's heritage, but in fact Joseph was the *son in law* of Heli, Mary's father. Therefore in the book of Luke we find that Jesus' actual biological trace is directed through David's son Nathan, rather than David's son Solomon. An interesting sidelight is that Bathsheba was the mother of both Solomon and Nathan.

Chapter 3

The Levitical law on naming a daughter as an heir is found in Numbers 27:8. Job (42:15) granted his daughters an inheritance along with their brothers. This was rare equal treatment for women in ancient times. During the time of Christ, the women of the Roman empire were the most liberated in history until now. Galilee had a large Gentile population. Many rich Jews had become Hellenist (Greek). Hellenist Jews sometimes adopted Roman customs when Rome became the major power.

A Jewish betrothal was as binding as a marriage and sealed by a special ceremony. The *mohar,* or bride price, was paid to the bride's father by the groom. An example of this is found in 1 Samuel 18:25-27.

Chapter 4

Betrothal normally lasted one year. Although fathers arranged marriages, their daughters were expected to agree to make the vow.

Joanna is a Hebrew name. Chuza ("Cuza") is an Arabian (Nabatean) name, according to the *Encyclopedia Biblica Dictionary of the Bible.*

In Exodus 34:16 the Lord through Moses instructed the Israelites not to marry pagans lest they be led away from the one true God. It was considered defilement for a Jew to visit a Gentile home. We find an example of this belief in Acts 10:28. However, they entertained Gentiles in their homes.

Chapter 5

The offered *mohar* could be forfeited without a contract of marriage if the woman was sexually compromised before the vows took place.

Bedouin life and marriage is described in "New Light on Nabateans," *Biblical Archaeology Review,* March/April 1981.

In ancient times, the sheet of virginity was standard proof of a woman's chastity before marriage. The bride's family would claim it after the marriage was consummated in case a disgruntled husband tried to slander their daughter's premarriage virtue in a writ of divorce. Deuteronomy 22:13-18 explains this measure that would protect a woman from being wronged by her husband.

Chapter 6

The Nabateans had a multitude of gods.

A rebellious child was considered dead in the eyes of a Jew, and would be disowned. In Luke 15:24, Jesus tells of the father of the Prodigal Son, who said, "this son of mine was dead, and is alive again," to show the father's great love and forgiveness.

Herod Antipas's first wife was the daughter of King Aretas IV of Nabatea. Although God instructed the Jews not to marry foreign wives, it was done by many of the kings and rulers through the ages as good political liaisons. Herod Antipas himself had Arabian ancestry.

Chapter 7

Manaen was a schoolmate of Herod Antipas when they were educated in Rome.

Chapter 8

Exodus 22:28-29 says that if a man seduces a virgin who is not under contract to be his wife, he must pay the bride-price and marry her, without the option of a later divorce. If her father refuses to give her to him, he must still pay the *mohar.*

In Roman society women were liberated both socially and economically. Sometimes marriages were made "with manus," where the woman retained control of her own inheritance. This freedom could be experienced by Hellenist Hebrew women as well. Obviously, Joanna had her own funds with which to support Jesus' ministry; Luke 8:3 says that she and other women did this. Chuza is only mentioned in relationship to his wife. This seems a clear indication of his inactive role at that time, although oral tradition says that later he was a prophet of the early church.

Chapter 9

Tiberias became Herod's capital in A.D. 23 Herod ran into difficulty building Tiberias because of the ancient cemetery, but the problem was solved by giving incentives to the slaves who built it, and tax breaks to investors. A clever idea, undoubtedly suggested by his financial adviser. Chuza was Herod's steward, according to Luke 8:3.

God's mandates about touching the dead (Numbers 19:11-13) were given for health reasons and also out of respect for the deceased. Coupling God's law with a natural fear of death, the Israelites' traditions about cemeteries bordered on superstition. Building on burial grounds was tantamount to living among and "touching" the dead continuously.

Images were forbidden in Jewish households (Exodus 20:4), but Herod had them in his new palace. They were popular in Roman culture.

Sadducees did not believe in the resurrection of the dead, but they held strongly to the Levitical law. They did not believe in angels or spirits. They were opportunistic, cosmopolitan, and politically influential aristocrats.

Chapter 10

Herod divorced the Arabian princess to marry Herodias and was denounced by John the Baptist, so he had John imprisoned at Machaerus (Luke 3:19-20). John was exciting the godly Jewish people to sympathize with the Arabians, according to Josephus, a historian of those times. In light of King Aretas's anger, John's denunciation was politically explosive, swaying public opinion against Herod Antipas. Insurrection and treason were common to the times, and execution often occurred with little provocation. John's death was over more than a moral issue.

Chapter 11

Susanna was healed by Jesus of an unmentioned illness, according to Luke 8:3. Jesus' words from the Sermon on the Mount are found in Matthew 5–7.

Chapter 12

Jesus never visited Tiberias. The neighboring city of Magdala was known as a city of prostitutes. Scenes by the Sea of Galilee are based on Matthew 8.

Chapter 13

When the Arabian princess heard that Herod planned to divorce her, she escaped to her father in Nabatea. She was assisted in her flight by Arabian "governors" (sheiks). Josephus records that Herodias told Herod Antipas to "get rid of her." Her life was certainly in danger.

Sejanus, commander of the Praetorian Guard for Tiberius Caesar, was assuming more and more authority at this time in Rome and was later executed. Herod was a friend of Sejanus.

A woman did not initiate divorce but could influence her husband to divorce her as Herodias did.

The rising of the widow's son in Nain is found in Luke 7:11-16.

Chapter 14

Christ's rejection at Nazareth is found in Luke 4:16-30, and the visit of John's disciples in Luke 7:20-28. Jesus speaks of spiritual birth in John 3:5.

Jesus' influence reached beyond Palestine, according to Luke 6:17.

Jesus' teaching on life and eternal values is based on Matthew 6:19-34. His teaching on divorce is found in Mark 10:4-12. "The kingdom is within you" is taught in Luke 17:21.

The friendships between the Herodian family and the Caesars are factual and spanned several generations.

Chapter 15

The Decapolis was comprised of ten Greek cities east of the Jordan River; they were free to govern themselves as long as they paid taxes to Rome.

Agrippa was Herod's city administrator for a short time after returning from Rome financially depleted. The job was granted him because of his sister's pleas to her husband on his behalf.

The account of the demonic swine is found in Mark 5:1-17.

The charge to seek first the kingdom of God is made in Matthew 6:33.

Alexander Jannaeus built the fortress at Machaerus. Herod the Great, father of Herod Antipas, built the palace. Holes for cells were commonly used in ancient times.

The bath resorts are factual, and they were very popular in Roman times.

Chapter 16

Herod's birthday party and John's death are recorded in Matthew 14:3-11.

The Scripture that spoke to Joanna's raging heart, My ways are higher than your ways, is recorded in Isaiah 55:9.

Chapter 17

Jesus' seamless robe must have been a gift from some wealthy follower. Reference to the garment is found in John 19:23.

Joanna's quote of her Lord's words, "No man, having put his hand to the plough," is found in Luke 9:62.

Joanna's song of praise giving thanks unto the Lord is Psalm 105:1. That she actually toured with Jesus' company is found in Luke 8:1-3.

The parable of the sower appears in Luke 8:4-15.

Judas Iscariot's mercenary nature is referred to in John 12:6.

Seeking a special place in the kingdom—and the cost of such an honor—is found in Matthew 20:20-28.

John's teaching of sharing an extra coat is recorded in Luke 3:11.

Jesus' words on "hiding your light," are found in Luke 8:16.

Chapter 18

The twelve apostles were sent out by twos with power to do the miracles that Jesus himself did, according to Matthew 10:1.

The right words for defense of our faith in Christ are promised in the face of any opposition a disciple encounters. See Matthew 10:19.

Herod's concern over Jesus' activities is recorded in Mark 6:14-16.

Jesus was accused of breaking the Sabbath in Luke 6:1-5.

The account of Jesus feeding of the five thousand is found in John 6:1-15.

Chapter 19

The materialism of the people is recorded in John 6:22-52. After this incident, Jesus lost followers (John 6:66).

Herod made many threats to intimidate Jesus (Matthew 14:1-2), but actually was unnerved by him after the death of John the Baptist (Luke 13:31-33).

The visit of the Jerusalem religious leaders is recorded in Matthew 15:1-6.

Jesus was slandered in many ways. The accusation that he had a demon is recorded in Matthew 12:24-26.

The fact that among the followers of Christ would be some who showed no steadfastness is predicted in the parable of the sower, which concerns rootless disciples (Matthew 13:21).

Jesus traveled and ministered in Phoenicia (Matthew 15:21).

Manaen was a believer and active in the early church, according to Acts 13:1.

The birthplace of the Messiah was prophesied in Micah 5:2 and was known by the common people (John 7:41-43) as well as the scholars of Jerusalem, who knew the ancient text of Isaiah 9:7. It was also prophesied that he would be a man of sorrow (Isaiah 53:3).

Chapter 20

Herod's temple took forty-six years to build, as mentioned in John 2:20.

It was tradition to make a procession to the Pool of Siloam on the first day of Succoth reciting the *hallel*, a song recorded in Psalm 118:1, 21-22, 25. Succoth was a happy festival with feasting, dancing, and drinking. The Menorah is a seven-branched lampstand fashioned after the one in Zechariah's vision (Zechariah 4:2).

Jesus had not planned to go to the Feast of Tabernacles, for his time had not yet come, but he changed his mind and went in secret, as recorded in John 7:1-11. During this time his own brothers did not believe in him. Jesus told his disciples of his coming death, but they were unable to accept it (Matthew 16:21-23).

Chapter 21

Solomon's porch and the Treasury were two of the places where Jesus usually taught in the temple. Background Scriptures for the chapter events are found in John 7:12-32 and John 8:31-59.

The Hebrews considered themselves sons of God by virtue of their faith (Hosea 1:10). They understood that the name God gave himself was "I AM," or Yahweh. He declared this to Moses in Exodus 3:14.

Chapter 22

The tour of Perea beyond Jordan is mentioned in Mark 10:1 and Luke 10:1-20. And the rising of Lazarus is in John 11:43-46.

The story of Zacchaeus is found in Luke 19:1-10, followed by the parable of the nobleman, Luke 19:11-27.

Jesus' teaching on counting the cost of following him is recorded in Luke 14:26-33.

Chapter 23

Jesus' followers still did not have a clear understanding of his kingdom. The question about marriage in heaven was answered in Mark 12:18-25.

Jesus had many trials. One before the Sanhedrin, one before Pilate, one before Herod Antipas, and another before Pilate. His trial before Herod is recorded in Luke 23:6-11.

"Hear O Israel, the Lord our God is one Lord" is the declaration of faith known by every Hebrew and is found in Deuteronomy 6:4.

Chapter 24

Jesus' second trial by Pilate is found in Luke 23:13- 25.

Jesus' crucifixion is correlated from portions of Matthew 27, Mark 15, Luke 23, and John 19.

Chapter 25

The fact that the tomb was sealed and a the guard set is recorded in Matthew 27:62-66. The events of Easter morning from Joanna's viewpoint are correlated, based on all accounts found in Matthew 28, Mark 16, Luke 24, and John 20.

Chapter 26

Salome married Philip the Tetrarch about A. D. 34.

Jesus appeared many times to his followers before his ascension, once to five hundred, according to 1 Corinthians 15:6.

After leaving Herod's employ, Agrippa attached himself to the Syrian governor Flaccus.

Luke's account is the only Gospel that mentions Joanna and Chuza by name, includes the trial by Herod, and places Joanna at the cross during the crucifixion and at the tomb on the morning of the Resurrection. Luke undoubtedly received his information from Joanna.

Sejanus was executed for treason in A.D. 31 when Tiberias Caesar discovered that he was usurping power.

Chapter 27

The problem of uncircumcised Gentile followers enjoying full fellowship with Jewish believers was not settled until twenty years after Jesus' resurrection (Acts 15).

The account of Ananias and Sapphira is found in Acts 5.

Many of the priests of that day were saved, according to Acts 6:7.

Gamaliel, recognized as a great rabbi, advised tolerance toward the disciples of Christ, according to Acts 5:34-39.

Stephen's death is recorded in Acts 7.

Philip, Salome's husband, died soon after their marriage in A.D. 34.

Agrippa went to Rome to seek imperial favors when he was no longer able to live off of other benefactors. He was a personal friend of Caligula, who was in line to become Caesar.

Chapter 28

The first great persecution of followers occurred soon after Christ's death and the establishment of the church (Acts 8:1-3).

"I go to prepare a place for you" is quoted from John 14:1-2.

Chapter 29

Caiaphas's corruption was evident with his bribery of Judas. Bribes were commonplace in those times, according to Acts 24:26.

In Matthew 10:19-20, Jesus taught that arrest gives an opportunity to witness. Saul's conversion is found in Acts 9.

Chapter 30

King Aretas finally went to war against Herod in the fall of A.D. 36.

Chapter 31

The final battle took place in the spring of A.D. 37.

Before his death, Tiberias ordered Vitellius to back Herod's army and bring King Aretas's head to Rome. The 8,400 troops were en route when Vitellius learned of Tiberius's death, and because of personal animosity toward Herod Antipas, Vitellius withdrew his support.

Research References

Alexander, David and Patricia, eds. *Eerdman's Handbook to the Bible*. Grand Rapids, Mich.: Eerdman's Publishing Co., 1973.
Alexander, Patricia, ed. *Eerdman's Family Encyclopedia of the Bible*. Grand Rapids, Mich.: Eerdman's Publishing Co., 1978.
Bowen, Barbara M. *Strange Scriptures That Perplex the Western Mind*. Grand Rapids, Mich.: Eerdman's Publishing Co., 1944.
Buttrick, George A., ed. et al. *Interpreter's Dictionary of the Bible*. New York: Abingdon Press, 1962.
Cheyne, T.K., MA., D.D. *Encyclopaedia Biblica Dictionary of the Bible*. New York: Abingdon Press, 1899.
Eiselen, F.C., E. Lewis, and D.G. Downey, eds. *Abingdon Bible Commentary*. New York: Abingdon Press, 1929.
Ferrero, Guglielmo. *The Women of the Caesars*. New York: G.P. Putnam's Sons, 1925.
Hammond, Philip C. "New Light on Nabateans," *Biblical Archaeology Review*, March/April, 1981.
Hoehner, Harold W. *Herod Antipas*. Cambridge: University Press, 1972.
Maier, Paul L. *First Easter: The True and Unfamiliar Story*. New York: Harper & Row, 1973.
Maier, Paul L. *Pontius Pilate*. Wheaton, Ill.: Tyndale House Publishers, 1973.
Marsh, Frank B. *Reign of Tiberius*. New York: Barnes and Noble, Inc., 1959.
Mazar, Benjamin. "Excavations Near Temple Mount Reveal Splendors of Herodian Jerusalem," *Biblical Archaeology Review*, July/August 1980.
Miller, Madeleine S., and J. Lane. *Harper's Bible Dictionary*, New York: Harper & Row, 1961.
Stalker, James. *The Life of Jesus Christ*. Englewood Cliffs, N.J.: Fleming H. Revell Co., 1949.
Tenney, Merrill C., ed. *Pictorial Encyclopedia of the Bible*. Grand Rapids, Mich.: Zondervan, 1977.
Wright, Fred A. *Manners and Customs of Bible Lands*. Chicago: Moody Press, 1953.

About the Author

It was during work on a research paper about women of the Bible that Rosemary Upton became fascinated with one particular, little-known woman—Joanna of Herod's court. Equally intriguing was her husband, Chuza, a man of strength and character in his own right. While researching and plotting the book, Rosemary completed her Bachelor of Theology and Master of Biblical Studies degrees at Christian International University in Florida. She is the mother of two and grandmother of three. She and her husband, Hugh, grew up in Michigan but have made their home in Florida for twelve years. She is the author of *Glimpses of Grace: A Family Struggles with Alzheimer's* (Baker) and numerous articles, plays, short stories, poetry, and radio commentaries. *Joanna* is her first novel.

A NOTE TO THE READER

This book was selected by the book division of the company that publishes *Guideposts*, a monthly magazine filled with true stories of people's adventures in faith.

If you have found inspiration in this book, we think you'll find monthly help and inspiration in the exciting stories that appear in our magazine.

Guideposts is not sold on the newsstand. It's available by subscription only. And subscribing is easy. All you have to do is write Guideposts, 39 Seminary Hill Road, Carmel, New York 10512. For those with special reading needs, *Guideposts* is published in Big Print, Braille, and Talking Magazine.

When you subscribe, each month you can count on receiving exciting new evidence of God's presence and His abiding love for His people.

Guideposts is also available on the Internet by accessing our homepage on the World Wide Web at http://www.guideposts.org. Send prayer requests to our Monday morning Prayer Fellowship. Read stories from recent issues of our magazines, *Guideposts*, *Angels on Earth, Guideposts for Kids* and *Positive Living*, and follow our popular book of daily devotionals, *Daily Guideposts*. Excerpts from some of our best-selling books are also available.